The
Harlot's Tale

Also by Sam Thomas

The Midwife's Tale

The Harlot's Tale

A MIDWIFE MYSTERY

SAM THOMAS

MINOTAUR BOOKS ✿ NEW YORK

www.minotaurbooks.com

Design by Omar Chapa

Library of Congress Cataloging-in-Publication Data

Thomas, Samuel S.
   The harlot's tale : a Midwife mystery / Samuel Thomas.—First edition.
      pages cm.
  ISBN 978-1-250-01078-0 (hardcover)
  ISBN 978-1-250-01079-7 (e-book)
  1. Women detectives—England—Fiction.   2. Serial murderers—England—Fiction.   3. Great Britain—History—Civil War, 1642–1649—Fiction.
4. York (England)—History—Fiction.   I. Title.
  PS3620.H64225H37 2014
  813'.6—dc23

                           2013032884

Minotaur books may be purchased for educational, business, or promotional use. For information on bulk purchases, please contact Macmillan Corporate and Premium Sales Department at 1-800-221-7945, extension 5442, or write specialmarkets@macmillan .com.

First Edition: January 2014

10 9 8 7 6 5 4 3 2 1

To the students, faculty, and staff of University School

Acknowledgments

As nearly any author can attest, the six months before and after the release of a novel are quite insane. I'll not bore you with the details (Copyediting! Line editing! Blurbs! Reviews! Blogs! And, heaven help me, Twitter!), but rest assured that in some ways the existence of a second novel is more miraculous than the first. All of which is to say that I could not have gotten through the past year without the help of a lot of people.

First and foremost, I am grateful to my wife and children for tolerating the many occasions upon which writing has pulled me away. I have asked a great deal of them, and cannot thank them enough for their love and support.

I am also extremely grateful to the book clubs, booksellers, and librarians in and around Cleveland. Their encouragement over the past year has been nothing short of amazing. As the saying goes, *Cleveland Rocks!* (I am also partial to *Cleveland 'til I Die* and *Cleve-Land that I Love.* Which I do.)

I would also like to thank my agent, Josh Getzler, and the entire editorial and publicity team at Minotaur/St. Martin's Press.

Acknowledgments

They have been fantastic every step of the way, putting up with my occasional (frequent?) panic attacks, and accepting last-minute requests, like this acknowledgments page.

Finally, I am and will remain in deep debt to Laura Jofre, without whom none of this would have been possible. If you like the book, credit her. If you don't, blame me.

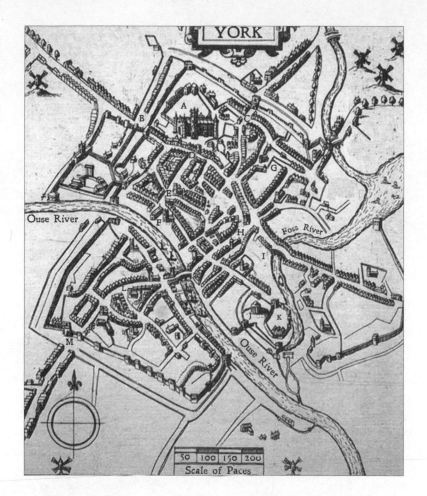

YORK

Ouse River

Foss River

Ouse River

Scale of Paces
50 | 100 | 150 | 200

A. York Minster
B. Bootham Bar
C. St. John-del Pyke Parish
D. Corner of High Petergate and Stonegate
E. St. Helen's Stonegate Church
F. St. Martin-Coneystreet Church

G. Hungate Parish
H. All Saints-Pavement Church
I. Foss Bridge
J. Clifford's Tower
K. York Castle
L. St. Martin Micklegate Church
M. Micklegate Bar

The
Harlot's Tale

August, 1645

YORK, ENGLAND

Chapter 1

"Jane! Listen to me, Jane! Can you hear me?"

With visible effort, Jane Moore lifted her head from the pillow. Sweat streamed from her brow and tears trickled down her cheeks. Time was short and she had little left to give. She tried to focus on my face, tried to listen to me, but after a moment her eyes rolled up and her head dropped to the pillow.

"Christ almighty," I said. "Fetch some pepper; we've got to bring her back to us." One of the women dashed away and returned with a small dish. I took a pinch of pepper and forced it up Jane's nose. Her eyes flew open and she cried out in surprise.

"Jane, look at me," I said. Her gaze was sharper than it had been since I'd arrived nearly twelve hours before. I thanked the Lord for giving her this moment of strength, but I also knew that He would not give her another chance. I cupped her face in my hands and looked into her eyes. "Jane, the baby is growing weak. If he is going to live, if *you* are going to live, he must be born soon."

Fear flashed in her eyes, but then it was gone. She breathed deeply and nodded.

"Good," I said, and returned to my work.

The child who had seemed so weak when Jane was in travail came squalling into the world just before the Minster bells called the faithful to the afternoon service. Jane collapsed into her gossips' arms, sobbing with exhaustion and relief. I left the infant to Martha Hawkins, my deputy midwife, and slipped out of the room to tell Jane's husband what had happened.

John Moore leaped from his chair as soon as I entered the parlor. His haggard face told me that the concern he felt for his wife ran deep into his bones. She was a lucky woman to have found such a husband. "Lady Hodgson," he said, and stopped, his mouth open but empty of words. I knew from experience that he feared the worst and dared not hope for the best. Through my own exhaustion I mustered a smile, and his face relaxed. "Oh, thank God!" he cried. "My Jane is well?" I nodded. "And the baby?" he asked. "I heard a cry, but then nothing."

"They are tired, but both are fine," I said. "You should wait a moment before going in. My deputy is wrapping the child and then he must suck. Once he has had his fill, you can hold him."

A sound somewhere between laughter and tears bubbled up from John's throat, and I could see two days of fear drain from his body.

"Thank you, my lady," he said. "Jane asked me to send for you earlier, but Mrs. Pike refused to have you in. She said she did not need your help to deliver the child. I should have insisted."

"Mary Pike is a capable midwife," I said carefully. This was not always the case, but I could not wantonly slander one of my sisters, however prideful. "It is hard for any of us to admit when a task overwhelms us. She had been with your wife for nearly two days and fatigue fogged her mind. I have had the same experience."

"What if I had waited to call you?" he asked. The lines of his face betrayed the guilt he felt at having placed his wife and child in peril. "What would have happened to my Jane?"

I knew the answer that was true, and I knew the answer that he needed to hear. I chose the latter. "Had I not come, the Lord's will still would have been done, and Mrs. Pike would have delivered your wife and child safely." He may have looked more relieved at this news than when I had told him that Jane and the child had survived, but I could not fault him for that. I knew many parents who blamed themselves when their children died, and it was a terrible burden. Some nights I was haunted by the memory of my own lost little ones, and by the nagging question of whether I somehow might have saved them.

Stepping out of the Moores' home felt more like entering a well than a courtyard. Buildings surrounded Martha and me on four sides, and the sky was reduced to a bright blue square some fifty feet above. The saving grace was that the courtyard seemed cool compared to the rest of York. Martha and I ducked through the low passage that led to one of the narrow streets that wound their way through the city with neither rhyme nor reason. Among the most difficult tasks for a city midwife was finding her clients in the warren of streets, as the close-built houses hid the city's landmarks. This, combined with the mad twists and turns of York's alleys, meant that even longtime residents could find themselves in unintended and—as Martha and I had discovered to our peril—dangerous neighborhoods.

Martha and I found our way from a side street on to High Petergate, and there we were met by the full fury of the August sun. For the last month, York had suffered from a heat more merciless than anyone could remember. The oldest among us said that a blast such as this had come in the time of Queen Elizabeth, but even they agreed that it had not lasted so long. Cowherds lamented that the grass outside the city walls had turned brown and that their animals would soon starve, while brewers worried that without rain their wells would run dry. I knew not what the Lord meant by sending this terrible summer season, but I felt quite sure that every sermon preached in the city that day would ask the question, and that every minister would have an answer.

Petergate was wider than most of the city's avenues, and it usually would be thronged with merchants and travelers flowing through the gate at Bootham Bar and into the heart of the city. On market days, walkers would have to compete with merchants, market women, horses, carts, pigs, and kine. But because it was the Sabbath and the afternoon service had not yet ended, Martha and I had the street to ourselves, save a few slow-moving pigs and the occasional lad rushing to the afternoon service in the fond hope of avoiding a whipping by his master.

Before the city had fallen into Parliament's hands, not all of its residents were so careful to attend services at both ends of the day, but our new Puritan masters made a point of punishing those who violated the Lord's Day. Even as godly preachers roared against plays, dancing, and other sinful recreations, the constables and beadles stormed into alehouses to harry their inhabitants to church. At long last the Puritan dream of uniting the Word of God and the Sword of Justice had come true.

Martha and I fell into our habit of discussing the birth and the lessons it could teach her. She had come into my service just over a year before and—in addition to saving my life on more than one occasion—had proven instrumental in solving a series of murders. Thanks to her quick mind and strength of character,

I took her on as my deputy as well as my maidservant and began to train her in the mysteries of childbirth. For nearly a year, we had been lucky; none of the labors she'd attended as my deputy had been difficult or dangerous. But I could tell that Jane Moore's brush with death had shaken Martha, for rather than talking exuberantly of how Jane's labor had compared to others, and pushing me to reveal more secrets of the trade, she kept her eyes fastened on the street before her.

"What would we have done if the child hadn't come when he did?" Though the street was quiet, I could barely hear her words.

"The child did come," I said. "That is what matters."

"No, it isn't," she insisted. "I need to know what to do if everything I try fails. What then? What haven't you told me?"

I had no ready answer, and no desire to tell her the horrible truth. If the child had not come on his own accord, we would have had to put aside his life and dedicate ourselves to saving his mother whatever the cost.

"It is not something we should discuss so soon after the birth," I said at last. "You must be able to think clearly, without worrying over 'what if' or 'what might have been.' Mother and child were saved, and for today that is enough."

"All right," she said. "How will you handle Midwife Pike? She was none too happy when you arrived, and she left in a fury like I've not seen in some time."

"In all but the most ordinary cases she is unfit to deliver a mare," I replied. I remained aghast at the care Jane had received at her hands. "But you must never say so aloud."

"What?" Martha cried. "She didn't even know the child had come shoulders first, and she screamed at Jane while gossips dragged her from the room! Surely we must do something."

"We will let the gossips tell tales of her inadequacy. That will be enough. However, you and I must soothe her anger as best we can. Today I will send her a note of thanks." Martha started to object, but I continued. "And when you are in the shops, you will tell the wives that Mrs. Pike prepared the way for the child's birth, and allowed me to step in when she grew tired."

"Why in God's name would I do that? Why would you? You yourself said she is unfit to be a midwife."

"And the gossips saw that," I replied patiently. "Soon enough all York will know of her carriage, and mothers will stop calling her to their bedsides. She will have a license to practice midwifery, but no mothers to practice upon, all without our uttering a word. There is no sense in angering a neighbor needlessly." Martha nodded grudgingly, and I knew she would do what I'd asked. In the year we'd been together we had learned to trust each other, both in the delivery room and out.

Even before we reached Stonegate, the street that would take us home, I could tell something ahead was amiss. The crowds had flowed out of St. Michael's church, but rather than continuing on their way, they had stopped and surrounded a man preaching in the street. While some listened intently, to my ears he sounded like a lunatic.

"In the midst of our nation's divisions, distractions, and desolations, the Lord our God has seen fit to smite us with war, with fire, with pestilence, and now with a terrible and torturing heat. The crying sin of our nation, the door through which Satan has entered our realm, is the profaning of the Sabbath with piping, with dancing, with dicing, and with other such devilish pastimes!"

The man wore all black with a white collar draped across his shoulders; the collar was plain, of course—such a one as he would view lace as mere frivolity. He held a large Bible with gilded edges over his head, and periodically jabbed it with his finger to emphasize a particular point. He faced away from us as we approached, but his voice was loud enough that we could hear him perfectly.

"Some of you will object to my words," he thundered. "You will say, 'We have spent part of the day in the House of the Lord; surely we should make merry in the afternoon. Why should we not dance? It is only good neighborliness.' But to you I say, why do you go straight out of God's church and into the devil's? Did the Lord say unto Moses, '*Part* of the seventh day is the Sabbath of the Lord'? Did he say, 'Do what you will in the afternoon'? Or, 'Thou shalt spend the Sabbath in the alehouse'?"

Martha tittered at the image of Moses on an alehouse bench, and the preacher whirled around to find the miscreant. Despite his age—I would have guessed him to be near fifty—he moved with the agility of a younger man, and seemed ready to pounce on whomever had had the temerity to laugh at his sermon. He stared into the crowd with such intensity, it took me a moment to notice the milky white pearl within one of his eyes; the man was half-blind.

"Oh, you may laugh now," he roared into the crowd. "But your screams will echo through the ages when the Lord comes to punish you for your sins. You must repent, and you must keep the Sabbath holy, for the Lord demands it!"

I took Martha's arm and gently steered her through the crowd toward home. Though I did not think the preacher had noticed me or Martha out of all those in the crowd, I could not help feeling that he watched us as we slipped away.

"Your brother-in-law will be pleased with the preaching that the rebellion has brought to York," Martha said disparagingly.

I would never have given voice to such thoughts, but I could not disagree with her sentiment. While the war between King and Parliament raged on to the south, York had been at peace ever since the rebel armies took the city and expelled the Royalist garrison, along with their allies in government. The change proved a blessing for the city's Puritans, including my brother-in-law, Edward. Rather than hiding their Puritanism—under a bushel, they would say—the godly were now free to do as they pleased.

Edward and the other Aldermen replaced the King's priests with ministers who loved the sermon above all else and disdained the beauty of holiness. In their fervor, they stripped the cathedral of its silver candlesticks and destroyed the memorial to Thomas à Becket. Nor was the Minster alone in its suffering: the godly had pulled the stained glass windows out of Coneystreet's church, and ordered crucifixes—"idols," they called them—be taken down throughout the city. I had been able to protect my parish of St. Helen's from such thefts, but most had not been so lucky.

Nor had the godly's efforts to transform the city stopped with churches, for they also sought to reform the churchgoers and to drive both sin and sinners from the city. In this matter, I found myself of two minds. I could not deny that a magistrate who suppressed vice did God's work; who but the devil would defend adultery and Sabbath-breaking? And if a sermon could save one of York's maidens from falling into bastardy, it was well preached.

But from the beginning it seemed to me that some among the godly would take their reformation further and faster than seemed prudent. I had no quarrel with those who would punish fornicators or brawlers, but their interference in harmless pastimes such as playing at bowls, which I quite enjoyed, seemed to do more harm than good. God would not damn me for my bowling or my silk skirts—as some of the wilder clergy claimed—any more than He would damn the goldsmiths for loaning money to the city.

When Martha and I entered my home, Hannah met us at the door. Hannah had been with me for more than twenty years, since

I was a girl in Hereford. She had seen me married and widowed twice, and attended me upon the birth and burial of both my children. I could not wish for a more constant and faithful servant. But Hannah was growing old, so Martha's arrival had come as a relief, as she shared Hannah's household duties and assisted me in my midwifery. By now, she and Martha had become close. As I listened to the two of them chatting in the kitchen while they prepared supper, my mind drifted to the day Martha had appeared at my door just over a year before.

She had slipped into York even as Parliament's armies laid siege to the city, and claimed that she had been a servant for my cousin in Hereford. When she produced a letter testifying to her honesty and diligence, I took her in. I should have been more suspicious of her, of course. How many young women could evade two different armies and sneak into a walled city?

Not long after she arrived, the truth about Martha's past began to come out. While Martha *had* come from Hereford, she'd never served my cousin. Rather, she had fled a lecherous and abusive master only to fall in with her brother, a notorious housebreaker and highwayman. She came to York in order to escape the criminal life into which he'd lured her, but she brought with her the skills of a burglar and cutpurse.

These were not abilities she needed often, but they proved useful the previous year when my friend Esther Cooper was wrongly accused of petty treason for the crime of murdering her husband. The Lord Mayor demanded her conviction to show the fate that awaited all those who "rebelled against their natural lords" (as he put it), and the city council, including my brother-in-law, Edward, obliged, sentencing my friend to burn. I was horrified at such an injustice, so Martha and I took upon us the task of finding the real murderer. Our search led us from the city's most dangerous and disreputable brothel to the parlor of its most powerful man, and might have killed the both of us, had it not been for Martha's "special skills." In the end, Ellen went free and Martha became my deputy.

I don't know if Martha ever regretted her decision to pursue a more respectable life, but she had proven herself a capable apprentice, and I knew that in time she would be a fine midwife. What struck me most when I considered the past year was that despite the difference in our ranks, which could hardly have been greater, we'd become fast friends. I would have thought such a transformation impossible, but the dangers we'd faced together as we hunted for a vicious murderer and the hours we'd spent together talking about childbirth had acted as a philosopher's stone, turning a maidservant and her mistress into comrades.

My reverie was broken by someone rapping urgently at my door.

"Hannah!" a voice called out. "Martha, Aunt Bridget, open the door!"

I recognized the voice of my nephew Will, and rushed to see what was the matter. I opened the door and he tumbled in, slamming the door behind him. Without a word, and barely slowed by the cane he used to walk, Will rushed past me into the parlor and peered between the curtains onto the street.

"Will!" I cried. "What in heaven are you doing?" He didn't answer but continued staring intently out the window. "Will!"

"It's all right, Aunt Bridget," he said. He glanced over his shoulder and I saw that he had been fighting again. His left eye would soon be swollen shut, and a trickle of blood oozed from a cut on his forehead.

"For God's sake, Will, what is going on? Who is after you?"

Will laughed derisively and I could smell the liquor on his

breath. "Who isn't? The sons of bitches who hit me from behind, the churchwardens seeking Sabbath-breakers, the beadle trying to find whoever brawled in the alehouse . . . it could be any of them. It looks like they lost the trail, so there's nothing for you to worry about." He turned away from the window and walked past me. "Do you have any wine? I'm not drunk enough yet."

Chapter 2

"Will, you drank me dry the last time you were here," I said. "You'll have to go without." It wasn't true: I had hidden several bottles of wine in the buttery—but I had no desire to see it disappear down his gullet, not when he was already so drunk. Not entirely convinced, he poked his head into my pantry, but when he didn't find anything he returned to the parlor, fell onto the couch, and closed his eyes. I retreated to the kitchen and returned with a basin of water and a clean cloth. Will ignored me as I wiped the blood from his face and cleaned the dirt from the cut above his eye.

Will's descent into drunkenness marked a sad turn for a year that had begun so well. In his youth, Will had been a bit of a brawler. At heart he was a kind and gentle lad, but other boys seized on his clubfoot and mocked him mercilessly as a cripple. Will silenced such derision with his fists, but, to his unending sadness, the one man he could not convince of his worth was his own father. Edward loved Will fiercely, but for years he could not see past his son's deformed body. He treated Will more as a daughter to be protected than as a son to be groomed for power. All this seemed to change when war broke out and Will's elder brother, Joseph, left the city to join Cromwell's cavalry. In Joseph's absence, Edward brought Will into the business of governing the city, and he'd been particularly impressed after Will helped Martha and me solve the previous years' murders. At long last, Edward took notice of the man Will had become rather than the boy he'd been. It even had been said that when Will reached his twenty-fifth year, Edward would make him constable. After that, there seemed no limit to how far he could go in politics or business.

But if the wars have taught us anything, it is that Fortune is a fickle mistress. Will's hopes for the future came crashing down when Joseph returned to York as a champion of the godly cause. Soon after the Battle of Marston Moor, Joseph and one of his sergeants were surprised by a squad of the King's footmen. The sergeant escaped, but a pistol shot cut down Joseph's mount, and he had to face his attackers by himself. By the time help arrived, Joseph stood alone, bathed in the blood of the half-dozen men that he had killed. One of the many wounds that Joseph had suffered became infected, and the surgeons said he would die. Edward nearly went mad with grief, but the Lord answered his prayers, and Joseph recovered and returned to York to a hero's welcome.

While never so quick of mind as Will, Joseph had the twin advantages of a body unmarred by defect, and the many honors he'd earned while in Parliament's service. Joseph also had changed with the times in a way that Will had not. Because of his intimacy with Cromwell's chaplains, or perhaps thanks to his miraculous survival, Joseph returned to the city with a new zeal for religion: he sought out sermons wherever he could find them and often spoke of the need for England to become a more godly nation. To Edward's immense satisfaction, Joseph joined in the effort to reform the city's sinners. He volunteered for the office of constable, and then worked tirelessly to find the city's whores, drunkards, and swearers and bring them into court for correction. Will, in turn, found himself increasingly frustrated as it became clear that any hope of following his father into city government had vanished when his brother returned. Now Joseph accompanied Edward to meetings of the city council, and when business drew Edward away from the city, he turned his affairs over to Joseph.

I knew Edward still loved Will, and I tried to warn him against turning his back on his own son, but made no headway. Edward insisted that while he loved Will, Joseph was better suited for the business of government. When Will realized that he had lost his place at his father's right hand, he returned to the more unruly courses of his youth. He knew that drinking and fighting would both infuriate and embarrass his father, and he took to these pastimes with the same enthusiasm Joseph brought to his Puritanism. I wept to see both Will's dissolution and the growing anger between father and son.

Even as I cleaned his wounds, Will succumbed to the drink and began snoring softly. I shook my head in despair and went to dinner.

We had just finished eating when the beadle came for Will. At first he pounded on the door with great authority, but the sound quickly fell to a timid tapping. Perhaps it had dawned on him just whose house lay behind the door. Martha answered his knock, and from the dining room I could easily hear what followed.

"I'm here to take Will Hodgson," a voice announced. I knew that Martha had more love for Will than she had respect for a petty official, so I stayed out of sight for the moment.

"I don't know who that is," Martha replied.

"Will Hodgson," the beadle said again, as if that would clarify matters.

"You can say the name as many times as you like, and I still won't know who you mean. And for that matter, who are you? Do you have a writ for his arrest? If so, I should very much like to see it." Martha's impudence could sometimes get the better of her, and I decided to intervene before the beadle summoned his superiors or decided to arrest her in Will's stead.

I squared my shoulders and swept into the foyer. Martha heard me coming and stepped out of my way. As soon as the beadle saw me striding toward him, the color that Martha's insolence had brought to his cheeks drained away. He'd come looking for a brawling youth, and while he was willing to argue with a serving-maid, facing someone of my stature was another matter entirely.

"Sirrah, what do you mean, thundering at the door to my house?" I asked. "What business could you possibly have with me?"

The beadle opened his mouth, but he could not find his voice. He looked as if he'd just eaten a meal of rotted mutton.

"Well, what is it?" I cried. "Are you here to call me to a birth?"

"N-N-No, my lady," he stuttered, grateful for a question he could answer. "I am looking for Will Hodgson . . . your nephew."

"I know who my nephew is, rascal, but *Mister* Hodgson does not live here. Seek him elsewhere."

"My lady, he was seen coming this way. The constable wishes to speak with him about an assault."

"When I see him, I shall give him the message," I said. "Until then, you should leave me in peace, or *I* shall call the constable to speak with *you*." This was an empty threat, of course, but one that I thought likely to work. The beadle peered over my shoulder, hoping to catch a glimpse of his quarry, before mumbling an apology and starting back to Stonegate.

I secured the door, spun on my heel, and strode into the parlor. The noise had woken Will, and I found him sitting on the couch looking at me groggily. "Thank you, Aunt."

"Don't you dare thank me," I hissed. "I did not do that to protect you, and if you say one more word, I'll drag you to the constable myself!" His mouth snapped shut. "I have a good reputation in this city," I continued, "and I'll not let you ruin it with your foolery. The beadles and constables rely on me, and I on them. I shall not lose credit for the sake of your debauchery. If you come to my home again in such a state, you'll find the door barred to you. If you think you can cajole Hannah or Martha, I urge you to try, but they are as disgusted with your carriage as I am."

At this, Will's face fell. Hannah, Martha, and I were the only people in York who loved him without reservation, without thinking less of him for his deformity. If he lost us, he would have no one.

"Aunt Bridget," he said.

"I'm not through yet. What do you think this sort of idiocy will achieve? Do you think getting drunk and fighting will convince your father that he's made a mistake? Do you think he'll welcome you back as if you were the Prodigal Son? Do you not know your father? He is many things, but nobody has accused him of tolerating weakness."

Will opened his mouth to speak, but I ignored him.

"Yes, your father has turned away from you and toward your brother. Such is the nature of fatherhood. Have you forgotten that my father sent me north to marry your uncle Phineas and in that instant made me the most miserable woman in England? Fathers make decisions—bad ones sometimes—for their own reasons. Your lot is that of the second son and that will not change. The question is how you will answer the challenge."

Will hung his head in shame. He seemed contrite, but I'd sung this song before, and he'd joined in the penitential chorus, swearing off drinking and fighting. Then he'd gone back to the alehouse. Whatever devils had ahold of Will would not be prised off by a few hard words from me. Will made his ritual apologies and swore—again—to reform his behavior, and after checking that the beadle was not lurking on my doorstep, he went on his way.

Hannah and Martha joined me in the parlor and together we watched as Will disappeared down the street.

"What will we do with him?" Hannah asked. She had known Will since he was a boy, and the two of us had helped to raise him after his mother died. Our love for Will and our sorrow at his decline were the same.

"I don't know," I replied. "If he doesn't mend his ways, the city may do it for him. I've no desire to see him in the stocks, but if he continues on this path, I see no other fate."

"A gentleman's son in the stocks for drinking and a scuffle?" Hannah asked. "Surely not!" Even maidservants were scandalized at the disorder that the Puritans had sown in our city.

"It is a new world the godly have made," I replied. "They that once were down, now are up; Edward will see his own son in gaol if need be."

"He will mend his ways," Martha said. "He must." I thought I heard a note of despair in her voice. In the time since Martha had come to York, she and Will had grown close, and she joined Hannah and me in the effort to pull Will back to sobriety. If he were not from so wealthy a family and she but a maidservant, they might have made a fine match.

As evening fell, I went up to my chamber. I had intended to write letters to my family in far-off Hereford, but the insufferable heat made it impossible for me to think clearly. I opened my windows, hoping that a cool night wind might provide some relief, but I found it as calm as it had been all month. With no hope of writing, I set myself to scripture-reading and prayer. As I sought out my Bible, my eyes fell upon the picture of my daughter that sat next to my bed.

My mind turned from God to my lost husbands, Luke and Phineas, and my lost children, Birdy and Michael. I looked down at the ring I wore on my right hand. It was of the finest gold and had my coat of arms and Luke's engraved on either side. He had given it to me as a token when we married, saying that our children would come from doubly strong stock. But he died before we had even one child. Then had come Phineas, a worse man than Luke in every way. But for all the scorn I heaped on Phineas, I could not deny that he had given me two beautiful children, a boy we named Michael and a girl we christened Bridget but called Birdy for all her flitting about.

Birdy had come first and given me hope for the future. I taught her to read and even to write a little, and dreamed that someday I would train her in the art and mysteries of midwifery. Then came Michael, the male heir that we all had wanted. But the Lord would not have it, and in the terrible year of 1642 He scythed down all my household kin. He took Michael soon after he was born, then Phineas, and finally Birdy.

Though I knew I could not fathom the Lord's will, I wondered at the mercy He showed to some of the city's most sinful citizens, and the swiftness with which He had destroyed my little family. I pushed such impious thoughts away and began to pray. I prayed for

Will and asked God to have mercy on York and its suffering people. But in the end, He denied my entreaties for York, and in the weeks that followed, the Lord God, in His eternal wisdom, blasted the city with curses far worse than the mere heat of the sun, causing many to wonder if hell itself might have come into the world.

The following afternoon, I directed Martha to read in my medicines book and try her hand at making some of her own. To protect my herbs from terrible heat, we had stretched a cloth over my little garden; but even so, my plants had begun to wilt. It would be better for her to use my herbs in practice than to let them die from the sun. While she worked, Hannah and I crossed over the Ouse river into Micklegate Ward for my weekly supper with Edward, my brother-in-law. I first met Edward upon my arrival in York to marry his brother, Phineas. While I came from an ancient family of gentry stock, and still owned several estates in Hereford, the Hodgsons were more recently wealthy, making their fortune in the cloth and wool trade. Phineas and Edward's father had served as Lord Mayor, and had hoped his sons would follow the same path; in this, as in so much else, Phineas disappointed him, as he proved no less incompetent as a merchant and officeholder than as a husband.

The meals with Edward were a ritual dating back to my marriage to Phineas. At first we were four, as Phineas and I dined with Edward and his wife. But soon Edward was widowed, and we remained three until Joseph came of age. This quaternion, however, fared no better than the first, as Phineas died soon after and Joseph went off to the wars. Will took his brother's place, and Edward and I carefully ignored the mounting evidence that death was an invisible guest at his table. When God answered our prayers for Joseph's safe return, he rejoined these meals and we were four again, at least until Will's drinking and fighting became so common that Edward excluded him from these gatherings as unfit for civil company.

When Hannah and I arrived at Edward's, she retired to the kitchen with the other servants and Edward's footman ushered me into the elegant, book-lined study, where Edward sat working on the city's business. He was not quite so tall as I but had lost little of the strength that had characterized his youth, when—like Will—he had been something of a fighter. Perhaps such behavior was in the Hodgson blood. The past year had added to the gray in his beard, for as an Alderman, he bore much of the responsibility for ensuring the safety and provisioning of the city. I sometimes worried that the work would overwhelm him.

When I entered, he embraced me warmly, then called for a bottle of French wine, and we fell to talking of the business of the city. Such talk was hardly idle chatter, for Edward and I worked together whenever city women encountered the law. In the case of witchcraft or rape, midwives searched women's bodies for signs of a crime, and how could city officials hope to find and punish York's bastard-bearers without the midwives' help? I took no satisfaction in a young mother's whipping, especially if it was her first child, but the city also ordered men who fathered bastards to support their children. I considered the whipping to be a mother's second labor, one that ensured that the child escaped a lifetime of hunger. While Edward was less merciful than I might have liked, I pushed him when I could, and sometimes he yielded. As we drank, we also talked of the war, the weather, and more pleasant news of the city . . . every subject we could imagine except Will's sad state. I dared not ask if Will had come home the previous night.

Just as Edward's servant announced that supper was ready, I

heard someone enter the house. I turned, hoping it would be Will, but instead Joseph entered the room. He was taller than his brother, and projected strength even beyond his stature. Whether he had acquired this authority from his time at Cromwell's side or learned it from his father I did not know, but it seemed clear that Joseph was well prepared to join Edward in city government. I gazed at his face and recalled his bloody deeds in the war. His pale skin and the warmth of his eyes belied the fact that he had single-handedly hacked six men to death.

Edward, Joseph, and I had only just begun to eat when a visitor arrived for Edward; he excused himself, leaving Joseph and me alone. The two of us sat in awkward silence for a few minutes, the only sound the clink of our forks and knives as we ate. Finally I could stand it no longer.

"Joseph, how goes the business of governing?"

He gazed at me for a moment before answering, as if he were giving the question serious consideration. "It is a life of constant toil for those who work in the vineyards of the Lord," he said at last. "I do what I can in His service."

"I hear you have jailed many of the city's harlots," I said.

"Not just them," he replied. "We'll whip the whoremasters who frequent them if we can, and I've imprisoned drunkards as well. The word of God, rightly preached, will awake the fear of the Lord in some men. But the law must correct those who are too old in their sins to be reached by sermons. If we are to transform York into a city on a hill, the minister and magistrate must work together." While I had my qualms about the Puritans' efforts to reform the city, I found Joseph's sincerity quite touching.

"So you are your brother's keeper?" I asked, with a small smile.

"Do you mock me, Aunt Bridget?" he asked. He seemed genuinely hurt by my words.

"No, no, not at all," I replied. "Perhaps I've spent too much time with the city's sinners to think that York can ever be changed."

"But the Lord demands it," Joseph insisted, and once again I found myself impressed by his earnestness. *Shall a trumpet be blown in the city and the people not be afraid?* In his goodness, the Lord has sent this terrible summer. He is begging for the city's reformation. If the people could see this, they would leave off their evil ways and turn to Him."

"And this is your duty? To reform the entire city?"

"God has placed the welfare of the city in our hands." Joseph nodded. "If we do not do His work, His vengeance will fall on the entire city, not just on its sinners."

When Joseph put it this way, I could not refute his argument, nor could I deny that the magistrate had a place in suppressing sin. But I had met too many magistrates who were themselves steeped in debauchery to believe that Joseph's "reformation" would mean anything more than punishing the poor while the wealthy wallowed in their sin. I started to reply, but Edward returned and Joseph turned his attention from me to his father.

"Was it city business?" Joseph asked, obviously eager to be included.

"Of a sort," Edward replied. "It was Henry Johnson." Henry Johnson owned the Angel, York's oldest inn and one I visited on occasion. "Henry's furious because Hezekiah Ward chose to spend the afternoon preaching in front of his entrance. He says Ward chased off a dozen customers before he was through, telling them they were damned if they didn't mend their ways. When Henry told Mr. Ward to move along, he called him a groomsman to the Whore of Babylon."

"What are you going to do?" I asked.

"They are both good men," he replied evenly. "I cannot demand that Mr. Ward stop preaching, but Henry is no great sinner. I'll send word that Mr. Ward should not trouble him in the future. It is a big enough city that he can find other places to preach."

"Who is this Ward?" I asked. "Is he new to the city?"

"He just came from Manchester," Joseph said, nodding. "He's as fiery a preacher as I've ever known. After I heard one of his sermons, I helped him get a license from the Minster so he could preach throughout the city."

"And you agreed to this?" I asked Edward.

"If he can bring the city closer to God, then it is all for the best," Edward replied. Joseph smiled at his father's approval.

"Did you invite him to the city?" I asked. Edward had hired godly ministers in the past, but usually moderate men.

Edward shook his head. "He seems to have come of his own accord, but I thank God for it. He has brought many a Christian to his senses, and I can only hope he will continue such work here. He is a powerful man indeed."

At that moment I realized that I might know Hezekiah Ward after all. "Tell me, Edward, what does Mr. Ward look like?"

"Oh, you'll know him when you see him," Edward assured me. "He'll be the one thundering about salvation and damnation. And he's got just one good eye, the poor man."

Chapter 3

As Hannah and I crossed the Ouse Bridge on our way home, I heard a familiar voice ahead, crying up damnation and the wrath of God. I could see Hezekiah Ward even from a distance—someone must have put him on a pedestal. Between the crowd there for the sermon, people trying to cross the bridge, and customers moving in and out of the bridge's shops, Hannah and I became captive members of Ward's audience.

"Yea, the Lord God has decreed eternal tortures of both soul and body, in those easeless and endless flames of fire and brimstone," he roared. "This is the very doom that God has denounced against the dual sins of uncleanness and filthiness for whoremongers and their whores."

As Hannah and I fought our way through the crowd, I saw that Ward was dressed exactly as he had been the day before, and despite his heavy black coat, he seemed unaffected by the afternoon's searing heat.

"There are some, nay many, in this city who take their pleasure from the beastly sins of whoredom and fornication! Such

26

ones should heed this warning: the Lord gives sour sauce to such stolen meat, and God wields a heavy hand in revenging and punishing this sin of uncleanness."

The crowd behind us suddenly surged forward, and I found myself separated from Hannah and pushed within a few feet of Ward himself. I turned to search for Hannah, but someone behind me toppled over and knocked me to the ground. As I clambered to my feet, I realized that the men and women around me were so enraptured by Ward's sermon that they had no idea I'd crashed into them or fallen at their feet.

"What a pitiful massacre followed the deflowering of Dinah by Shechem, the son of Hamor! What a heavy time it was, what a black day in the congregation of Israel when Zimri and Cozbi perished, and twenty-four thousand Israelites were swept away by the hand of God."

The men and women closest to Ward wept in terror, even as they stared at him with unnerving intensity. As my eyes searched the rest of the crowd, I was startled to see a pair of familiar figures standing near Ward: Rebecca Hooke and her son, James. Rebecca gazed at the crowd with a look of satisfaction on her face, as if the sermon were her doing. James stared intently at the preacher, but every few seconds he glanced at a beautiful dark-haired lass next to him. He seemed equally entranced by each.

Not long ago the Hookes' presence at a midweek sermon would have seemed unlikely, to say the least. When the King's men had ruled York, Rebecca had been a Cavalier and supported the Church of England with all its ornaments. But now she donned the drab colors of the godly, and made a great show of her piety by leading the charge to remove the stained glass from her church of St. Michael. What her new friends did not know—and I could not prove—was that Rebecca was a coldhearted murderess. She had confessed as much to me in private, but I'd never been able to find evidence sufficient to convict her in court. My failure to see her hanged still gnawed at my soul.

In the months since this murder, Rebecca's husband had died as well. Had he not been kicked to death by his horse in full view of his neighbors, I might have suspected her in that killing, too, for he was a useless man and she made no secret of her disdain for him. Rebecca had not even removed her mourning clothes before she began to push James, her dim-witted son, toward positions of power within the city. By a mix of flattery, extortion, and bribery, she had placed James in line for a seat on the common council, and she'd already begun to fill her pockets from the city's coffers. Such corruption was no secret, but none had the courage to face down such a vicious woman.

James's presence at Ward's side was less mysterious, or at least less hypocritical. From his youth, James had been a weak and silly boy, inclined to drink but nothing worse. But James had a hand in the crime his mother had committed, and while Rebecca was most to blame, James felt more than his fair share of guilt. Shaken by his role in the killing, James experienced a religious transformation worthy of the apostle Paul himself. He'd begun to seek out godly ministers wherever he could find them, gadding about the city, its suburbs, and far beyond, always in search of a soul-quaking sermon. I could not help hoping that he would find whatever comfort the Lord might see fit to offer.

"How long will God allow York to wallow in this sin before He visits His terrible justice on the entire city?" Ward continued. *Not long!* cried out the crowd. "If the Lord will strike down the Israelites, His chosen people, by the thousands, why should He not destroy all of York?" *Yea, He should! He should!* cried the crowd. "Is not this terrible summer a sign of things to come? Does our great God not warn us of the fires of hell?" *He does, He does!*

Rebecca's presence on the bridge and her proximity to Ward made me suspect that she had brought him to York. I knew that she had seen the advantage of throwing in her lot with the godly, so it would not be out of character, and I could not help being curious as to what her plan might be. Edward sincerely believed that a preacher like Ward might do some good, but Rebecca had never concerned herself with the good of the city. Every one of her actions was intended either to advance her place in the city or to destroy one of her enemies. If she had made Ward her creature, it must have been to some malefic end.

I was struggling back through the crowd in search of Hannah when I heard Ward shouting "Amen! Amen!" and his hearers took up the cry. To my relief, the crowd quickly thinned and I saw Hannah on the north side of the bridge, trying to find me among the multitude. Ward was between us, now standing at the center of a small circle. He had been joined by two women and two men. One man I took to be Ward's son—he was dressed similarly, held a Bible identical to Ward's, and had very nearly the same visage. The other man was an entirely different creature, standing a full head taller than anyone around him, with shoulders as broad as two men's. He stared wide-eyed over the crowd with what seemed to be the beginnings of a snarl on his lips. Those crossing the bridge gave him a wide berth.

The women with Ward seemed to be his wife and daughter, for the older one took his hands when they met and embraced him warmly. She was nearly as tall as Ward, with a powerful body and a barrel chest that she used to clear the way before her. The younger woman was the one whom James Hooke had found so enticing, and she was a mirror of her mother, tall and strong. James appeared at the girl's side, gazing at her face with the same rapt attention he'd given her father while he preached. She greeted him with a smile, and James turned such a bright shade of crimson that I feared he would faint. That certainly added a new wrinkle to things—did Rebecca know of her son's fascination with the girl? Or was that somehow a part of her scheme?

I turned away before James saw me—not that he would with the girl there—and found my way to Hannah. When we reached my house, we found a note from Martha: *Prudence Hewley in St. Wilfrid's parish has begun her travail. Her maidservant said it is early yet. I went to her with your medicines and birthing stool. I will tell the gossips to expect you this evening.*

"Good girl," I said and went up the stairs to change into a dress appropriate for the work that lay ahead.

Eli Hewley opened the door as soon as I knocked, and I stepped into the small room that served as both a parlor and a second bedchamber. A handful of men had settled in to await the arrival of the child, and all seemed to be in good spirits. Eli worked as a glover and did well for himself, but his family nevertheless occupied the same two rooms they had when I'd delivered Prudence of a baby girl eighteen months before. The child now lay sleeping in Eli's arms.

"Your deputy says that everything is proceeding apace," he whispered. "She seems a capable girl."

"She will make a fine midwife," I said. "Prudence has been in good hands." I ducked through a low doorway and into Prudence's birthing chamber. The size of the room meant that only a handful of gossips could assist in her travail, and they sat on the bed or stood talking quietly. I found Prudence pacing the room, her arm around Martha's shoulders. She seemed completely at ease with her travail; thus far, Martha had handled everything perfectly.

After greeting the women, I laid Prudence back on her bed so I could better examine her privities. While Martha could prepare Prudence for her travail and manage the gossips, a deputy could never lay hands on the mother; that was the midwife's domain. Thankfully, the child lay with his head down, and while he was still several hours from being born, all seemed to be in order. I stood, then helped Prudence back to her feet so she could continue to walk the room. "Is the child still kicking?" I asked.

"As if he wants out through my navel." She laughed. "He'll be a lively one, that's for sure."

And so he was, welcoming the dawn with cries that put the most audacious roost-cock to shame. The birth went so smoothly, Martha and I could find little to discuss as we walked home, so I told her of my suspicions about Rebecca Hooke and Hezekiah Ward.

"Why would she want to bring a hot gospeller such as him to York?" Martha asked. "I was surprised when James turned godly, but surely Rebecca hasn't as well."

"Not in her heart," I replied. "But Ward can attract a crowd, and Edward said that he preached outside the Angel and frightened away some of the guests. If she suggested he preach against one of York's citizens, he'd find many who would listen. There's no doubt that she's got something in mind, and she certainly needs watching." When Martha and I neared home, the sun had only begun to scorch its way across the morning sky, but as we walked down Petergate we could already feel its searing heat on our faces.

"Jesus," Martha said. "God's got it in for us again today. Probably because we missed the sermon on Sunday. I knew I'd regret it." Martha paused. "Do you think the preachers are right about that? If we go to church this Sunday, will God send rain?" I refused to answer so impudent a question. "I'd make that deal," Martha continued. "But if He were to accept it, He'd be a bit of a dupe, wouldn't He?"

Since I'd taken her on as my servant, I'd tried to convince Martha to keep such irreverent thoughts to herself. In the past I might have beaten her for such words, but the loss of my children had robbed me of my belief in a loving God who cared for His earthly children. Michael and Birdy had certainly committed no crimes against Him, and while I sometimes fell into the sin of pride, the slaughter of my children seemed a high price to pay for such small offenses. Some nights I prayed for God's mercy, and asked Him to lead me back into the comfortable faith of my youth, but thus far He'd not seen fit to grant my petition. Until He did, the most I could do in response to Martha's blasphemous words was beg her to be discreet, particularly around Edward and Joseph.

We'd turned off of Stonegate when not ten feet before us, a sow stumbled out of an alley and turned toward us. Her mouth hung open and she swung her snout from side to side as if in desperate search of water. She stopped and fell to her side before her entire body began to convulse most terribly and she voided her bowels onto the cobblestones. Martha and I stared in wonder at the terrible sight. "She died of thirst," Martha said at last. "I saw it happen once when I was a child. It's not something you forget." We gave the sow a wide berth and walked the last few steps to my door. That night I dreamed of a blazing sun and dying pigs.

The next morning I awoke to find Hannah at my door. "What is it?" I asked, trying to pull myself awake.

"Mr. Hodgson is here, my lady," she said. "He says he must speak to you."

"Edward?" I asked. He rarely visited, and the news was never good when he did.

"No, my lady. It's Joseph. He won't say what it is, but he seems serious."

"Well, that is his nature, isn't it?" I said. "Tell him I'll be down after I dress. And send Martha up to help me."

I found Joseph sitting in the parlor, a glass of barley water next to him, apparently untouched. When I entered, he stood.

"Aunt Bridget, my father needs you right away."

"What is it about?" I asked.

"I cannot say, but he seems upset," he replied.

"Where are we going?"

"St. John Hungate. He's meeting us there."

St. John's was one of the poorest parishes in the city, and I knew it passably from my work with the city's paupers.

"Wait here. I'll summon Martha."

"He said you should come alone," Joseph said.

"I'll bring her," I said. "If it's a matter important enough to involve your father, I might need her assistance." After a moment's consideration, Joseph nodded. I found Martha in the kitchen and told her that Edward had called for us.

"Will we need the birthing stool?" Martha asked. The city sometimes called on midwives to deliver bastards, and it seemed possible that this might be why Edward had summoned us. I looked at Joseph and he shrugged his shoulders.

"I don't know. He refused to say. He only told me to find you as quickly as I could."

"Bring both the stool and my valise," I said to Martha. "It is better to have them and not to need them."

A few minutes later, Martha returned with my baggage and the three of us started east toward St. John's with Joseph in the lead. "If it's a birth, who could it be?" Martha asked. "I've not heard of any singlewomen so far along."

"I told you, my father wouldn't say," Joseph replied, his aggravation showing.

I could tell that Martha shared my frustration. We were so often privy to the city's secrets that we could not help worrying when one escaped our notice. Either we had been remiss in our duties, or something more awful than an ordinary bastard birth had taken place. As we walked toward Coneystreet, I tried to imagine what turn of events would require such a degree of secrecy. A dangerous birth or a mother's death seemed the most likely explanation. Martha gave voice to my thoughts.

"If it's a birth, why didn't your brother-in-law insist we bring the stool?" Martha asked. "It must be something worse." I realized that Martha was right; visions of blood swam before me, and I felt my stomach churn. Had a midwife tried to remove a dead child with instruments and killed the mother, too? Edward could easily have been called in such an instance, and he would need a midwife to examine the corpse. I hoped that this wasn't the case.

We turned down a narrow street that wound its way into the bowels of Hungate parish. Many of the tiny cottages seemed on the verge of collapse, and small children peered at us through open windows, their eyes hollowed by hunger and a lifetime of want. I wondered if I had delivered any of them, and such a thought further darkened my mood. Joseph turned down an alley so small that I might have otherwise missed it. A man I had never seen before waved to Joseph when he saw us, and I knew we'd reached our destination.

I looked closely at the stranger as we approached. His clothes were plain but of good quality and covered a compact, powerful frame. He had cut his hair short in the style of Parliament-men, but even without this I would have guessed that he was a soldier. To my surprise, he and Joseph embraced when they met. When they did, I noticed that the stranger's left hand had only two fingers and a thumb. The other two, and much of the hand along with it, had been cut clean off.

"Aunt Bridget," Joseph said. "This is Mark Preston. We fought together at Marston Moor."

"And in many battles before that," Preston added with a broad grin. "But Marston Moor was my last at Mr. Hodgson's side."

A shiver passed through me when he continued to smile even as he held up his ruined hand for us to see. I glanced down at his belt and saw a long dagger hanging on his right side.

"I can still hold my own with a knife," he said when he noticed this. "It was loading the pistols that was a problem." He'd stopped smiling and now stared at me, daring me to contradict his claim.

"After Mark left the army, I recommended him to my father," Joseph said. "I thought he would be a useful man to have in his household." Preston's smile returned—still without humor—as he acknowledged Joseph's compliment.

"I have no doubt that he is," I murmured. I glanced at Martha and saw her eyeing Preston warily. It seemed that he had unnerved her as much as he had me. Preston turned and knocked on the door behind him.

While we waited, I looked over the tenement to which Joseph had brought us. At one time it had been a comfortable house, but it had been divided into several smaller dwellings, which were rented to York's poorer residents. They, of course, had no need to maintain the building, so the plaster walls had taken on a grayish color and begun to crack in many places. The building itself was no larger than any of its neighbors—I guessed that each dwelling had one room; two at the most. The horn windows would have allowed in little light under the best of circumstances, but a red cloth appeared to have been hung up inside to cover the windows. This struck me as very strange, and I tried to peer through. Whoever had covered them up had done a thorough job; I could see nothing.

After a moment the door cracked open. Edward slipped out and closed it behind him. I don't think I'd ever seen him so distraught, so pale, even after the deaths of his wives. He took a deep breath before he spoke.

"Thank you for coming so quickly, Lady Bridget," he said. He glanced briefly at Martha, but did not object to her presence. "Joseph," he continued. "Go to the Lord Mayor, and tell him I must see him this afternoon. I will be there by two o'clock." Joseph nodded, bade us farewell, and disappeared toward the city center.

"I cannot find words to describe what has happened here." Edward paused, gathering his thoughts, seeking the right phrase. "There has been a murder. Two murders. Terrible crimes. The blood is everywhere. I will tell you now that the scene is one that will haunt you until your death. If you do not wish to come inside, I will not insist. I can only ask for your help."

Martha and I glanced at each other nervously. We'd each been in blood up to our elbows, and Edward knew it. Whatever horrors the house contained must have been jarring indeed. I looked at Edward, struck again by his deathlike pallor.

"I'll help," I whispered. Martha nodded her assent. Together we ducked through the front door and into hell itself.

Chapter 4

As soon as we stepped into the doorway, the heat from inside poured over us. Whoever had closed the windows had turned the small house into an oven. While the curtains kept out prying eyes, they were less effective against the sun's fury: the room glowed with a crimson light, as if everything inside had been bathed in blood.

On the surface, the room seemed similar to many others I'd entered as a midwife. It served as both kitchen and parlor, with a dining table against one wall, a narrow bed against the other, and a hearth for cooking in the corner. But it was also clear that something terrible had happened here. An iron cooking pot lay on its side with the remnants of some uneaten meal spilling into the ashes of a small fire, and a straw mattress lay half on and half off the bed. The bed frame had been broken down the middle. As I entered the room, I nearly stepped on an iron poker lying on the floor. The handle was bent and it appeared to have dried blood on the end.

"The bodies are in the back room," Edward murmured, as if afraid to wake someone.

The second room of the house was smaller than the first—it had served as a bedchamber, but now it seemed like nothing so much as a slaughterhouse. Blood covered the uneven wood floor, a thin coating in some places, but pooled so deeply in others that it would take hours to dry. As I slowly raised my eyes to the bed, horror welled up and a scream clawed to escape my throat. Next to me, Martha gasped and leaned against the doorway to steady herself. Even Edward, who'd already seen the carnage, looked away. I heard a high wheezing sound and realized that it was my own strangled cry as I tried to comprehend the terrible scene before me.

Two figures lay upon the bed in a gruesome imitation of carnal copulation, a man, breeches pulled down to reveal ghostly white buttocks, sprawled on top of a woman; her legs were splayed open and her skirts pulled up above her knees. I could not see the man's face for it was buried in the nape of the woman's neck, but it was clear that she had suffered terribly before she died. Her eyes bulged in their sockets, more bloodshot than I'd ever seen. In life they must have been a striking blue, but now the color had faded and they stared vacantly at the ceiling. Her lips were drawn back from her teeth in a horrible grimace, and her killer had stuffed her mouth with a cloth of some sort, no doubt to silence her cries. Her wrists were bound and tied to the bedstead above her head. Because of the man on top of her, I could not see any wound, but unspeakable amounts of blood had poured from the bed onto the floor.

I closed my eyes, and leaned against the wall as waves of nausea roiled within me. I tried to drive away the image I'd just seen, but I could feel the woman's blood seeping between my eyelids, forcing its way into my imagination. I took a deep breath in the hope of steadying myself, but the choking scent of blood and the room's suffocating heat were too much. As my stomach rebelled, I fled the room. I threw myself against the front door and stumbled into the street. Fear and revulsion had so overcome me that I ran headlong into Mark Preston, who still stood guard at the door. He moved not an inch when I hit him, and it was I who crashed to the ground. He smiled mirthlessly when he looked down at me.

"Not a pretty sight in there, eh, my lady?" he said, extending his hand. "I sometimes forget that we soldiers have seen and done things that the rest of you cannot begin to imagine." I extended my hand, but instead he seized my forearm and—without any visible effort—hauled me to my feet. If he had done this in order to demonstrate his strength, he succeeded, for that night I had a bruise where he'd grabbed me. I had no doubt that even though he'd lost two fingers, he would have no trouble throttling a man if he so chose.

Before I had the opportunity to respond, Martha and Edward joined me. I was relieved to see that they were no less affected than I. Martha had seen terrible things in her time, yet even she had paled, and her hands shook as she wiped her palms on her apron.

"What in God's name happened in there?" I asked. I could hear my voice shaking.

Edward shook his head slowly. "We don't know much yet—we only found the bodies about an hour ago. When the neighbor came out this morning, he saw the door was open. He went in to see if anything was wrong, and found them there. He summoned a constable, who sent for me."

"Who are they?"

"The neighbor says her name is Jennet Porter. He heard someone crashing around last night, but said it wasn't too unusual." I looked at him, confused. "She was a whore. Sometimes the men she brought here treated her badly. If they became too violent, a neighbor would intervene, but usually they quieted down."

"How long has she been in York?" I asked. "I've never seen her before." It was not uncommon for one of the city's whores to call on me for aid in case of a difficult birth, and over time their faces became familiar.

"She just took the house a month ago, when another whore moved on," Edward said. "The building is owned by Helen Wright."

"Ah," I said, as some of the pieces came together.

"Ah?" asked Martha. "Who is Helen Wright?"

"She is one of the city's most notorious bawds," I explained. "She has a hand in satisfying every lewd appetite in York. God knows how many tenements she rents to women like Jennet."

"I've known such women," Martha replied. "They make a comfortable living from such work." Edward looked at her quizzically and I hurried to change the subject.

"Who is the dead man?" I asked.

"We don't know. I imagine he's a brotheller. What other reason could he have for being here? I'd have recognized him if he were a citizen, and he had neither letters nor a notebook with him, so it may be some time before we discover his name."

I looked down and saw that the soles of Edward's boots were rimmed with blood. My stomach clenched once again and threatened to empty itself in the street. I settled on my haunches and put my head in my hands. I felt a hand on my arm, but did not look up, strangely afraid it might be Mark's.

"I'll be fine," I said. "It's the heat." While the heat didn't make things easier, the sight of the two bodies would have been no less shocking in midwinter. After a moment I stood on my own and looked into Edward's face. "There. I'm better."

"Mr. Hodgson," Martha said. "Why have you brought us

here?" I didn't know if she was trying to draw Edward's attention away from me, but I was grateful all the same.

"You know the whores, and I need the two of you to question them. They might have seen or heard something."

"Why don't you send Joseph?" I asked, though I knew the answer. The city's governors, and Joseph in particular, had hounded York's sinners, especially the whores, without a shred of mercy. If a common doxie saw a constable coming her way, she'd run for her life rather than stay and talk to him. Edward ignored my question.

"Also, it would help if we heard what Helen Wright has to say," he said. "She'll not talk to a constable if she can help it, but she might be willing to talk to you." I nodded. "I also need you—both of you—to be discreet. It is inevitable that people will hear that murders have occurred, but if the citizens knew the horror of what happened here, it would put the city in an uproar."

"I'll help, of course," I said. "Is that all?"

"I also need you to inspect the whore's body and give your opinion of what happened to her."

Though I'd expected he would ask this, Edward's request weighed on me just the same. This was the darker side of service as a midwife. Most of our labor went into delivering mothers and infants, but constables and Justices also called upon us in more desperate situations. Midwives bore the burden of examining the wasted bodies of children who had been bewitched, and those of infants left to die under a haystack. On this day it was a slattern who had been stabbed to death. Such work was not why I or any woman became a midwife, but it was my duty. I gathered myself for the gruesome task ahead.

"Very well," I said. Edward nodded his thanks.

"Go ahead and start your search," he said. "I'll be in momentarily." He turned to Mark and spoke to him in low tones.

I took a deep breath, and looked at Martha. She nodded and the two of us went back into the house. I hoped that I would be able to control myself this time. When we entered the room, I was careful not to look too closely at the bodies; even so, I could not avoid signs of the carnage. There was the blood on the floor, of course, but somehow the subtle signs were more even disturbing: the bloody handprint on the wall, another spot where Jennet or the man had raked blood-soaked fingers, and—most horrible of all—a tuft of hair, ripped from her head, lying in a pool of blood. We began to look around the room. I had no idea what we hoped to find—all I could see was blood.

Martha crouched over a chest in the corner and examined the small lock that secured it. "If it were a better lock, I might need my tools," she said. "But in this case a couple of pins ought to do it." She hunched over the chest and after a few minutes, the lock clicked open. Martha opened the chest and sorted through its contents. "Nothing but clothes," she said. "Poor ones at that."

When I looked back at the bodies, my eyes came to rest on Jennet's hand. This time I noticed that she held a small piece of paper. "Martha," I said, and reached down to get it. She peered over my shoulder as I unrolled the paper. Printed in a plain hand was *Num. 25:8*.

"What is it?" Martha asked.

"It's a Bible verse," I said. "Numbers, chapter twenty-five, verse eight."

"What does it mean?"

"If it's Numbers, it's during the Israelites' time in the wilderness," I said. "But what part, I don't know." While I read the Bible regularly, I favored the loving God of the Gospels to the wrathful deity of the Old Testament. I looked about the room, but saw no books at all, which puzzled me.

Martha noticed the same thing. "If she doesn't own a Bible, why is she carrying about a verse such as that?"

"And could she even read?" I asked. Not many poor country girls could. "And why did she die with that particular verse clutched in her hand?" I tucked the paper into my apron. "We'll see what this means when we get home."

We heard the door to the house open, and Edward joined us in the bedchamber.

"Now to the bodies," he said.

"We should separate them first," I ventured as we crossed the room. It quickly became clear that there would be no avoiding the pools of blood that lay especially thick at the foot of the bed.

"Let's lift him up and roll him onto his back," Edward suggested. "I'll take his shoulders." I took a deep breath and seized the man's legs and we turned him over. Now the two corpses lay side by side and we got our first look at the man's face. He was older than I'd expected, perhaps forty. I stepped closer to examine his wounds. The left side of his head had suffered a grievous blow—perhaps more than one. The killer had also cut the poor man's throat, and there was a single stab wound in his belly.

"He was alive when his throat was cut," I said, pointing to the blood beneath that end of the bed. "Else he'd not have bled so much." Edward and Martha nodded in agreement. My eyes traveled down his body and I saw that his hand was closed in a fist. I reached down and pulled the fingers open. A small piece of paper sat nestled in the palm of his hand. I heard a sharp intake of breath, and knew that Martha had seen it, too. I picked it up: *Rev. 2:14*. I showed it to her.

"Revelations, chapter two, verse fourteen," I said.

"What do you mean?" Edward asked.

"He was holding this in his hand," I said, handing him the

piece of paper. His brow furrowed as he read. I thought I saw a flicker of recognition but could not be sure. "Jennet was holding one as well." I gave him the other slip of paper. I had known Edward for years, and I could tell he saw a meaning in the verses that had escaped me.

"They both held the papers?" he said. "Are you sure? You didn't find one on the floor?"

"Jennet's hand was slightly open, but it was in her palm," I said.

"If it had been on the floor, it would have blood on it," Martha added.

"The killer must have put the papers there after they died," I said. We both looked at Edward, awaiting his reaction. I could see the tension on his face. This development troubled him considerably.

"Like everything else, you'll keep this to yourselves," he said. "We don't know what this means, and I'll not have shop women spreading gossip." Martha and I nodded. There could be no mistaking how serious Edward was about this. "Let us examine the bodies," Edward continued.

I could not help being thankful for the cloth covering the windows, for I do not think I could have tolerated seeing the bodies in full daylight. The three of us bent over the man, squinting at his head. To my surprise, Martha took the lead as if she'd been examining corpses all her life.

"What shall we call him?" Martha asked.

I looked at her in astonishment. "Whatever do you mean?"

"We have to call him something," she replied. "Jennet has a name. Shouldn't he? 'Mr. Jones,' perhaps?"

Edward gazed at her in amazement. "If you must," he said at last. I could only shake my head.

"The killer hit Mr. Jones on the side of the head," she said, gently combing her fingers through his hair. "Look, he did it more than once. You can see the marks in his skull." She pointed to three distinct wounds, each one no wider than a finger.

"Probably the poker from the other room," I volunteered.

"Yes, that might be it," she said. "Could you get it?"

Well, I asked for that, I thought. I returned to the parlor and retrieved the poker. After all the blood in the bedchamber, the smear on the end of the poker seemed almost inconsequential. I handed the poker to Edward, who placed the end in the wound.

"Yes, that's it," Martha said. "Well done."

Edward straightened up, crossed to the doorway, and looked back and forth between the kitchen and the bedchamber. "So Jennet and . . . Mr. Jones were in here on the bed, and the killer came in through the front door."

"Mr. Jones leaped up, and ran to the door, hoping to escape," I said. "Or perhaps in the hope of securing the door."

"But he was too late," Martha said. "The murderer got in the house."

"Then he picked up the poker," I said, "and hit . . . Mr. Jones in the head."

"Mr. Jones fell back, breaking the bed frame," Edward concluded. "That all makes sense."

"But then what?" Martha asked. "The killer didn't cut his throat in there. He took the body into the bedchamber and *then* did it." The three of us looked about the room in search of answers. What *had* the killer done to them, and why?

We crossed the room and stood over the bodies as if they would stand up and speak. The front of Mr. Jones's shirt was soaked with blood, which seemed to have flowed more from the wound to his throat than from the one in his belly. Jennet's bodice was similarly stained, which was hardly surprising, given that he'd been lying on top of her. But when I looked more closely, I realized something was missing.

"What killed her?" I asked. Martha reached down and lifted Jennet's chin. Her neck was covered in blood, but bore no marks of violence.

"Here," she said, pointing to Jennet's stomach. She had been stabbed once.

Edward peered at the wound. "This didn't kill her," he said. "It might have eventually, but it would have taken days." He gazed at her body, no less puzzled than I was.

I looked down at Jennet's skirts and noticed that they, too, were soaked with blood. I pointed it out to Martha.

"Could it be her monthly courses?" Edward asked. Martha looked at him as if he were an idiot but held her tongue. The skirts were soaked through.

"It's unlikely she would bleed so much," I said with as much patience as I could muster. To think the man had been married twice! "I should examine her."

I reached down and closed Jennet's eyes for the last time. She did not deserve to see this final violation of her body. Full of trepidation, I pulled up Jennet's skirts. I stared at her privities, unable to comprehend the horror before me. I tried to speak, but found no ready words. Rather I pointed, and Edward and Martha came to look. The murderer had cut deeply into both her thighs, slashing again and again until he found an artery, and she'd bled to death from there. Uncontent with mere murder, the killer also cut into her privities, disfiguring them with a viciousness that could not fail to astound. What fury drove the killer to such lengths? If Jennet had been alive when the killer had done this, the pain would have driven her mad. I pulled her skirts down, covering the bloody scene as best I could.

"The murderer cut her and then threw them together," I said.

"They lay together and bled to death," said Edward. He took a deep breath and made a decision. "Wipe your hands before you go. I'll make sure they get a Christian burial."

I looked at him in shock. "That is all? You are dismissing us?" I cried.

"There is nothing else to be done. We know what happened to these poor souls. I brought you here for your keen eyes and mind, and I was right to do so. It is now the city's responsibility to find the murderer and see him hanged. And I'll remind you to keep to yourselves everything you saw here today."

"What about questioning the whores? What of Helen Wright? That was part of why you brought me here, was it not?"

"The situation has changed," he said. "That will not be necessary." I knew Edward was not telling me the entire truth.

"You're not even going to raise the hue and cry, are you?" I asked. "What is your plan?"

He took my arm and guided me toward the door, trusting that Martha would follow. I pulled free and stopped to look him in the eye.

"Edward, I can tell that you are hiding something from us. Do you remember what happened the last time you kept secrets from me in a matter such as this?" I knew he needed no reminder, for it nearly had resulted in the death of a guiltless soul. He returned my stare and refused to answer my question.

"You must go," he insisted. "Anything I tell you now would be mere gossip. I must learn more." When I hesitated he took my hands and looked me in the eyes. "Lady Bridget, please. I want to see whoever did this hanged as much as you do. Not to do so would be a terrible injustice and would leave a stain on York, on my family's city."

I considered Edward's words, and they rang true. He loved York more than anyone I knew, and while I did not understand what he intended to do, I knew he would not rest until he'd found the murderer.

"I'm trusting you," I said, giving his hands a squeeze. He nodded his thanks.

Martha and I ducked back through the low door and into the street. Mark Preston still stood watch, and when we came out, he slipped inside, closing the door behind him. God only knew how they would get the bodies out of the house and into a church-yard without attracting all the neighbors, but that was Edward's problem now and I had the uneasy feeling that Mark was the right man for such work.

We walked in silence until we reached Petergate, which would take us home. I looked down the street toward the Minster, at the striped awnings, the crowds of buyers, sellers, and passersby haggling, laughing, and arguing, all oblivious to the horror that lay just a few yards away.

"That is all?" Martha asked. "We are just going to walk away from those bodies? From whoever did that?"

"That would be the prudent thing to do, don't you think?" I replied evenly.

Martha understood my meaning and smiled. "But you don't plan to take the prudent course."

"You are as good a judge of the living as you are of the dead, Martha," I said. "I have no intention of abandoning Jennet or Mr. Jones after all they have suffered." I knew that Edward would be

furious if he knew what I intended, but I had proven myself useful in the past, even in the face of his objections. I was not his
maidservant, and would not act like it. "Come, we will see if my
Bible can help us understand those verses."

Chapter 5

When Martha and I reached home, we found an unexpected but entirely welcome guest in the parlor. The moment the door closed behind us, a small and very dirty boy flew to our side and wrapped his arms around Martha's waist and then my own.

"Martha! Lady Hodgson!" he cried.

"Tree!" I replied, and tried to scoop him into my arms. The boy wriggled to escape—he'd often told me that holding was for babies and he was *eight*—but I held him tight.

Tree was the bastard son of a woman who had died while imprisoned in York Castle, and he'd been taken in by the jailor, Samuel Short. I'd met Tree and Samuel the year before, and in the months since, Tree and I had become close. Samuel was a fine guardian, but Tree lacked a mother and I think he sought one in me. He still called the Castle home, but visited me regularly, sometimes just for a meal, sometimes for a few days at a time. To my sorrow, the summer's heat had driven Tree to spend more nights at the Castle, which he said was not so hot. While I knew that others in the city suffered far worse from the cursed weather, I counted this the cruelest blow that God had dealt to me, for I missed him sorely. I stroked the boy's hair, and reflected on my own lost children, and on Tree's ability to soothe the pain just a little. While we'd never said as much, Tree and I needed each other.

"Can we play at dice?" Tree asked once he'd freed himself from my embrace. "Samuel has been teaching me how to coz—" Tree stopped himself. "He's teaching me how to win."

"Cozen, eh?" Martha said in mock horror. From her former life, she knew a thing or two about cheating at both dice and cards, and said that Tree had become quite good at it.

"Well, I wouldn't take your money," Tree replied. "It would be just for fun."

Hannah bustled in from the kitchen. "I've got some bread just out of the oven," she announced. "Though in this heat, the rising was like nothing I've seen. I have no idea how it will be." Tree's eyes lit up at the prospect of fresh bread, and he dashed into the kitchen. I took Hannah by the arm.

"Keep him with you for the moment," I said. "We have some business to discuss that is not fit for a child's ears." Hannah nodded and followed Tree. I then sent Martha for some white wine—which we both needed after the afternoon's work—and she joined me in the parlor.

"Let us look to the verses first," I said. I pulled down my Great Bible.

"Numbers, chapter twenty-five, verse eight," Martha said from memory.

"Here we are," I said. "The Israelites are still in the wilderness, and the Lord has afflicted them with a plague because they have *begun to commit whoredom with the daughters of Moab.*"

"Whoredom?" murmured Martha. "Interesting."

I nodded and continued reading. "*And Moses said unto the Judges of*

Israel, slay ye every one his men, that were joined unto Baal-Peor." I ran my finger along the text. "One of the Israelites brought a Midian whore back to the camp. When another saw this, he picked up a javelin. *He went into the tent, and thrust both of them through, the man of Israel, and the woman, through her belly: so the plague was stayed from the children of Israel."* By the time I reached the end of the passage, my voice had fallen to a whisper.

"This Israelite killed two people because they were guilty of whoredom?" Martha asked.

"He stabbed them through the belly," I said.

"Just as Jennet and Mr. Jones were stabbed."

I nodded. "And then God lifted the plague."

"The murders were made to look like a story from the Bible?" Martha asked, still unable to believe what we'd found. "He slaughtered Jennet and that poor man as a part of a play?"

I nodded again, struck dumb by our discovery. I had met murderers before, and not just poor girls who had abandoned their infants in a churchyard, but truly evil people who had killed for money or merely to protect their reputations. But even the worst of them had motives I could comprehend: greed, revenge, anger. Having seen all this, the idea of killing someone in twisted homage to an obscure Biblical verse seemed to be madness. Did the murderer believe that killing Jennet would inspire God to lift the terrible heat that lay upon the city?

"My God," Martha said softly, giving voice to my own thoughts. "Who is this man?"

I shook my head to clear it of the image that the passage had painted in my mind. "Let us look to the other verse," I said, turning to the end of the Bible. "Revelations, chapter two, verse fourteen. Here, God is condemning the men of Pergamon *who taught Balac to eat things sacrificed unto idols, and to commit whoredom."*

Martha furrowed her brow. "What does that mean? Who is Balac?"

"I don't know," I admitted. "But I don't think that is the point. There's more: *Repent, or else I will come unto thee quickly, and will fight against you with the sword of my mouth.*" Martha looked at me and shook her head in confusion. I reread the passage.

"Both passages condemn the sin of whoredom," I said. "In Numbers, God lifts the plague when the Israelites kill the whore and the man who brought her to the camp. In Revelations, God renews His threat against those who taught Balac to commit whoredom."

"God demands that those who commit whoredom be put to the sword?" Martha asked.

I nodded.

"So the murderer thinks he is doing God's work?" Martha asked, her voice rising. "And you wonder why I resist going to church?"

I chose not to answer her challenge, for I had no ready response: the killer had indeed fashioned his crime after passages in the Bible.

"Lady Bridget," Martha said after a moment. "Why did Mr. Hodgson react so strangely when he saw these passages?"

I considered the question for a moment. "He must have recognized them, or at least he recognized what they meant," I said. "And he's afraid that the killer comes from the godly faction."

Martha nodded. "I'd not be surprised. None know the Bible so well as them." Her tone made clear her disdain for those who held such beliefs.

"Mr. Hodgson is in that faction," I said testily. "And there is no need to paint all the godly with that bloody brush." I paused. "But you are not wrong. If the killer does come from the godly, it would besmirch them all. Edward would want him hanged quickly and quietly."

"What do we do now?" Martha asked. "We can't very well ask all the city's Puritans if they murdered Jennet and her whore-monger."

"We'll let Edward worry about the godly. Tomorrow we will talk to the other whores and find out who knew Jennet. Perhaps one of them saw her last night."

"What will you say if your brother-in-law finds out?" Martha asked. "He said we are not to trouble ourselves with this crime."

"I'll not abandon the search for Jennet's murderer simply because Edward asked me to," I replied. "She deserves more. Besides, the whores and the constables are not on good terms, and we will be discreet."

Martha smiled a little. I think she enjoyed the prospect of disobeying Edward.

Tree joined us for supper, providing a welcome diversion from that day's bloody business, but all too soon he returned to the Castle. After he left, I gazed out the back window of my house. The sun hung low in the sky, and bathed my small garden in a red light that reminded me of nothing so much as Jennet's blood-spattered chamber. Even this late in the day, I could feel the searing heat as if I were standing in a smithy rather than in my own home.

I retired to my chamber earlier than usual, so I could reflect on the day's events. I closed my eyes and let all the horror of the day wash over me—I knew that if I did not, Jennet and Mr. Jones would haunt my dreams. I tried to imagine what had brought Jennet to her awful end. I knew many of the city's doxies, of course. I provided advice and medicines to help them avoid becoming pregnant, and I tended them when their efforts failed. Some were maids who had fallen into whoring when the world turned its back on them; for these women I felt sympathy. Other whores seemed wholly unredeemable, not caring if they became pregnant, and then seeking medicines to destroy the children in their wombs. These I refused to help. If Jennet was new to the city, she had likely come to York in the hope of finding work as a servant but her luck or money had run out. Did she have family who did not yet know of her fate? Would they ever find out? I imagined a mother's weather-beaten face as she stood on the northern moors, gazing toward the city, wondering what had become of her daughter.

I thought too of Mr. Jones—or whoever the poor man was. He was too old for his whoring to be mere sport and that galled me. He likely had a wife and children. Had he abandoned them for a night with a whore? Did he think of them as he lay dying? Or only of himself and his horrible death? If he was not from the city, we might never know his name, and his family, too, might never know of his fate. He would simply have disappeared.

I also tried to imagine the killer himself. How had his brain become so fevered as to think that God demanded such a bloody reprisal for sin? How had he chosen his victims? I pictured him waiting outside an alehouse, following Jennet and Mr. Jones to her house, and then forcing the door open. Mr. Jones would have been terrified of discovery, so he tried to run, only to be knocked senseless the moment he reached the door. Then what? Did the killer lecture his victims, or just go about his gruesome work? Did Jennet cry out? What strength must the killer have had to kill two people and then heave their bodies about as if they were dolls! Did the killer truly draw his strength from the mad belief that he was doing God's work? I had faced a savage killer before, but the demons that drove this murderer were of another order entirely. I prayed that he would be found and hanged quickly, for I could not believe that the blood he'd spilled that night had quenched his fury.

I awoke the next morning to a frantic pounding on my front door. I raced downstairs just as Will stumbled in, his chest heaving from the journey. He had the smell of old ale on him, but he seemed sober enough.

"Will, what is it?" I cried as soon as he entered.

"Have you read this pamphlet?" He handed me a single sheet of paper. At first glance, I took it to be a ballad or a jest, but as I read it became clear that merriment was far from the author's mind.

"Martha," I called out. "You should see this."

Martha hurried in, drying her hands on her apron. I showed her the title of the sheet. *God's Terrible Justice in York.* Her eyes widened as she read. "My God," she gasped. "Surely it's not about Jennet. So soon? How?"

To answer her question, I read from the pamphlet. *"The Lord God visited his terrible justice on the city of York, as a common whore and her whoremaster died a monstrous but much deserved death last night."*

"So you know about the murders?" Will asked.

"Of course," I answered. "Your father asked me to examine the bodies. Didn't he send you here with this?"

"No," Will spat. "I overheard him telling Joseph that someone had killed a doxy, and I guessed that he would call you. When I asked what had happened, he said it was city business and I ought not concern myself."

I could hear the anger and pain in Will's voice and marveled at what Edward's neglect had begat in his son.

"Will . . ." I said.

"That's not the worst of it," Will continued. I could see his knuckles whiten as he tightened his grip on his cane. "I had to beg the details from a new servant, the three-fingered dog that followed Joseph home from the wars."

"Mark Preston," I said. "He was at the site of the murders."

"Then you know what pleasure he took from seeing me grovel."

I imagined the shame Will must have felt at having to abase himself before one of his father's servants. I resolved to speak with Edward about how he treated Will. I had done so before to no great effect, but when I saw the anger in Will's face, I knew I could not abandon the fight.

"Will, where did the pamphlet come from?" Martha asked. She put her hand on Will's arm in the hope of comforting him and it seemed to help. I said a prayer of thanks that she'd found a way to steer the conversation away from Will's latest humiliation.

"We don't know," Will said. "My father is furious. He sent Joseph to arrest the printer, so we should find out soon enough. But I thought you should see it as soon as possible."

I nodded and continued reading the pamphlet aloud. *"The principal cause for God's punishment was for the terrifying of all such whores and whoremongers so they might be assured that they could not sin secretly. They shall be discovered and punished as God sees fit. The bodies of these wretches died last night, but God will see that their souls suffer eternally in easeless and endless flames of fire and brimstone."*

I stopped for a moment, scrambling to remember where I'd heard those words before . . . *easeless and endless flames of fire and brimstone.* Then I remembered.

"The preacher!" I cried. "Hezekiah Ward. When I saw him on the bridge, he cried out for 'easeless and endless' punishments for whores and whoremongers."

"Then whoever wrote this pamphlet heard the sermon," Martha said. "He must have been in the crowd with you."

I continued to read, now more closely and with a greater sense of urgency. My eyes caught a note printed in the margin. *Num: 25:8.*

"Dear Lord," I said. "Will, how thoroughly did your father read this?"

"I don't know. He flew into a rage as soon as it arrived, and sent Joseph out. What is it?"

"This," I said, pointing to the note.

"Numbers, chapter twenty-five, verse eight?" Will asked. "What does that mean?"

"It's the same verse that the murderer put in Jennet's hand after he killed her," Martha said. "The murderer and the author must be the same man."

Without another word, the three of us rushed to the door.

As Martha, Will, and I hurried across Ouse Bridge toward Edward's home, I described for Will what we'd seen at Jennet's the previous day.

"And you think the murderer is also behind the pamphlet?" Will asked.

"He must be," Martha replied. "How else is it that the killer and the pamphleteer cited the same verse?"

We moved to the side of the street to make room for a carriage as it crossed the bridge to the north. When we reached Edward's home, his servant ushered us into his study immediately. He sat behind his desk, his face pale and drawn. He glanced at Martha and Will when they followed me in, but he did not question their presence.

"Lady Bridget," he said with forced cheerfulness. "What brings you to this side of the river?" I could tell that he hoped my visit was unrelated to the murders.

"We saw the pamphlet about Jennet Porter's murder," I said

without preamble. "The author used the same verse that the murderer placed in Jennet's hand."

Edward offered a thin smile. "Why am I not surprised you noticed? You'd have made a fine Justice of the Peace."

"I'm a better midwife and do far more good than any Justice," I replied. I was in no mood for his compliments.

He looked again at Will and Martha, before returning his attention to me. They'd proven themselves valuable in the past, and by letting them stay he admitted as much. But he would never say so in their presence.

"You knew I would recognize the verse," Edward said. "Why have you come?"

"There is more to it than just the verse," I said. "The pamphlet says that whores will suffer *easeless and endless flames of fire and brimstone*." I paused. "The day before the murder, I heard a sermon by Hezekiah Ward. He used exactly those words. Edward, the murderer and the pamphleteer are the same man, and he is one of Mr. Ward's followers. He is one of the godly."

Edward considered what I had said before he answered. "The murderer is a madman, that is clear enough," he replied at last. "But he is hardly one of the godly." He paused again, choosing his words carefully. "However, it is possible that a lunatic has sought refuge among Mr. Ward's people. If that is so, we must ensure that justice is swift and sure. It would be a terrible thing if good men were tarred by a lunatic's murderous actions."

Will laughed scornfully. "The only reason you want justice to be *swift and sure* is that half the Aldermen have wrapped their arms around Hezekiah Ward and preachers like him. And you are chief among them, aren't you? The last thing you want is for the murderer to splatter mud on your godly suit."

"Will, please," I said. "Now is not the time."

"Not the time to speak the truth, Aunt Bridget?" Will replied with a sneer. "You know as well as I do that he doesn't care about the murders. The man was a stranger to the city, and the woman just a whore. If anything, he believes that they received their just deserts." Will turned and addressed his father. "But you do care about power, don't you? The city is already chafing under your rule, for the people—the reprobate, you call them—prefer dicing to preaching. If the city learned that a Puritan had killed two people, and had done it in the name of God, all of York would turn against you."

"Will, stop," I said. "Please." I could see the color rising in Edward's cheeks, and knew that he would not tolerate much more of this lecture before lashing out at Will. But Will was in no condition to listen.

"You can no more force the people into goodness than you can hound me into sobriety," Will continued.

"The Lord used the whip to correct Israel, His chosen people," Edward replied through clenched teeth. I could see him struggling to control his wrath, and said a prayer that he would succeed. "It is what He demands of me and all who have authority over His people."

When I saw that Will was prepared to continue the argument, I tried to intervene, but someone else spoke before I could.

"Our father is right, brother," Joseph said. I turned in surprise, for I'd not heard him enter the room. "We can turn York into a city on a hill, set an example for all England to follow. Think of it: a city without drunkards and whores defiling their bodies and souls." He looked at me. "Aunt Bridget, can you imagine a city without masters getting their maidservants with child? Without bastard-bearers abandoning their children in privies or throwing them in the river? That is all we want." He spoke with such sincerity I wanted desperately to believe that so perfect a city was possible. After a moment I shook my head.

"I do not think the people will be so easily reformed," I replied. "Free use of stocks and whips would not have kept Jennet Porter from her whoredom. Such women fear hunger more than the lash, and men will always be slave to their passions." I paused and turned to Edward. "Have you considered the possibility that the murderer will kill again? If he believes he is doing the Lord's work, he will not stop."

"That is my fear," he said, nodding solemnly.

"Then Martha, Will, and I will do our best to stop him," I replied. Edward started to object, but I would not let him. "The whores will never speak to you or any of the constables. You need us."

Edward hesitated before nodding. "But talking to whores is all you will do," he said. "You will not disturb Mr. Ward or his people. And if you learn anything, you must tell me or Joseph."

I agreed. I had no intention of serving as one of Edward's beadles, but knew I could never persuade him to agree to anything more than this. It seemed that Martha, Will, and I would be working on our own, just as we had the year before.

"Joseph, have you brought the printer?" Edward asked.

"Better than that," Joseph replied. "We have the author."

Edward's eyes widened in surprise.

"Already? How?" Edward was clearly impressed by his son's efficiency.

"The printer led us straight to his door," Joseph said. "And the man doesn't deny it."

"Send him in," Edward said. "We will question him immediately." It seemed we were dismissed.

Will, Martha, and I followed Joseph into the entry hall. I

gasped aloud at the sight of the prisoner. He was the same giant of a man I'd seen with Hezekiah Ward after the sermon on Ouse Bridge, but he seemed even larger now that I found myself near him. He must have weighed nearly as much as the beadles together. His hands twisted and turned in the manacles, though I wondered if he could simply have broken the chains with one swift pull. My skin crawled as his small, black eyes slid over me before settling on Edward, who stood in the doorway. The prisoner radiated violence and malice in every way imaginable.

"You had your men bring me here?" he demanded of Edward.

"You wrote a pamphlet about a murder, and I will know how you heard of it," Edward replied.

"Will you imprison me for doing the Lord's work?" the stranger hissed. "What word in my book is not the truth? Were those two not sinners? Were they not struck down by the hand of God?"

Edward ignored the questions. "Take him to my study and sit him down," he said to the beadles. "And keep him in his seat." Edward followed the men into his study and closed the door behind him.

"What do you know about him?" I asked Joseph.

"He's John Stubb," Joseph said. "The printer said he brought the pamphlet last night, and demanded he print it immediately. Stubb let him print and sell however many copies he wanted, so long as he got a hundred. Stubb had only a few left when we found him. The rest are spread throughout the city."

"Who is he?" I asked. "He's not from York."

"He came here with Hezekiah Ward. He said he's been following Mr. Ward for six months now." Joseph paused. "It's strange—I knew Stubb a little when I was with Cromwell, but I never thought I'd see him again. He was a godly man then, but certainly not like this."

"How did he know about the murders?" I asked.

"I demanded that of him, but he refused to say. He said he wrote to glorify God, and would not answer to any man. I should attend my father," he said, and disappeared into Edward's study.

I looked at Will and raised an eyebrow. He nodded. "I'll see what I can find out and send word to you immediately," he said, before following Joseph.

Chapter 6

"What do you make of Mr. Stubb?" Martha asked as we approached the Ouse Bridge. "Could it be so easy to find the killer?"

"Perhaps this time the simplest explanation is the correct one," I said. "Stubb knows more about the crime than he should, and he used the same verse we found in Jennet's hand in the pamphlet. And he surely is big enough to have killed two people by himself." I paused, examining the idea of Stubb's guilt in my head. "But why would he announce his guilt so publicly? Surely he must have known *someone* would notice the verses."

"Perhaps he thought God would conceal him," Martha said. I thought I detected a mischievous lilt in her voice. She meant to mock him, but she could also be right.

"Perhaps he did," I said. "Men who believe they are doing the Lord's work can convince themselves of many things."

As we crossed the bridge I heard a voice calling my name. I looked up to find a girl of perhaps sixteen years running toward me. "Are you Lady Hodgson?" she asked breathlessly. I nodded. "Thank the Lord I found you!" she cried as she curtsied. "My

64

mistress sent me. I came first to your home, and your maidservant said you had gone to Mr. Hodgson's. I couldn't find his house, so I waited on the bridge."

"Who is your mistress?" I asked. "What is the hurry?"

"I am with Dorothy Mann," she said. "She asks for your help with a woman in travail." At her words, I felt my pulse quicken. Dorothy was a longtime friend and sister midwife in the city. We had worked together on many births, and I knew her to be skilled in the art. If she needed help, either the labor had gone on for days and she was exhausted, or something had gone terribly wrong. Whatever the case, I knew it would prove to be a difficult delivery.

"Where is she?" I asked.

"With one of her neighbors in the Pavement," the girl said. "She asked you to come straightaway. The mother lives in an alley near the church there. I can take you." I turned to Martha.

"Go home and get my bag. I'll send the girl for you as soon as I arrive." Martha nodded and disappeared into the crowd.

The girl and I crossed Coneystreet and turned down an alley. The relative cool of the shadows made the stench rising from the gutter a bit more bearable. With no rain to cleanse the streets, some parts of the city smelled more like a jakes than a neighborhood. We came to a low door and the girl knocked before opening it. As soon as I stepped into the home, I knew that the mother and child were in grave danger.

The woman—girl, really—lay closer to death than life. Her arms were little more than bones with skin hanging off them and her face bespoke the difficulty of her travail. Were it not for the greatness of her belly, I would have put her age at perhaps twelve years. Dorothy sat on the bed holding her hand. Even though the girl seemed to be asleep, Dorothy whispered words of encouragement in her ear. When she saw me, Dorothy gestured me over to the bed. When I sat, the girl didn't even open her eyes.

"What has happened?" I asked Dorothy.

"I only arrived an hour ago," she said. "The girl—Sarah Stone's her name—hoped to give birth in secret, with just her mother attending her." She nodded toward an older woman sitting on a stool against the wall, asleep.

"The child is a bastard?"

"Aye. A local boy promised her marriage but was taken into the army. She's not heard from him in months. She was afraid of the whipping that would come if she were discovered to be with a bastard. Her mother tended her as best she could, but the child wouldn't come. When she lost hope of delivering the child herself, she summoned me."

The girl moaned as a labor pang struck her, but she did not wake. Dorothy gazed at the girl to ensure her eyes were closed, looked at me, and shook her head slightly. She held out no hope for the child.

"Can you tell the problem?" I asked.

"It could be the heat," she said. "It constricted a woman I delivered last week, and I had to use goose grease."

I nodded. I hadn't noticed abnormal tightness in my clients, but it would not surprise me.

"Do you have what we will need?" I asked.

"Need?" she said, but I could tell from her expression that she knew what I meant. In cases in which a mother could not deliver her child, it fell to the midwife to do so using crochets, hooks, and knives. I had delivered only two mothers in such a fashion, and none since Martha had come to my house, but memories of these women still came to me as I slept. In my dreams I heard the dying child crying out from within his mother's womb. I would awake to find the infant's cries were my own. I never tried to go back to sleep on such nights.

Dorothy shook her head. "I don't keep my tools in my bag," she said. "It's an ill omen. I can send my girl for them."

"There is no need," I said. "Martha will be here soon, and she will have mine. Pray God we will not need them. How long has she been asleep?"

"About half an hour. The labor pains have lessened some."

"We should wake her. There is nothing to be gained by waiting." It took some doing, but Dorothy managed to bring Sarah to her senses. She looked at me in alarm, her sunken cheeks and bulging eyes giving her a look more gargoyle than human.

"Why are you here?" she asked. "My mother and Mrs. Mann are going to deliver me. Why have you come?" Her voice rose as she gradually realized that if Dorothy had brought in another midwife, something must have gone wrong.

"Hush, child," I said. "Mrs. Mann and I often work together—you will be safe."

"What about my baby?" she said. "Will he be safe?"

I could not tell her the truth, of course. If she lost hope, she might prove unable to deliver the child at all, and then her life would be in danger as well. "We will see," I said. "The most important thing is that we deliver him as quickly as we can. You are both weakened."

The girl bit her lip and nodded. I admired her courage and lamented the sorrow that the rest of the day would hold for her. I felt her breasts and despaired when I found them slack; Nature provides no milk for a stillborn child. Her belly was not so cold as I would have expected if the child had died, but with the summer heat, it could not mean much. When I examined the girl's privities, I noticed that the humors were not corrupted. I felt a flicker of hope that the child might not be dead, but reprimanded myself for entertaining such fanciful thoughts and pushed them away before they made their way into my eyes. If the child had died earlier that day, many of the signs would be wanting, and I did not want to give the girl false hope.

"Do you have an eaglestone?" I asked Dorothy. Before I made the decision to use tools, I would give Sarah one more opportunity to deliver the child—dead or no—without resorting to instruments. Dorothy brought me her eaglestone. I held it out to Sarah and shook it. She offered a wan smile when the stone rattled.

"What is it?" she asked.

"It's an eaglestone—a stone inside a stone, so it mimics the child within you."

Sarah smiled again at the idea. "What does it do?"

"It is said to help speed labor if the child is weak." I did not tell her that most midwives doubted it worked, or that her child probably was beyond saving. I also knew it couldn't do any harm, and if it gave her hope enough to survive her travail, then it had served its purpose. I asked Dorothy for a mix of pepper and hellebore. When everything was ready, I turned to Sarah.

"The next time you are in the throes of labor, you must snuff up this powder. It will help the child to come. Between now and then, you should stand." She nodded, and Dorothy and I helped her to her feet. Within a few minutes, Sarah gasped and tightened her grip on my shoulders.

"Here it comes," she said. Dorothy and I took Sarah to the bed, and she leaned into Dorothy's lap while I anointed her passages and my hands with lily oil. I laid the eaglestone on Sarah's belly and Dorothy put the powder under her nose. Without a moment's hesitation, the girl inhaled sharply.

"Jesus God!" she howled, throwing her head back into Dorothy's chest. "What have you done to me?"

"It is some spices to help you," I said as I reached in to find the child's head. "When the next pain comes, hold your breath."

She looked at me, her eyes watering and shot through with blood, and nodded. Sarah's shouts had at last roused her mother and she crept to the side of the bed. I found the child's head, but he was not as far along as I'd hoped. At that moment, Martha arrived. She set down my bag, and without a word took her place next to Dorothy. She looked at me, hoping for some reassurance. I knew Sarah was watching as well, so I dared not betray my fears.

As Sarah's throes waned, Dorothy helped her up and began to walk her around the room while Martha and I huddled over my valise.

"Will you need your tools?" she breathed.

"Probably," I said. "You should get them ready. I won't tell the girl until just before I start. It is better that way."

Martha paled and looked at my bag doubtfully. She'd never had to do this before.

"Martha, the child is not coming of his own accord. He is likely dead already and we must save the mother." She nodded and opened my bag. I motioned for Dorothy to bring Sarah back to the bed so I could begin my work extracting the child.

I positioned myself between Sarah's legs and felt inside her to see how she fared, and to find purchase for my tools; the mouth or jaw was best. I felt the child's eyes, and tried to turn him for purchase on the mouth. I found it with my finger and breathed a sigh of relief. If I secured the hook there, the horrible business would pass quickly. Martha appeared at my side, holding the box that contained my tools. I breathed deeply and tried to find the words to tell Sarah what I was about to do. I looked up at the girl, and could tell that she knew something was wrong.

"What has happened?" she asked. "My baby?" I opened my mouth to answer, and managed to half contain the scream that welled up inside.

"He's sucking!" I cried. "The child is sucking on my finger!"

Dorothy stared at me, stunned, and I heard Martha gasp.

"Are you sure?" Martha asked.

"Absolutely—he's weak, but he's sucking. I can feel it as we speak."

"Oh, thank God," Dorothy said, and she crossed herself.

Sarah's eyes shifted uneasily between me and Martha, and then she looked over her shoulder at Dorothy. "What is it? What is going on?"

I regained command of myself as best I could. "Nothing at all," I said, only a little too quickly. "Let us get this child born. Dorothy, at the next throe, give Sarah some more of the pepper."

Perhaps the child responded to the surprise and joy in the room, but once I was able to turn him just a bit more, he was born within minutes. From the bruises on his tiny face you'd have thought he'd been born in the midst of an alehouse brawl, but his lungs were strong enough and he had no trouble feeding.

It was only then, with the child safe in his mother's arms, that the reality of what I had nearly done overcame me. I felt a roiling in my guts, as if a serpent had just loosed itself in my belly. Without a word, I stumbled through the kitchen toward the door that led into the courtyard behind the building. My foot caught on the threshold, and I fell forward into the garbage that tenement residents had cast there. My stomach had just finished voiding itself when I felt hands helping me to my feet. Dorothy wiped my cheek with a handkerchief while Martha put her arm around my waist and ushered me into the kitchen. When I saw Sarah nursing her child, blood rushed from my head and my knees buckled again. Martha and Dorothy helped me to a chair. I lowered my head between my knees until the roaring in my ears abated.

"Should I call for a physician?" Martha asked when I looked up. "You look unwell."

I gazed back at her but could not find words to explain what had happened to me. I had become a midwife to save lives. But thanks to my haste or poor judgment, I had nearly slaughtered an infant before he'd even taken his first breath. The irony was that if I *had* killed the child, I would never have known of my guilt. I would have left that day secure in the belief that the child I'd cut to pieces inside his mother's womb had already died. My mind scrambled back to the other stillborn children I'd delivered in this way. Could any of them have been alive when I began my gruesome work? I told myself they could not. One had already begun to decay, and the other had been a monster, not long for the world. But what if I was wrong? Or what if tomorrow I made the same mistake but was not so lucky?

"I should like to go," I said at last, and Martha helped me to my feet. If Sarah Stone had noticed my condition, she was kind enough not to say anything about it. Her mother thanked me profusely, and tried to press a few pennies into my hand, but I could not take them even for politeness's sake.

By the time I stepped into the street behind Dorothy and Martha, I felt as tired as I ever had in my life. I goggled at the evening sun hanging low in the western sky. It felt as if we'd been inside for days; how could it still be daylight? Even at this hour, the sun's rage against the city endured, and the buildings seemed brittle in the heat. An orchard—or what was left of it—lay across the street from the Stones' house, but the fruit had shriveled to nothing and the leaves had started to brown for want of water. Such a price the poor would pay for the loss of these trees.

Dorothy and I bade each other farewell—the words were short, but we gazed at each other with hollow eyes; we both knew that we'd come within seconds of a most horrible error.

For the second time that week, Martha and I had difficulty discussing the child we'd just delivered. "What are you thinking of?" Martha asked.

"Sunday, when we nearly lost Jane Moore," I said. "And the child today."

"Why are you thinking of Jane? You've delivered women from greater peril than she suffered."

"Jane walked hand in hand with death before God brought her back. And only He knows what would have happened if we'd not roused her that last time. Today, I nearly killed a child with my own hands. What if I'd decided to cut him at the shoulder instead of bringing his head down to reach him with my hook? What if my finger had found his eye instead of his mouth? What if he'd not sucked at that moment? What if?" I paused, knowing full well that she would not accept what I was about to say. "Martha, we had a full year without trouble, and in just a few days we almost lost a mother, and I nearly murdered a child even before he'd been born."

"These were not the first difficult cases you've had," Martha replied. "And surely they will not be the last."

"Edward would say that God Himself intervened to save this child's life. He'd say that he sucked my finger at that moment by divine providence. He would insist that I search my heart to discover what He meant by these portents." I'd never been one to seek His providence in unremarkable events, but I could not help wondering if He'd sent these difficult cases for a reason.

"A Puritan sees God's hand in a loose shit and then he lies awake half the night praying on it," Martha sneered. I was not surprised when Martha rejected the idea—that was probably why I'd told her. "We had a good year," she continued, "and we both know that misfortune may strike at any time. It is our job to overcome this misfortune, not to accept it because God is the author. If God is telling us anything, it's to keep up the good work."

I could not help smiling. Here the deputy was teaching the midwife.

"I hope you're right," I said. But I resolved to pray on it all the same.

When we arrived home, we found Will stretched out on the parlor couch snoring softly. In the evening light he looked like the same youth who began appearing at my door when I married his uncle many years before. Martha gently shook him awake and I marveled at the soft, sweet smile that crossed his face when he saw her standing next to him. At that moment I recalled the nights he'd stayed at my house after my beloved daughter died. He was but a boy then, but somehow he knew I could not have survived without the comfort that his presence offered.

"Hannah fed me well while I waited," he said. "I was just having a moment's rest. How was the birth?"

I glanced down at my hands and pushed away the memories of the disaster we'd so narrowly avoided. "It was fine," I said. "What did you learn about our pamphleteer?"

"Good Master Stubb? He's as fanatical as any man in England," Will replied. "Even my father seemed skittish around him. If he'd seen fit to break out of his chains, he certainly could have, and we'd not have subdued him without spilling much blood."

"What did he say about the murders?"

"Well, he says he's innocent, of course," Will said. "He claims that last night he was at a young men's prayer meeting until midnight, and then went to bed. He's lodging with another of Ward's followers, so if he's lying, my father will find out soon enough."

"Unless his friend will lie on his behalf," Martha said acidly. "If he's innocent, how did he know about the murders? Who besides the killer would have known what happened there?"

"He refused to say," Will said. "Swore that it was God's will that he tell the truth, and he would not betray his brother any more than he'd betray Christ himself."

"Did your father enquire about the Bible verse?" I asked.

"Aye. He says Mr. Ward preached and prayed on it for two days and it was read aloud at the young men's meeting. All in attendance would have had God's vengeance against whores and whoremasters pounded into their heads."

"And is he now in the Castle?" I asked. I could not imagine Edward would tolerate Stubb's refusal to explain how he learned of the murder.

"You'd think so," Will said. "But Joseph spoke up on his behalf."

"What?" Martha and I cried out together.

"Why would he do that?" I asked.

"Joseph reminded my father that he served with Stubb under Cromwell. He said they met at prayer meetings led by the army chaplains." That made sense. The chaplains serving the Parliamentary armies were renowned for their fevered godliness. "After he swore to Stubb's innocence, my father released him. He trusts Joseph, and if Joseph trusts Stubb, that's enough."

"So what will we do now?" Martha asked.

"I think we need to question Jennet's bawd," I said. "Since

Jennet was her whore, she will have good reason to help us." I hoped. "And if you want to join us, Will, you'd best be here early and without the stink of liquor on you."

Will considered my demand and then nodded.

"I'd planned to meet friends at the Black Swan, if only to prove my father right about my debauched nature," Will replied. His bitterness was sweetened by the barest hint of a smile. "I'm sure he will be sorry to forego his morning speech urging me to be more like Joseph. But a day with you searching for a murderer? I wouldn't miss it for anything."

Chapter 7

Though it was early when Will arrived, I found the iron door handle hot to the touch when I let him in. It would be another brutal day.

To my relief, Will had stayed true to his word and had neither the smell nor the look of liquor upon him. Without further ado, Martha, Will, and I set out in search of Jennet's bawd.

"Now, how is it that you know where to find a bawd?" Will asked with a glint in his eye. "I understand why she might want to keep a midwife on hand, but you hardly seem like the kind she would seek out." Even at this early hour the sun had a razor-sharp edge, and we shaded our eyes as we walked east along Coneystreet.

"I don't know her myself," I explained. "But I've delivered enough of the city's whores to have learned something of her business. In truth, I know more about bawdry than I'd care to."

"She lives in Micklegate?" Martha asked. The southern part of the city was home to York's wealthiest families, and a bawd would have seemed out of place. We had crossed the Ouse and were walking toward Micklegate Bar, the southernmost of the city's gates.

"She's just outside the city walls," I said. "Her kind prefer not to live in the city itself. So long as she's out of sight and pays whatever fines the city sees fit to levy, she can live in peace."

"She's outside Micklegate Bar?" Will asked. A worried note had crept into his voice. "What is her name?"

"Helen Wright," I said.

"Do you know her?" Martha jumped in.

"Er, no," Will replied. "I've never met her."

"But you know *of* her?" Martha enjoyed few things quite so much as vexing Will, and she knew she'd stumbled onto a secret worth knowing.

"Well, yes. Many people in York do." He clearly hoped to end the conversation there, but Martha was having none of it.

"And when she sees you at the door, what will she think we've come for?"

Will's ears turned pink, as they usually did when Martha teased him, and he decided—wisely—that silence would be the best defense. Martha continued to question him, but he held his tongue. Will was a young man, so it would not surprise me to learn that he'd visited York's whores before. He was not yet ready to marry; it was better he seek out a whore than corrupt a respectable woman. Such behavior was common among York's youth, and winked at by their elders.

When we passed through the gate, it seemed as if we'd entered a different country. During the siege, the King's men had set fire to the suburbs, and scorched earth and burned-out buildings still ringed the city more than a year later. Some of the lower sort had scavenged wood, stone, and brick from the ruins of the fire and put up small hovels. Other houses stood half-built. But most of the neighborhood was no less blasted than it had been the summer before. The slow pace of rebuilding meant that we had no trouble finding Helen's home, for it stood out from its neighbors both for its size and its quality. It had the same half-timbered frame as houses inside the city, and while it was not so large as mine, it made clear the profits to be had from bawdry.

Martha's eyes traveled slowly up the face of the building, passing three stories before settling on the tiled roof. "This is a bawd's house?" she gasped. "She can't have earned this much just from matching an apprentice with his whore, can she?"

"Ah, she does far more than that," I said. "Bawdry is just the beginning. When merchants come to the city for months at a time, they want more than a few thrusts in an alley with a tavern drab. They want a woman for the whole stay, one who can read, and doesn't have the pox. A woman like Helen Wright can find such a one, and they'll pay handsomely for it."

"Yes, I suppose . . . ," she said, still not convinced.

"But even that's still just the start," I continued. "Remember, she owns buildings in the city like the one where Jennet lived. Some are for her whores; some rooms she keeps empty, renting them for a day at a time to adulterers who need a place to hide." Martha nodded, if not in approval then at least in appreciation of her ingenuity. "And if a woman finds herself pregnant with a bastard and wants to avoid a licensed midwife, Helen will find her a place to have the child in secret; for the right price, of course." Martha whistled softly. "She'll even arrange a lying-in of sorts if the father will pay for it. Some of York's leading citizens send their maidservants to Helen with the regularity of the seasons."

"And the city doesn't stop her?" she asked. "Surely the godly must object."

"She's called to court a few times each year and charged with all manner of lewd behavior. She pays her fines—and perhaps a little extra to a cooperative judge—and returns to her business. The city fills its coffers and officials can claim that they carried on the battle against sin, so all the players profit. Only God's law is impoverished." I glanced up at the sun as it continued its remorseless work of burning the city one day at a time, and worried what it might mean for women who neared the time of their travail. "Perhaps this summer's heat is His reward for such flaunting of His will."

"Oh, nonsense," Martha scoffed. "Just look around you. The farmers are suffering far more than the citizens." She gestured at the sun-burnt fields that stretched off to the south. "Wealthy men like your brother-in-law will have their bread no matter how dear it becomes, so if this is a message from God, He's speaking in the wrong ears."

I could not deny Martha's logic, and such doubts troubled me. If the summer heat had been sent by God, why had He done so? What could His message be? I pushed away these thoughts and turned my attention to the task at hand. I climbed the steps and knocked on Helen Wright's door.

We didn't have to wait long before the door opened to reveal a tall and strikingly handsome young man. He was a full head taller than Will, with slate-gray eyes that lent his face a certain coldness. I could not help feeling that he was a dangerous man when crossed. I also noticed the quality of his clothes. Despite the fact that he was her servant, Helen had dressed him in a suit that was nearly a match for Will's.

"How can I help you, my lady?" he asked, inclining his head slightly to acknowledge my rank.

"I am Lady Bridget Hodgson, and we've come to see your mistress," I said.

"Mrs. Wright is occupied with several very important matters," he replied. "Perhaps you could come back another day."

"We are here about the murder of Jennet Porter," I said. "She died in a building owned by Mrs. Wright." Referring to a bawd as "Mrs." nearly choked me, but I knew this was not the time to start a quarrel. The purpose of our visit surprised him, and his eyes narrowed as he considered his response.

"Yes, we heard about that. It's a terrible thing, but she was simply one of Mrs. Wright's tenants. It really has nothing at all to do with her." He paused. "If you're here only to discuss the murder, I do not think you need to return. Mrs. Wright has nothing to say on the subject."

I had not expected to be turned away so abruptly, and found myself at a loss. He started to close the door, but Martha stepped past me and blocked it. Anger flashed across the servant's face, and my heart leapt in my chest. While I knew that Martha could defend herself against some men, she would be no match for this one.

He placed his hand on Martha's shoulder and tried to guide her back outside. At that moment I saw that his fine clothes concealed well-muscled arms and a powerful chest. Martha tried to shrug off his hand, but he tightened his grasp. The tendons of his forearm jumped beneath the skin, and Martha gasped in pain. From the corner of my eye, I saw Will step forward, his jaw clenched, and I knew that we were moments away from violence.

"We have reason to believe that your mistress may be in danger," Martha said between clenched teeth. "We believe that Jennet's murderer will kill again, and next time he might not settle for a whore."

"Stephen, who is it?" a woman's voice called from inside. He relaxed his grip on Martha's shoulder, and she slumped slightly in relief.

"A Lady Bridget Hodgson. She wants to see you about the murder in the city," he called out. "Her maid says you might be in danger."

"Does she?" the voice said. "Very well, see them to the parlor. I shall be with them presently."

Stephen opened the door and led the three of us into a spacious room at the front of the house with a fine view of Micklegate Bar. I have to admit that the interior of Helen's house surprised me. It was not so much that the furnishings were expensive—they clearly were—but that they were so restrained. I expected a cacophony of whatever baubles had caught her eye: gold leaf here, satin pillows there, silk hangings covering whatever space she could find. Such furnishings would have been appropriate for a low-born woman who had come into great wealth. Instead, the parlor seemed no less dignified than my own. The couch was in proportion to the room, and carefully covered in red silk with a subtle gold thread. The sideboard seemed to have been wrought from oak by the same joiner who crafted the couch, and the edge had been beautifully carved. I noticed a few books on a table, and wondered that a bawd would take the trouble to read.

"Lady Hodgson," a voice came from behind me. "It is good of you to come to my home." She spoke with a distinct Yorkshire accent, but not so thick as the one carried by the rough country folk. She looked older than me—I put her age around forty—but I knew I could be wrong by some years; the life she'd led would have taken its toll. She was not quite pretty, but carried herself in such a way that most men would think that she was. High cheekbones and a sharp nose gave her a severe appearance, but the deep brown of her eyes softened her visage. I noticed a thin and fading scar running from below her left ear nearly to her chin and instinctively raised my hand to the scar that marred my own cheek. As in the case of her home, Helen's clothes would not have seemed out of place on a gentlewoman of far better birth. She curtsied and I nodded in response.

"Stephen said that you are here about Jennet," she said. "I was very sorry to hear of her death. She'd only just come to the city."

"And she died horribly," I replied. "I have been charged by the city to help find her murderer."

"It's been a year since the city's done something other than arrest and whip its whores," she said bitterly. "I wondered how much violence could be done to a whore before the Justices intervened. It appears that murder breaks the pale. That's some comfort, at least."

"How well did you know Jennet?" I asked, declining her invitation to debate godly efforts to reform the city.

"Not well." She shrugged. "As I said, she'd not been here long. One of the other whores brought her to me. She'd come to York in search of work but had found none. She needed the money." Helen described Jennet's descent into whoredom as if it were no more remarkable than the rising of the sun in the east. I felt anger begin to rise within me and I pushed it back down.

"Did you find men for her?" I asked.

"I'm not in any danger, am I?" she asked. "Your servant lied." She looked at Martha, who stared back unblinking.

"We don't know," I said. "We think Jennet's killer is influenced by the godly. He believes he's doing God's work."

"And God's work won't be done until the return of King Jesus," she said. "I know these fanatics well enough. But when your servant said the murderer might come for me ..."

"My deputy may have overstated the case," I said. "We simply do not know. But we do need your help to find the killer."

Helen shrugged at Martha's deception. A woman who took small lies to heart would not survive long as a bawd.

"Jennet only rented a room from me," Helen said, answering my original question. "She was so new to the trade that she still sought business from apprentices and drunkards. I don't trouble myself with such poor payers anymore. Do you know the man who died with her?"

"Not yet," I said. "We don't think he was from the city, so we may never know."

"Whoever he was, they probably met in a tavern or alehouse, or even on the street. Beyond that, I can't tell you anything. I hardly knew the poor girl."

"You said one of the other whores brought her to you," Martha said. "Who was it?"

"Isabel Dalton," Helen replied. "She lives up in Hungate. She keeps an eye out for maidens coming in from the north who might need my help."

I examined her face for even a trace of irony but found none. I clenched my teeth in the hope of restraining my tongue, but I could not do so for even a moment longer.

"Need your help?" I asked. "The last thing these poor girls need is help from a woman such as you!" Helen stared at me for a moment. I expected anger to match my own, but instead she smiled at me indulgently, as if I were an unruly child.

"And there she is, the true Lady Hodgson," she said as if to herself. "I knew your judgment would come out eventually. It must have galled you to speak with me as if I were anything other than a common jade. I am relieved that you were able to speak your mind, Bridget." At this familiarity, my vision narrowed and I felt myself choking on my fury.

"How dare you?" I sputtered, completely out of control. "I am a gentlewoman and a licensed midwife."

"Yes, I can see that, can't I?" she said, gesturing to my silk skirts. "You're certainly doing well for yourself. Tell me this, *my lady*—how much of what you have did you earn by your own labor? Or did your parents give you land? And what of your husband? Surely you profited from his estate."

I was so overcome by wrath that I had no ready words to respond to such impudence. I felt my mouth working, but no sound came forth.

"If you are short of cash," she continued, "do you not have friends who can loan it to you? Does your family keep you safe from predatory men in your widowhood? Can you imagine what most women would give for such advantages? What Jennet would have given?"

I looked at her in shock, still unable to respond, but now my wrath had been joined by hurt, for her words had begun to cut.

"You started your life with money, land, and family," she said. Her voice now had an edge of steel to it. "I started with nothing but a child in my belly and my master's lash on my back. I came to this city alone, and I found my way with none to help me. I laid beneath more men than I can remember. Some beat me because they could, and I robbed them whenever *I* could. I had my head shaved for being a whore. In my youth I was whipped by men whose sons had lain with me the night before." At this she stared furiously at Will, and I saw the color rising in his cheeks. He looked down to escape her gaze.

"The simple truth, *my lady*, is that I earned everything I have: this house, these clothes, these furnishings, everything including the French wine I drank last night. And the scorn that people like you heap upon me for it makes the wine taste that much sweeter." By now her eyes were blazing and I realized that my first judgment of Helen Wright was wide of the mark—thanks to her strength, she was astonishingly beautiful.

She turned from me to Martha. "I hope you find Jennet's murderer. If I can help in any way, tell me."

Martha looked from Helen to me and back again, her mouth agape. "I . . . I will," she stammered at last.

"Stephen will see you to the door." She swept out of the parlor and disappeared up the stairs. Stephen returned and led us to the front door. He gave no indication that he'd heard any of his mistress's outburst. Before we departed, he held out his hand to Martha. In his palm lay a small and exquisitely carved wooden serpent. Martha accepted it and looked at him in wonder.

"I work with knives," Stephen said with a smile that chilled my heart. Visions of Jennet's pale and bloodless body leaped into my mind. Martha nodded her thanks and slipped the snake into her apron.

As we walked back toward the city, Will and Martha kept their eyes fastened on the ground in front of them, not daring to look at me or even at each other. I counted it a blessing that the wagons, horses, and cattle threw up clouds of dust from the sun-baked road, for it kept us from having to discuss our visit. I'd never been spoken to in such a disrespectful manner, and they'd never seen anyone—a bawd, no less!—insult me so viciously. Indeed, they may have felt more embarrassed by the scene than I. We all remained silent until we passed through Micklegate Bar.

"We should find Isabel Dalton," I said. "I know where she lives in Hungate, so it shouldn't take too long. Will you both join me?"

I could see the tension run from their bodies at my words. At that moment, we silently agreed never to discuss Helen's reprimand.

"Well, from a bawd to a whore in a single morning?" Will said. "Why not?"

Chapter 8

Isabel Dalton lived in Hungate parish, the same one where Jennet had lived and died. The parish lay along the city's northern wall, and even the most hard-hearted observer would have wept to see the poverty of its residents. The roads were more dirt than stone in some places, and the houses were small and in various states of disrepair. In the shimmering heat and dust, the children seemed like ghosts as they darted in and out of the maze of alleys that made up the parish.

"Where will we start?" Martha asked. Many a gentlewoman's maidservant would have felt ill at ease in such a place, but Martha had survived much worse.

"Isabel Dalton has been in York long enough that I know her," I said. "She sometimes attends other common women in their travail, and in the past she would call for me if she needed help with a difficult birth." I reflected for a moment on the strange fact that a gentlewoman and a whore could share the work of a midwife, and were it not for this, I should never have met Isabel.

But if midwifery could bind me to a maidservant such as Martha, why could it not bind me to a doxy? I peered down the street, trying to get my bearings. "It has been some time since I've been to her home, but I should be able to find it."

We set out again, and after a few wrong turns I found the house I'd been searching for and knocked on the door. I waited a few moments and knocked again. As was his wont, Will made to pound on the door, but I bade him wait. I did not want Isabel to think we'd come to her house with a mind to arrest her. A woman's knock would do for now.

A moment later, we heard the bolt slide back and the door opened a few inches. A child's pale face peered up at us, her delicate features framed by red hair that blazed in the sunlight. She was a beautiful girl, with porcelain skin and clear blue eyes. The girl looked me up and down, as if a visit from a gentlewoman were no new thing. I had to suppress a smile at her naked impudence—Birdy had reacted much the same way when she'd met the Lord Mayor in his robes and regalia, asking why he wore such strange clothes.

"Mum, there are some people here to see you," the girl called over her shoulder before returning her gaze to us. "She'll be here in a minute. What d'you want?" I opened my mouth to reply but a voice from inside cut me off.

"I told you to leave us alone, you godly whore!" The voice was that of a woman who'd had her fill of whoever she thought was at the door. "I told you I'd call the constable if you troubled us again. Close the door on her, Elizabeth."

"It's not them, Mum," said the girl. "It's a lady."

The door opened a bit more to reveal a rather plain woman in her late twenties. Elizabeth had gotten her red hair from her father, it seemed. Isabel's ears pinked when she saw it was me. "Oh,

God. Lady Hodgson, I am *so* sorry," she stammered with an un-usually low curtsy. "I thought it was someone else. How are you? What brings you here?"

"I'm very well, Isabel, thank you," I said, suppressing a smile. I decided to save for later the question of who the godly whore was, and why Isabel thought I might be her.

While we had known each other for some time, Isabel seemed reluctant to open the door any wider and let us into her house. I could not blame her for it. While I sometimes helped whores in labor, I also reported their bastards. The city had been so unkind to them of late that for some women I had become more enemy than friend, and I regretted the change.

"I am not here about your work," I said, hoping to put her at ease. "I've come with questions about Jennet Porter."

At the mention of Jennet's name, Isabel's face fell. She opened the door and ushered us inside. Her home consisted of a large room with a kitchen in one corner. The bed that Elizabeth and Isabel shared—with Isabel's men, I could not help thinking—stood in another corner, with bits of straw poking through the rough cover-let. Two wooden bowls with the remnants of a pottage breakfast sat on the trestle table. As we came in, Isabel scooped up the dishes and dropped them into a bucket of water near the hearth.

Isabel had been one of my first clients after I finished my time as a deputy midwife. Her master had gotten her with child and dismissed her from his household when he learned of her condi-tion. He said he could not have so lewd a woman in his home. With a child to feed and no easy route back into service, Isabel soon fell to whoring, sometimes with her former master. I had heard that he often sought her out on the Sabbath between the morning and afternoon services. Isabel owned only two stools, so we stood in a small circle in the center of the room. When

Elizabeth asked what was happening, Isabel wrapped a protective arm around her shoulders and bade her hush.

"Helen Wright told us that you brought Jennet to her when she came to the city," I said. Before answering, she stared at Will for a moment, not trusting him, but unwilling to challenge his presence.

"Yes," she said, and once again looked in Will's direction.

"I have been charged with finding Jennet's murderer," I said. "Mr. Hodgson is my nephew and he's with me. We worked together last summer."

She nodded, apparently satisfied with my explanation. One of the murders we had solved had taken place in a nearby brothel and caused quite a sensation among York's jades, making the three of us famous in the city's poorer parishes.

"I didn't know her very well," Isabel said. "She'd come to the city but couldn't find work. She tried begging, but the beadles chased her off. She wanted to go home, but hadn't the money. She was from Durham, I think. I took her to Mrs. Wright. I thought Jennet might get a room from her." Tears filled her eyes. "I helped her as best I could," she wept. "I'm so sorry."

She took a step forward and buried her face in my shoulder. Martha reached out and put a hand on Isabel's arm. *She is thinking about how close she came to the life of a whore*, I thought. It took a few minutes before Isabel recovered herself.

"Do you know who might have killed her?" Isabel asked as she wiped her eyes on her sleeve.

"Not yet," I said. "We're trying to find anyone who might have seen her the night she was murdered. Were there any men who troubled her before she died?"

"I didn't see her often," she said. "She lived in Hungate parish, but she mostly sought men in the inns down on Coneystreet."

"Where do you work?" I asked.

"Mostly men come here. I've worked long enough that men know where to look for me. I take them elsewhere, or we arrange a later meeting." She paused and then her face lit up. "I've started spinning." She gestured at a wheel in the corner. "I don't have any wool to work right now, but I'll buy some soon. It means I can spend more time here with Elizabeth, and perhaps I can start spinning full days instead of whoring." She seemed genuinely hopeful at the prospect of leaving off her old trade, and I said a prayer that she would find a way.

"Isabel, is there anyone who might have seen Jennet on the night she died?" I asked. "It's our best hope for finding the murderer." Isabel's face fell at the reminder of the reason for our visit.

"Aye," she said. "Talk to Barbara Rearsby, if you can find her. I've not seen her since the Sabbath but she and Jennet were fast gossips. I heard the women saying that the constable took Barbara to the gaol."

I thanked Isabel and was preparing to bid her farewell when I remembered her strange and profane greeting when we'd arrived.

"Isabel, whom did you think it was when I knocked on the door?"

"Just one of them godly women who've started coming to preach us up of late," she said with a harsh laugh. "They were after Barbara, too. She'll tell you."

"What do you mean?" Martha asked.

"They seek us out in taverns and alehouses, just as men do," Isabel spat. "But they want to preach rather than lie with us. They tell us of our evil lives. As if we didn't know. As if we'd taken up the comfortable life of a nun. They offered me many fine words and gospel passages, but gospel passages won't fill Elizabeth's stomach, will they? I told them that, and they called me a blasphemer."

I felt Isabel's pain and bitterness in my heart, and cast about for something I could offer her, something other than fine words. My eyes settled upon the spinning wheel in the corner.

"Will, could you have one of your father's factors bring Isabel as much wool as she needs? I'll pay for the first bag." Once Isabel had spun a bag of wool into yarn, she could trade it for more wool and a few pennies.

Before Will could answer, Isabel turned to him and bowed her head in thanks. "Mr. Hodgson, I would be so grateful for your help. I'll be the finest spinster you've seen, I promise."

Will looked at me in surprise before stammering out his assent to the arrangement. That business complete, I asked Will to step outside so Martha and I could discuss more secret matters with Isabel.

"Have you been caring for yourself, Isabel?" I asked.

"As best I can," she said. "The herbs you suggested have kept me from getting with child." She looked down at Elizabeth. "I love this little one, but could hardly afford another."

"And you can get the necessary herbs?" I had heard that some of the apothecaries had become afraid to sell their wares to the city's jades for fear of angering the magistrates. I marveled at such shortsightedness. Perhaps the godly thought the one thing York lacked was more bastards born to whores.

"Aye. One of the apothecaries comes to me monthly. I get my herbs from him in trade. And if I can get the wool you've promised, perhaps I won't need them at all." We bade Isabel farewell, and I prayed that she would soon find her way out of whoredom. But I did not think God would hear my prayers.

As we went outside to meet Will, I considered the course that Isabel's life had taken. I didn't approve of her vicious ways, of course, and when I first became a midwife, cases such as hers drove me to long nights of prayer as I wondered whether I should serve such women. I would happily aid the deserving poor, but I thought that York's whores led evil lives, and believed that they deserved a difficult travail as punishment for their sins.

My thinking changed after I was called to a whore's bedside for a birth gone wrong. By the time I arrived, the poor girl—and she did seem a girl—lay near death, for the child within her had come sideways and could not be turned. I could not save her. When she died, the baby still unborn, I wrapped her body in wool for burial and accompanied it to the churchyard. The vicar absented himself, sending some traveling curate in his place, who stumbled through the service with only half his mind on the business at hand. The poor girl had no family in York, and only a few other whores to mourn her. Of course there was no sign of the man who had thrown the child into her womb. That day I realized that I could not count as innocent the men who condemned York's whores to such a dreadful life, or paid them a few pennies for a rough grope in an alleyway. Many of them were respectable citizens who returned home from their frantic rut and laid the pox upon their wives. Such men.

Soon enough I got to know the whores and hear their stories. Most were like Isabel, good women who had fallen into evil lives. I also had come to see that while they traveled a sinful path, their sins hardly yielded a life of luxury, as they lived out their time in one or two rooms, scraping by from day to day. Eventually I concluded that the poverty in which the city's whores lived and the humiliations they endured were punishment enough for their transgressions.

"If the constables took Barbara, there's no telling where she'll be." Will's voice interrupted my thoughts as we approached Peasholme Green. "She could be at the Castle, one of the gatehouses, or even a working-house. It could take days to find her."

"Well, we can't concern ourselves with that," I said. "We'll start our search and hope fortune is with us." Despite my words, worry filled my heart, for the delay of even a few days before we found Barbara could mean the death of more innocents.

"Perhaps we should separate," Martha suggested. "Will can head west toward Bootham Bar and the Minster. We'll head south and meet at the Castle." Will agreed and started off on his own.

Martha and I first stopped at St. Anthony's Hall. During the siege it had housed sick and wounded soldiers, but since then it had been repurposed as a working-house for poor women and beggars who'd run afoul of the law. If a prisoner had no skills and no master, she would be put to spinning to earn her keep.

"I can go in by myself if you'd like," I said. The summer before, Martha had entered the hospital and gazed into Death's eyes. I knew she could not have fond memories of such a place.

"No," she said. "I'll go with you. If Barbara is here, she may be more willing to talk to a servant than a gentlewoman." I couldn't argue with that.

We stepped through the low gate and climbed the stairs. In the year since we'd last been in the hall, St. Anthony's had changed entirely. Gone were the beds with their moaning patients. Gone, too, was the stench of infected wounds, the smell of patients' waste, and the scent of death that underlied all the others. The floor had been scrubbed, the walls whitewashed, and rather than beds, the room was dotted with spinning wheels and bags of wool the city had purchased for the residents to work. A few elderly women sat at the wheels, spinning wool into thread, but none seemed young enough to be Barbara Rearsby. A middle-aged woman crossed the room to greet us.

"Good afternoon, my lady," she said with a bow. "What brings you to St. Anthony's?"

"We are in search of a woman taken recently by the constables," I said. "Her name is Barbara Rearsby."

"I don't know the name, and these are all the women we have today," she said. "I am sorry, my lady."

I thanked her for her time and attention, and slipped a tuppence into her hand before departing. Martha and I turned south toward the Pavement, and faced into the blazing heat of the sun. After the relative cool of St. Anthony's, it burned double. "Christ," Martha muttered. "It will never end, will it?" We shaded our eyes as best we could and went on our way. As the lantern tower of All Saints church came into view, I heard a familiar but unwelcome voice.

"Listen, O children of God. There is nothing that causes such boldness in sin as the failure of justice! If the sentence against an evil work is not speedily executed, the hearts of men are set to do still more evil. So sayeth the Lord. Is there anyone here who can deny that sin reigns where justice is delayed?"

"Oh God, again?" Martha moaned. As we neared the church, we found ourselves caught up in a crowd. Hezekiah Ward stood on the steps of All Saints in the Pavement, gesturing wildly at his hearers. Martha and I seemed to be the only two in the crowd not overcome by his words. As he had on the bridge, Ward had surrounded himself with his closest followers. James Hooke stood to his left, and again he seemed entranced with Ward's daughter. Ward's son stood next to James, holding his Bible up for all to see. On Ward's other flank stood his wife, whose eyes swept the crowd as if she were a sentry rather than his helpmeet. She certainly had the bulk to stop any but the stoutest of men.

"Come on," I said, trying to force a path through the mass before us.

"Did we not, this very week, see God's terrible justice visited upon the city?" Ward continued. "Yea, the failure of rain and the burning sun are sign enough of God's wrath, but have we not seen worse of late? Have we not seen the wonderful spectacle of a whore and her master struck down for their sins?"

I froze. It took me a moment to grasp that Ward had made Jennet's life and death into grist for a sermon. I suppose I should not have been surprised. If John Stubb would do such a thing in a pamphlet, why wouldn't Ward use her in a sermon? In life and in death, men used poor Jennet as they saw fit.

"God will not tolerate such a thing." Ward's voice rose and fell, capturing his audience with a hypnotic rhythm. "The hope of escape from God's justice draws men to sin, draws them bare-faced and bold—but the Lord will not have it! The reason God punished this whore, the reason He cast her down to a bloody death, was for the terrifying of all such filthy wretches. This is God's warning to all York's beastly sinners that they cannot escape unpunished."

I pushed aside a man who—by his stench—must have come from the Shambles, and to my horror nearly crashed into John Stubb. He stared at Ward, his eyes wide and sweat streaming down his face. I could see his lips moving as he muttered to himself. A push from behind forced my face into his massive chest, but he paid me no mind. I realized that he was repeating Ward's sermon even as it was delivered, uttering each word mere moments after Ward had. I pulled myself away, afraid that he might recognize me, but his eyes never strayed from the preacher.

"The Lord demands the reformation of the city and the extirpation of sin. If we fail in this duty—if the magistrates, God's vice-regents on earth, fail to suppress whoredom—then God Himself will act. Have we not seen the bloody spectacle of His justice? Amen! Amen!"

The crowd echoed Ward's cries and surged toward him, carrying Martha and me toward the church steps. As I veered to the right to escape the throng, I seized Martha's arm and brought her along in my wake. A few steps before we would have broken free, I thought I caught sight of a familiar face. I stopped and searched the crowd. I wanted to be sure my eyes had not fooled me. Then I saw him.

Mark Preston—Edward's man and Joseph's three-fingered comrade—stood in a doorway not far from Ward, staring at the preacher with the same intensity Stubb had. The only difference was that Preston's visage lacked the mania I'd seen in Stubb. He looked like the soldier he'd once been, and I wondered if he still saw himself as a soldier in the Lord's army.

"My God," Martha gasped when we finally burst free. "Say what you will, he does bring in a crowd. And did you see Stubb, the hulk of a pamphleteer? He seemed right fanatical about the sermon."

I nodded, and once again I wondered how far the giant's zeal might take him. Ward preached death to the city's whores; might a man like Stubb have decided to act in God's stead?

"Perhaps his size will help us," I said. "If anyone saw him near Jennet, they would remember such a creature."

Martha nodded, and with one final look back at the crowd surrounding Ward, we resumed our search for Barbara Rearsby.

Chapter 9

Martha and I wound our way south and east until Clifford's Tower came into view. For centuries the keep had stood guard over York Castle, the walled compound at the heart of the city's defenses. We spied Will as we neared the drawbridge that led into the Castle.

"Did you find her?" I asked as we approached.

"I checked Ousebridge Gaol," he said. "They had a beggar, two debtors, and a poor soul who made the mistake of drinking to the King's health, but no whores."

"We can check with Samuel and if she's not here, split up again." The city maintained a half-dozen prisons, and while inmates had often been separated based on their crime—debtors in the gatehouses, felons awaiting execution in the Castle—order broke down after the city fell, and there was no telling where Barbara Rearsby might be. The Castle gate stood wide open, now guarded not by soldiers but by a sleepy youth who waved us through with only a glance. We arrived at a tower in the southeast corner of the wall and Will rapped on the door with his cane.

The small window in the door popped open and Tree peered

out. When he recognized us, the boy smiled broadly. The window snapped shut, and Tree dashed through the doorway, wrapping his arms around my waist for a moment before beginning to poke at my apron in search of an apple or a package of cakes.

"Have you brought any food?" Tree asked.

"I'm afraid not," I said with a laugh. "If I'd known I was coming, I would have brought something. Perhaps Will has a penny or two." Tree looked expectantly at Will, who fished a few coins out of his pocket for the boy. The two often gambled at cards or dice, with Will always coming away much the poorer. He swore that someday he'd figure out how Tree cozened him, but so far he'd had no luck.

"Is Samuel here?" I asked.

"Aye," said Tree. "He's in the jakes. He should be out soon, though." As if Tree had summoned him by magic, Samuel Short appeared. The two made a strange pair indeed. While Tree was long, lean, and beautiful, Samuel had the wizened face of an impossibly old man, and stood no higher than my waist.

"Lady Hodgson," he said. His warm smile revealed only a few teeth, none of which seemed too securely moored in his head. "What brings you to my manse? If one of my guests is with child, she's not told me."

"We have other business," I said. "Is Barbara Rearsby here? We heard that a few days ago the beadles took her up as a strumpet."

"Aye," Samuel said, raising an eyebrow in surprise. "I imagine Mr. Hodgson told you she was here. There are few secrets from you."

I looked at Samuel in confusion. "Which Mr. Hodgson brought her in?"

"Joseph did," Samuel replied. "He said I'm to hold her a week and then turn her out with a warning that she'll face a whipping if she is taken again."

This struck me as strange. Joseph had been in the room when Edward charged us with questioning the city's whores, and he must have known we would start with those closest to Jennet. Why had he not told us he'd sent Barbara to the Castle?

"I don't know what good he thinks jailing a few doxies will do," Samuel continued. "There are still whores in the city, so it won't stop the men from their doings. And once she leaves here, this one will rejoin their numbers." He shook his head at the folly of the godly magistrate.

"We'd like to see her," I said. He looked at me warily.

"If she's not with child, what is your concern?" he asked. "I'm not looking for trouble with the city."

"We're here on city business," I said. "My brother-in-law sent us." I hesitated before saying more. If the man who'd killed Jennet thought that Barbara was helping us search for him, he could set his sights on her. I knew all too well that if a man killed once, he would not hesitate to kill again. Samuel nodded.

"All right," he said. In the year I'd known him, I'd earned his trust. I paid him the customary fee for visiting a prisoner, and we followed him to the upper cells. When Samuel stopped, I turned to Will.

"I think Martha and I should go in alone," I said. He started to protest, but I interrupted.

"You saw how you unnerved Isabel. Barbara is already in gaol and faces whipping. She'll not say anything in your presence." I could tell that Will resented my words, but he also knew I was right.

"I'll go and lose the rest of my pennies to Tree," he said, and retreated down the stairs.

Samuel unlocked the cell door, and Martha and I slipped in. We found Barbara sitting on the pallet that served as her bed. She looked up when we entered. She must have been attractive before poverty, the pox, and dissolute living had taken their toll, but now sunken eyes and hollow, pockmarked cheeks marred her face. After looking us over, she curled her lips back in a sneer.

"Try giving me your gospel and you'll have a turd in your teeth," she hissed.

Martha and I burst out laughing.

"We're not with the godly crowd," Martha volunteered. "So you can keep your turds to yourself."

"Then why are you here?" Barbara looked as us warily and then stared at me more closely. "I've seen you. You're a midwife. What do you want from me? I ain't done nothing wrong. At least nothing I'm not already in gaol for."

"We're here for the city," Martha said, "but not with an eye to punishing you. Isabel Dalton suggested we talk to you. She said you knew Jennet Porter."

At the mention of Isabel's and Jennet's names, Barbara's face softened a bit.

"I know Jennet," she said. "She's new to the city. What's she done, gotten herself with child?"

Martha froze when she realized that Barbara hadn't heard about Jennet's murder.

Barbara immediately knew that something was wrong. "What is it? Has something happened to Jennet?"

I could hear the ache in her voice and feel it in my own chest. Martha was still struggling for words, so I stepped in to help.

"She's dead, Barbara."

Tears filled her eyes before she looked down to hide them from view.

"What happened?" she asked without looking up.

"We still don't know much," Martha said. "She was with a man. They both were murdered."

"Someone killed both of them?" Barbara looked up at us, her brow furrowed. "Who would do that?"

"That's why we're here," I said. "We haven't learned much. The only sign the murderer left behind was Bible verses. He wrote them down and left them with the bodies."

She looked at me blankly. "I don't know about that," she said. "I don't even read."

"The verses came from a sermon that was preached here in the city," Martha said. "And we heard that some of the godly sort had been preaching to you and Jennet. We thought there might be a connection."

"Oh, them," she said with a harsh laugh. "I know who you mean. Mr. Ward and his people sought us out, wanted to convert us."

"The minister himself?" Martha asked.

"Just the women at first," she replied. "His daughter and wife were the worst of the lot. They started by preaching redemption, said I could be sanctified. I asked if they had honest work for me, or if one of their number might marry me." She smiled bitterly at the memory. "They want us to change but will do nothing for us save talk, talk, talk. Like men, trying to bed us, eh?" she said to Martha.

"Then what?" I asked.

"And then their honey turned to vinegar. First they sent the younger one. They call her 'Silence,' though I know not why— she never stopped her mouth. She came to me with that giant of a man, told me God would not suffer me to continue in my 'sinful courses.' I asked what He would do if I didn't listen, and she said

101

that His justice would be done, and I should not be surprised if it was visited upon me soon. The constable took me soon after."

"Did Mr. Stubb say anything?" I asked.

She looked at me in confusion.

"The big man," I said. "Did he threaten you?"

"No—he never said a word. Just stood in the corner, staring at me with the most hateful expression. I don't frighten easily anymore, but he scared me some." She paused for a moment. "Do you think *he* might have done in Jennet? Is that why you're asking about him?"

"We don't know," I replied. "We're just trying to find out who was with her in the days before she died." Now that I said the words aloud, I realized how little we had learned. We were like drowning men catching at straws.

"But you said it might be one of the godly." She leaped to her feet, her eyes ablaze. "And he's one of that crowd. He's probably the one who done it. You have to do something."

Martha crossed the room, took Barbara's arm, and gently guided her back to the bed before sitting beside her. "We have to find out more before we do anything," she said. "Mr. Ward has powerful friends in the city. We can't just accuse one of his men of murder."

Barbara considered Martha's words and calmed herself.

"You said that Silence Ward was the first woman who came to you," Martha continued. "Did others come as well?"

"His wife came," she said, nodding vigorously. "Said the same things as her daughter. But she was more cruel."

"Did she bring Stubb?"

"No—a different young man. Her son, I think. He didn't say anything either. Just stood there while she told me of the punishments that awaited me in hell. That was last Friday. The constable took me on the Sabbath, and I've been here since."

"Did the Wards treat Jennet in the same way?" I asked.

"She said they did. The women didn't frighten her. At least that's what she told me. But the giant did. And she said that Mr. Ward did, what with that crazy eye. She feared he had the evil eye, might curse her."

Before I could reply, I heard a commotion from downstairs where we'd left Will. I could hear Samuel's voice and that of a woman, and both seemed to be at the height of fury. I thanked Barbara for her help, and Martha and I dashed down the stairs to see what the matter was.

When we arrived, we found the entry room in utter chaos, most of which seemed to have been provided by the newly arrived visitors. I stood on the stairs staring at the scene in amazement. Samuel, Tree, and Will had been joined by a half-dozen others, and everyone seemed to be shouting at once. I knew immediately what the tumult must be about, for nearly all of Hezekiah Ward's party stood below me: his wife, son, and daughter were there, as were Stubb and James Hooke. There were a few others, who seemed to be birds of the same fanatical feather.

As soon as he saw us, Tree dashed up the stairs, taking them two at a time in his haste to escape the tumult below. He grasped Martha's hand, and slipped behind her skirts. Martha knelt next to him, and took him in her arms.

"What in God's name is going on?" she asked.

"The High Sheriff's man let them in," Tree said. "He said they could preach to the whore. And they didn't have to pay!" His horror at the prospect of visitors seeing Barbara without payment matched his unease at the shouting. "Samuel says that she's *his* prisoner and he'll be the one to decide who sees her and how much they'll pay."

I turned my attention to the shouting below. Tree seemed to have gotten it right.

"I don't care who you are, whose work you *think* you're doing, or what the Sheriff said." Samuel's face was bright red as he roared up at the trespassers. "This is *my* jail, and *I'll* decide who comes in and goes out. I say it's two shillings for each of you, and if you say another word, it'll be four!"

I could not help smiling at the ridiculous fee he demanded. Samuel was not usually so difficult a man—they had simply enraged him beyond all reason. Will stood behind Samuel, his cane at the ready, but the dwarf showed no signs of needing help.

"If you will not cooperate, the Lord will know of it, and you will feel His wrath!" Ward's wife shouted back. "You will learn what terrible fate awaits those who would thwart His will."

"And I shall inform the Sheriff," Ward's son added lamely. His voice was high and reedy, more suitable for a child than a man.

"It looks to me as if the Lord has already punished this one, Mrs. Ward," sneered Stubb. "Surely a shriveled dwarf with so weak and crooked a frame can mean little else."

Behind me I heard Martha gasp, not at Stubb's cruelty, but in anticipation of the storm that would surely follow such an insult.

"That's it! That is all!" shouted Samuel. He plucked a small cudgel from his belt and swung it with both hands at the nearest set of knees, which happened to belong to Ward's son. The young man squealed in pain and toppled to the ground like a wind-blown tree.

"Praise God!" cried out Silence Ward, and she rushed to her brother's side.

It took me a moment to realize that rather than rejoicing in his suffering, she'd called out his name. Ward had named his daughter Silence and his son Praise-God. Such were the names with which the godly burdened their young; may the Lord save us from ourselves.

Stubb took a lumbering step forward, and for a moment I feared that Samuel had gone too far and the giant would crush him. Then I heard the hiss of a blade being drawn and Will stepped forward, extending his sword toward the giant's throat. Everyone in the room froze at the sight of the blade and the prospect of blood.

"If you want to attack the dwarf, you'll have to fight through me first," Will said softly. Will's tone must have convinced Stubb that he was serious, for after a moment's hesitation, he stepped back.

"Mrs. Ward," Will continued, "I suggest you take your people and leave." I marveled that in just a few moments, Will had seized control of the chaotic scene; how was it that Edward could not see this side of him? This seemed an ideal moment to introduce myself to the situation, so I descended the last few steps.

"Hello, Will," I said. "What's the matter here?" I turned to Ward's wife without waiting for an answer. "And who are you to cause such trouble?"

My sudden appearance had caught her off guard. Torn between her anger at Samuel and the respect she owed me, she could only offer an awkward curtsy.

"I'm Deborah Ward," she replied. "I am wife to *Mr.* Hezekiah Ward, minister of the Gospel. If you've not heard him, he's newly come to the city." She stared into my eyes, the very soul of impudence, as if her marriage to a clergyman somehow made us equals. I would have none of that.

"Well, Deborah, you seem to have wandered some way from the city and its pulpits. I think it is time for you to return. Don't you?"

There was, of course, no way for her to object. Samuel had refused to let her into his tower, and while she might have blustered through that, she could no more overrule a gentlewoman than she could refuse the King himself. When Deborah realized that I'd cornered her, her cheeks turned bright red. She took a deep breath to recover herself and then sought an honorable way out.

"There are other whores who need us no less than this one. We shall tend to them." By now Stubb had hauled Praise-God to his feet, and Deborah led her godly crew into the Castle court-yard.

Samuel hung his cudgel on his belt and turned to me. I could tell he still smarted from Stubb's insult, but he'd regained command of himself. "Thank you, my lady," he said. "But I did not need your help."

I realized that he'd taken my intervention as an attack on his manhood, and tried to repair the damage as quickly as I could.

"I've no doubt of that," I replied. "I feared more for them than for you. The last thing this city needs is more spilt blood. What is more, I had my own reasons for confronting Mrs. Ward and her crowd. I needed to test their mettle and make sure that they knew of mine."

"Fair enough," he replied with a curt nod. If he wondered what business I might have with godly newcomers to the city, he kept it to himself.

"Samuel, what will you do if they return?" Will asked. His sword had disappeared back into his cane, and he once again appeared a model young man.

"Increase the fee to four shillings," he said with a laugh. "I'm nothing if not a man of my word."

"Shall I make another offer?" I asked. "I'll match their best price if you *don't* let them in."

"You'll pay me to keep visitors *out?*" Samuel asked.

"These visitors only," I said. "If her true friends come, they are welcome." I wanted to keep Barbara safe from Stubb, just in case he proved to be the murderer, but I also had to admit I took some pleasure in thwarting Deborah and her gang. Whore or no, Barbara had done them no harm.

Samuel smiled and we agreed to terms.

"Samuel," Tree chirped as he skipped down from his perch on the stairs. "Might I have supper at Lady Hodgson's today?"

"Well, pug," he said, "if she agreed to it, how can I deny you?"

I could not help smiling. I'd made no such offer, but as surely as I'd trapped Deborah Ward, the boy had bested me.

Tree dashed out ahead of us as Martha, Will, and I reflected on our encounter with Ward's followers.

"Will," I said, "what did you make of Stubb? You heard him at your father's and looked him in the eyes today. Is he the kind of man who would kill?"

"He meant to do real harm to Samuel," Will said. "And even with a sword at his throat, he seemed ready to assault me; I feared I would have to use it in order to save myself. I can't imagine what my father would say if I had killed one of the godly for trying to preach to a whore."

"Never mind that," I replied. "You did nothing wrong. The question is what we do now."

"I could watch him if you like," replied Tree from behind us. We turned in surprise. A moment before he'd run out in front us, but somehow he'd slipped in behind. "Such a fellow wouldn't be hard to follow."

"You'll do no such thing," I ordered. "If he snatched you up, who knows what would become of you."

"Ah, but he'd never catch me, would he?" Tree replied tartly. "Besides, he is so big I wouldn't even have to get close. Where's he staying, Will?"

"At the Three Crowns on Coneystreet," he replied.

"Will, no!" I cried.

"He won't even notice me," Tree said.

"Promise you'll stay in the alley by the river," Will said before I could object. "If he comes out, see where he goes, and then come tell us." He held out a shilling coin. "But you must promise that you won't go near him. If he sees you, run. When night comes, go back to the Castle. Don't follow him down alleys where he might trap you. Don't even walk on the same side of the street. If you lose sight of him, just return to the inn and wait. You know he'll be back."

Tree nodded his agreement, snatched the coin from Will's hand, and dashed off toward Coneystreet. As I watched him go, I felt my heart rise up in my throat. What had we just done?

Chapter 10

While I knew that Will was right—Tree was hardly fool enough to let Stubb catch hold of him—I could not help worrying. If Tree did fall into Stubb's hands, he would last no longer than the chicken Martha had cooked for supper. That night I went to sleep praying for Tree's safety, and I cannot think it mere happenstance that I dreamed I heard my daughter, Birdy, scampering through the house. Tree's visits had helped ease my grief and made such dreams less frequent, but the merest thought of losing him—never mind that I would be responsible for his death—made me regret my failure to stop him.

When Tree appeared at my door the following morning, I felt no small measure of relief, and I offered a prayer of thanks.

"He didn't go out before I left yesterday, but he's up and about early this morning," he said. Tree peered past me in the direction of the kitchen, his nose twitching. "I'd only just gotten to the inn this morning when he set out. Is the bread done yet?"

Without my saying a word, Hannah appeared with two thick

slices of bread, slathered with butter. Martha came in, wiping her hands on a towel, no less eager than I to hear Tree's account.

"First place he went was to Mrs. Hooke's," he said through a mouthful of bread.

"Rebecca Hooke?" I asked. I wondered again if she might be behind Ward's presence in the city.

Tree nodded vigorously. "Well, he wasn't there for her, of course. He went to get her son."

"James?" I asked.

"Has she got another one?" I could not tell if Tree's innocent tone was entirely genuine—I suspected not—but I let him continue. "He didn't stay long. The two of them went back to the inn and right upstairs." Tree must have seen the worried look on my face. "Don't worry. I didn't go near him—I'm no lunatic. He's got a room on the first story, and from the roof across the street I could see right in the window, the whole crowd of them."

"What crowd?" Martha asked.

"I saw the giant Stubb and James Hooke, of course. Then two who were at the Castle: the woman and the skit-brained fool that Samuel thumped. It looked like he was still limping a bit," Tree added with a smile.

"What were they doing?" Martha asked.

"Dunno," Tree said. "They got in a circle, read from books, and talked to each other. When they settled down, I came here."

"Martha, a word?" I said, and we withdrew to the parlor. "What do you think?"

"If James is so close to Stubb, we should talk to him first," she said. "And perhaps the other young people. If they know what Stubb is up to, they might let something slip."

I agreed, and when Tree had finished his bread, I sent him for Will.

"Tell him to meet us here as soon as he can. We don't know how long they'll be at the inn."

Tree nodded and dashed off once again.

Within half an hour, Tree returned with Will. I was pleased to find him well-rested, sober, and even clean-shaven.

"Tree says Stubb and James Hooke are together?"

"Aye," I replied. "And Silence and Praise-God Ward are with them. It sounds like they've come together for prayer."

Tree looked up at me, his brow furrowed.

"Prayer? By themselves?" he asked. "At an inn?"

"For the godly, there can never be too much prayer," Martha announced as she joined us. "Inns, streets, alleyways, out on the moors, even a barn or brewery will do in a pinch. What is our plan?"

"Let's go to the Three Crowns and see if they are still there," Will replied. "Once we see how things lie, we can figure that out." Will had always been one for action over planning, but in this case it seemed a reasonable suggestion, so the four of us set out for Coneystreet.

When we arrived, Tree led us into an alley across the street from the Three Crowns. "Will, can I borrow your coat?" he asked. Will looked confused, but he handed it to the boy. "I'll need something to sit on if I'm on the roof," he explained as he scrambled up. "The tiles are devilishly hot already."

Tree peered in the window across the street.

"They're still at it," he called down. "It looks like James is shouting and crying," he added uncertainly. "Is he unwell?" Clearly he'd never seen the godly at prayer.

"He's fine," Martha called up. "He's just overcome by the Lord." Tree shook his head in wonder.

Will looked up and down the street and then pointed at the Angel, an inn that sat across the street from the Three Crowns.

"If we went in there, we could watch the front door without fear of being seen," he suggested. "And if any of them leaves alone, we can accost him three against one."

"Good idea," I replied and called Tree down to the street. "We are going to watch them from inside the Angel," I told him. "You go back to Samuel." He started to protest, but I was having none of it. "Tell him you're invited to supper tonight. *Really* invited this time."

This seemed to mollify the boy, and after wheedling a penny out of Will, he dashed toward the Castle. I smiled as he disappeared among the market women, shopkeepers, and customers who filled the street.

Martha, Will, and I climbed the small flight of stairs to the Angel, and requested a table by the window. From there we could look out over the crowds and keep an eye on the entrance to the Three Crowns. We ordered a second breakfast of small beer, bread, and cheese, and settled in to watch our quarry. Happily, it did not take more than an hour—and a second pot of beer—before we saw our chance when Stubb left the inn and walked south toward the Ouse Bridge.

"Let's question them while Stubb is gone," Will said. He stood and threw a few coins on the table. I nodded, and the three of us crossed the street and entered the Three Crowns.

We climbed the stairs to the first floor and found ourselves in a short hallway with doors leading to a half-dozen rooms. We looked about uncertainly, trying to determine which room might be the one we sought. Will shrugged, and knocked on the nearest door. When nobody answered, he tried the next. It opened a few inches and Praise-God Ward peered out. His eyes widened when he saw us but before he could react, Will lowered his shoulder and forced the door open.

Praise-God cried out as he tripped over his own feet and tumbled backward onto the bed. A squawk from beneath him alerted us to the presence of his sister, Silence. James Hooke stood stock-still, mouth agape, staring at the jumble of arms and legs thrashing about on the bed. Martha and I followed Will into the room, and I latched the door behind us.

"What is going on here?" Praise-God sputtered as he tried to disentangle himself from Silence. He struggled to his feet and faced Will. "You cannot come in here uninvited!"

"Sit," Will said. When Praise-God hesitated, Will put a firm hand on his shoulder. "Sit, now, before things get worse for you."

To his credit, Praise-God understood that Will did not speak in jest. Without another word, he dropped onto the bed next to his sister. Will turned to James and pointed to the bed. "Sit with them."

Once James, Silence, and Praise-God were seated, I stepped in front of them and looked each of them in the eye. Of the three, only Silence held my gaze; both James and Praise-God tried, but looked to the floor after a few moments.

"Do you remember me?" I asked. James did, of course, but like the other two, he remained silent. "I am Lady Bridget Hodgson. As you know, a terrible murder took place on Monday, and we have been charged by the city to find the killer."

"And what does that have to do with us?" Silence stared up at me, her eyes as black as her hair. Despite her youth—she couldn't have been much older than twenty—Silence showed none of the deference due to a gentlewoman. Such were the godly: overthrowing the King would never suffice—they would not rest until they had extirpated God's order, root and branch. In that moment, between her beauty and the steel that lay beneath the surface, she reminded me of Rebecca Hooke. I could see why James had taken to her. I decided to ignore her challenge for the present.

"There were signs at the site of the murder indicating that the killer comes from your faction," I said. James started to protest, but I held up my hand. "We do not think any of you are guilty of this terrible crime, but we must find out what you know of Mr. Ward's other followers."

"What signs do you have?" Silence stood and leaned toward me. "You've no right to be here. Get out before I summon a constable."

I felt rage rise within me, and as if it had a will of its own, my hand flew up and struck her across the face. I knew that in order to salvage the day, I had to remind Silence of her place, so I did not regret it. The blow did its work. Silence's eyes bulged, and her lips pulled back in a furious grimace, but she sat back down.

"As I said, there were signs that one of the godly—one who has lost his way—is behind the murder. The nature of the signs is unimportant." My body still hummed with the fury I felt at Silence's impertinence, but I regained control of myself as best I could. "It is enough to say that I have seen them with my own eyes, and they are real."

"What do you want from us?" Where his sister's voice carried admirable strength, Praise-God's wanted all authority. As much as Silence reminded me of James's mother, Praise-God seemed the very mirror of James himself, weak and ineffectual.

"We think you know the murderer," Will answered, staring at Praise-God. "It is one thing to hate the sin of whoredom. But who among you hated the sinner, too? Who among your number is a killer? You must know. You must have suspicions."

"God is the author of all things," Silence replied. She kept her eyes down, but there was no mistaking the anger in her voice. "The hand of God imposed His punishment on that whore and her whoremaster, and it was just. Coming from God, how could it be otherwise? I can only hope that through the destruction of the flesh, the souls of the dead may be saved when the Lord Jesus returns. God is merciful indeed." She spoke these last words through bared teeth, and seemed ready to sink them into Will's neck. Will had never wanted for courage, but even he seemed unnerved by her fury.

"It was not God who killed those people," Martha answered. "And we will see whoever did it hanged."

"God is the author of all things," Silence said again, her voice rising and falling as her father's did when he stood before a crowd. "He is riding a circuit that includes all the world, and He shall judge all men. He judges by Himself or by earthly magistrates, but if magistrates do not act, God will. Yea, He *demands* that we take vengeance and inflict punishment upon offenders. If we fail to do so, we are no better than the sinners themselves, and God will judge us no less severely.

"And when the Beast comes—and he *is* coming—the whores shall suffer most. The Beast will make them desolate and naked. And he will eat their flesh, and burn them with fire."

Martha stared at Silence, stumbling for a suitable response.

"You are a true fanatic," Martha said at last.

"You do not see?" Silence said with a bitter laugh. "God is daily burning the city to ashes for its sins, and you do not see. The sun is but a foretaste of the wrath and terror to come. It is far better for the sinners to suffer for their sins than for all mankind to die on their account."

"And John Stubb agrees with you on this?" I asked, hoping to wrest control of the conversation away from this girl. "Might he see himself as one of God's judges, sent to destroy the flesh of whores? To make them desolate and burn them with fire?" I expected a hot denial, a claim that he would do no such thing, that despite his size, John Stubb was as meek and mild as a lamb.

"John is a good man, and will do whatever God commands him," answered Praise-God. "It is not for us to question His will. God told Moses, *Honor thy father and thy mother*, and God is father to us all. There is no command greater than this one." He still had not looked up from the floor, but there was a new strength in his voice.

"How long has Stubb been with you?" I asked. "When did he join your father's company?" Praise-God seemed taken aback by such a simple question.

"He first felt God working on his soul after a sermon my father preached in Manchester. He came to my father, and confessed his sinful nature. He's been with us since."

"Was he from Manchester?" I asked.

"I don't know," Praise-God replied. "He had been a soldier for Parliament. He said that."

"And a soldier he remains," Silence added. "You'll not find a more courageous man in the army of the Lord." From the corner of my eye, I saw James wince as if he'd been struck. Could he be jealous of Stubb? Silence seemed intent on defending him, even to the point of justifying murder. Perhaps James would be my way into this crew.

"Stubb is back," Martha said from the window. "Will, your brother is with him." I looked out the window and thanked God for making Stubb so tall. He was impossible to miss, even from a distance. He and Joseph were engaged in an animated conversation, and Joseph seemed to be angry. I considered our options. I could not see any profit in confronting Stubb before I knew more, certainly not with Joseph present.

"We should go then," I said. "There is no sense in courting danger." I turned back to the trio on the bed. "You know more than you are saying, and I will find out the truth. If you are hiding anything, it will come out, and I will see you punished."

Will opened the door, and Martha and I followed him toward the stairs.

"I don't care what happened!" Joseph's voice echoed up the staircase. The three of us froze midway down the stairs. Were Joseph and Stubb coming up, or going to the inn's dining room? Stubb mumbled a response, but whatever he said did not satisfy Joseph. "Enough!" Joseph shouted. "I don't want to hear your excuses!" I had never heard such a sharp edge in Joseph's voice, and supposed it was his time with Cromwell that had made it so. When we heard the sound of boots mounting the stairs, it became clear that we would not escape that way.

I grasped Martha's arm and pulled her back the way we'd come. "Up," I hissed. "We'll hide on the story above." As we climbed the stairs, I said a prayer that Stubb hadn't taken one of the inn's garrets. If he and Joseph were going to the top, we would be caught for sure. The thought of Edward's fury if Joseph told him we'd troubled the Wards spurred me up the final set of stairs. We reached the top and slipped into the hallway. None of the doors was open, and there was nowhere else to hide. If Stubb lived on the third story, we were done for. We stood stock-still listening to Stubb and Joseph mounting the stairs, and my mind raced for an explanation as to why we had disobeyed Edward. None presented itself.

A door below slammed shut, cutting off Joseph's voice; we were safe. It was only then that I realized I'd been holding my breath. I exhaled softly, grateful for the reprieve. Before we could start back down the stairs, we heard another raised voice, this time much closer.

"I have had enough of it and you must stop!" a woman shouted. I looked at Martha. We'd heard the voice before, but where? "It is the rankest hypocrisy, and I will not stand for it," she continued. "And neither will the Lord. He will not be mocked." Then I knew.

"It's Deborah Ward," I whispered.

Martha smiled and nodded in agreement. "I only hope that it's Mr. Ward who's in there with her," she murmured. "He deserves such a lashing." God granted her wish.

"You must hear me, my chick," Ward pleaded.

Will's eyes widened at the crashing sound that followed Ward's plea, and Martha's mouth dropped open. I could not imagine what Deborah had thrown at her husband, but it sounded heavy.

"*I* must hear *you*?" Deborah demanded. "I have done nothing *but* hear you. I've heard your sermons, your excuses, your rank deceptions, and you will stop!"

"But darling, I am your husband." His voice was barely a whimper. I realized with a start that Hezekiah Ward's mewling sounded precisely like Phineas's as he tried to convince me to sell one of my estates to fund his harebrained business schemes. I could only hope I never sounded as malicious as Deborah did.

"We will continue this later and you will heed me," Deborah said. "But you must prepare for this afternoon's sermon." She paused. "Here. Wipe the blood from your nose before it drips on your Bible."

After a few moments of silence, I inclined my head toward the stairs and we hastened toward the safety of the crowds on Coneystreet. As soon as we were away from the Three Crowns,

Will turned into another of Coneystreet's inns, eager to discuss what we'd heard.

"My God, what a woman!" Will laughed.

"From his sermons, you'd never have guessed he's so timid," Martha replied with a smile. "If only other women were so sharp with their husbands, the world would be a finer place."

Will laughed again, this time more uneasily.

"Let us concern ourselves with the business at hand," I said. I had no desire to revisit my own unhappy marriage. "What do you make of the younger Wards?"

Martha needed no further prodding to vent her fury.

"Is this what Englishmen have come to?" she hissed. "Laying two murders at God's door, and washing their hands of the crime? Stubb is a soldier in God's army? God, what rot!"

"Control yourself," Will whispered. "If we start shouting about the Wards, my father will surely hear of it."

"Did you not hear what that girl said?" Martha objected. "*The Beast will make them desolate and naked. He will eat their flesh, and burn them with fire?*" She turned to me. "Have you forgotten how she treated you? Her impudence?"

"Of course not," I said. "But that is not the point—finding Jennet's murderer is. To that end, we should focus on Stubb. From what we've seen, he's the most likely suspect."

Will nodded in agreement. "Stubb fought in the wars, so we should take him seriously. He's fanatic enough to see fighting against sin as no different from fighting against the King. What better way to glorify God?"

"Praise-God said Stubb came to God after a sermon in Manchester," I said. "Will, can you write to one of your father's contacts there and see if they know of him?"

"I'll ask my father to send a messenger immediately. I should think he'd be happy to learn that the killer is a stranger to York."

"In the meantime, we need to question James when he is alone," I said.

"Aye," agreed Martha with ill-disguised pleasure. "Did you see the look on his face when Silence went on about Stubb's courage? If there is anything to learn about Stubb, James will tell us."

I nodded in agreement—I had seen the same thing.

"Can you find out when in the afternoon Ward will preach?" Martha asked Will. "If Silence is present, James will be, too. We can try to catch him afterward."

"I'll keep my ears open," Will replied. "I'm sure my father will hear something about it. When I do, I'll send word and we can meet there."

"Good," I said. For the first time since Jennet's murder, I felt like we were making progress in finding the killer.

Will departed for his father's house while Martha and I returned to Stonegate. Less than an hour later, Will appeared at our door, red-faced and sweating from the blazing sun.

"Well, you are a quick one," Martha joked as she brought him a glass of barley water. "You can't have heard from Manchester already, can you?"

Will mopped his brow and drank the water in two large gulps.

"My father did send the messenger," he said. "But I'm here about Ward—he's going to preach at four this afternoon."

"Oh, very good," I said. "Where will he be this time? Not on Ouse Bridge again, I hope."

"That's why I made the trip myself. He's going to preach in St. Michael le Belfrey." I looked at Will in astonishment.

"Surely not in the church itself," I said. "The vicar is a moderate man. How could he let such a zealot into his pulpit? *Why would he?*"

"According to Joseph, it's Rebecca Hooke's doing. She wants to make it clear that in parish affairs, her voice speaks the loudest. If that means forcing the vicar from his pulpit, even for a day, then she'll do it."

"How did Joseph find out about the sermon?" I asked.

"One of the godly sent him a letter," Will said, pulling a paper from his pocket. *"Mr. Ward will preach at four o'clock at St. Michael's church. The texts will be Deuteronomy 23:17 and 22:21."*

I went to the parlor and retrieved my Bible. I found the first passage and read it aloud: *"There shall be no whore among the daughters of Israel, nor a Sodomite among of the sons of Israel."*

"What is it with the Wards and whores?" Martha cried out. "Surely there are other sins they could root out."

"Perhaps he's turned his attention to sodomites," Will ventured.

"I don't think so," I said, and read the second passage. *"Then they shall bring the damsel to the door of her father's house, and the men of her city shall stone her with stones that she die, because she hath wrought folly in Israel, to play the whore in her father's house: so shalt thou put evil away from among you."*

"Oh, no," Martha whispered. "If he preaches on that text and the killer listens..."

"Then God help us," I said softly. "We must stop the sermon."

Chapter 11

"Do we have time to stop him?" Martha asked. I raced to the parlor to see my clock.

"It is almost four," I said. "It will be close." The three of us hurried from my home, to Stonegate, and then north toward St. Michael's church. The church was among the finest in the city, dwarfing St. Helen's in both size and magnificence. It had the added advantage of lying not a hundred yards from the Minster itself and was made all the more impressive by its proximity to the cathedral.

The moment we turned the corner of Petergate, I knew we would be hard pressed to prevent Ward from preaching, for the church and its surrounding streets resembled nothing so much as an Oriental bazaar, with a crowd seemingly in the thousands surrounding the church to hear Ward preach. With Will clearing a path before us, we approached the church's west doors, but within a few steps, the throng became too thick for us to advance any further. To make matters worse, as soon as we stopped, we were overtaken by those behind us and trapped in place.

"We'll not be reaching Ward," Will said. "I'm sorry, Aunt Bridget. If I'd come to you sooner..."

"From the size of the crowd, it would not have mattered," I said. "We simply would have gotten closer to the church before we became frustrated."

"I don't envy the poor souls inside," said Martha. "I cannot imagine the heat within. It must be akin to hell itself."

I had no doubt that she appreciated the irony of her statement, and she was right: the afternoon sun seemed hot enough to melt the church's leaded roof, and the interior of the church must have been unbearable. Will stood tall, looking over the crowd in search of a route by which we could escape the throng. He shook his head in dismay.

"We're not going anywhere for a while," he said.

At that moment the people closest to the church door fell silent, and the rest of the crowd followed suit. I could see the crowd ahead of us make room for someone coming out of the church, and then Hezekiah Ward appeared above the crowd.

"They've fashioned a stage of sorts in the doorway," Will said. "From there he can preach to the crowds inside and out."

Within moments, Ward had been joined on one side by Deborah, his wife, and on the other by Praise-God. I peered at Deborah's face, trying to find some sign of the woman who'd bloodied her husband's nose just a few hours earlier, but found none. She seemed as meek and mild as any man could have wanted. Once in place, Ward did not await any sort of introduction, but immediately began to preach.

"My dear and beloved people, this city, this city of sin, suffers under the lash of a righteous God, and we must ask ourselves: how long will we suffer? How long, O Israel? How long?

"The truth is that we will suffer until we transform York into a city on a hill. We will suffer until it becomes not a city of sin, but a city of God!" He spoke with the same power he had on the bridge, and with each call for reformation, with each exhortation to holiness, the cries of *Amen* became louder and more widespread.

"How is it that he can preach with such power in public, and suffer such abuse from his wife in private?" Will asked. I shook my head in wonder. Ward continued in this vein for some time; I quickly lost interest, but the crowd did not. Eventually he made his way to the texts for his sermon and began to rail against the city's whores, calling them unclean and blaming them in particular for God's wrath against the city.

"Women such as these," Ward roared, "with their lewd acts and unclean lives, beg the Lord to strike them down, and to punish those who permit them to sell their wares to all comers. And in days of late, we have seen the sad fruit of such acts. Who among us has not heard of the terrible judgment visited upon a whore and whoremonger just days ago? And who among us can argue that this fate was not just?"

If any in the crowd questioned the justice of slaughtering a young woman and disfiguring her privities, he did not say so, for the only cries I heard were *Amen! Amen!*

I looked at the crowd that had gathered to hear Ward preach. They were a strange mix indeed: respectable shopkeepers and merchants, hoping for both personal salvation and the moral regeneration of the city; ignorant servants and apprentices caught up with godly enthusiasm; citizens who wanted nothing more than deliverance from the terrible heat. Others seemed to be there simply for amusement, for they stood on the edges of the crowd and whispered behind their hands.

Closer to Ward, I saw members of his party. Stubb stood out above the rest, of course, but I'd started to recognize others. There was a tall, cadaverous man with a crooked nose, and a woman who seemed his opposite, short, plump, and pretty; both had been with Deborah Ward when she came to the Castle to preach to Barbara Rearsby. These two stared at Ward with a fever burning in their eyes, repeating Ward's sermon to themselves just as Stubb had at the Pavement.

"How do the wicked become so bold and presumptuous as to fall upon their sin with the greediness of pigs at the trough?" Ward asked. "I tell you this: Whores, whoremongers, and adulterers are so cunning in their uncleanness that they believe that nobody knows of their sin. It is a mystery of their iniquity that they think they are safe if they can sin in secret. But I ask you, is *any* sin hidden from the Lord?" *No! No!* cried the crowd. "No, it is not," Ward confirmed. "The Lord sees all sin and condemns all sin!"

"Well, at least he's turned against the adulterers," Martha said. "Perhaps the killer will follow suit, and leave the whores to themselves."

"In the book of Deuteronomy," Ward continued, "God says that there shall be no whores among the daughters of Israel. Yet here in England, in this new Israel, we are overrun with such baggage, such vile streetwalkers. And we well know that God will be revenged on such carrion. I hope, I truly hope and pray, that by the destruction of their flesh, their souls may be saved."

I looked at Martha, and could tell that she, too, recognized these words—Silence had said the same thing in the Three Crowns.

"Has he preached this sermon before?" she murmured to me. "How else would she know what he would say?" I shook my head but did not respond. I now wanted to hear more from Ward.

"There are some who will have pity on such whores. To these people I say that we should find joy not only in God's mercy, but also in the terrible and just punishment of his enemies. And you should make no mistake: whores are enemies unto God, for they draw good men into sin! It is no cruelty to rejoice when whores are subjected to God's justice, however bloody. Nay, in God's mind, cruelty lies in the foolish pity of men. We should not pity the sinner; rather we should hate him. But that hate must be a special hate."

Ward paused. The audience hung on his every word as if he were the Apostle himself rather than a half-blind old man with a fevered brain. "Your hatred must be a charitable hatred. It must be a *Christian* hatred." The crowd burst out with another chorus of *Amens*, this one louder and longer than the last. Apparently they approved of bloody justice and Christian hatred.

"Has the city gone lunatic?" Martha cried out, unable to contain her outrage. "This man is a madbrain!"

I elbowed Martha hard in the ribs. "This is not the time or place," I hissed.

She nodded, rubbing her side where I'd hit her, but my warning came too late.

I watched in horror as those around us who had heard her words began to point her out to others and whisper behind their hands.

"A madbrain, is he?" A stout man stepped forward to speak for the group. They'd become more intent on defending Ward than on hearing his words. "What kind of woman says such things?"

From his fine clothes, I took him for one of the better sort rather than some rogue unconcerned with the law or with manners. Ordinarily I would have stepped in, claimed Martha as my own, and put an end to the business. But the feverish glint in his eye told me that on this day, in the midst of this sermon, the old order meant nothing to him. Only the word of God—as he understood it—mattered.

"I'll tell you what kind of woman," he went on. "A whore."

The blood rose in Martha's cheeks, and I could tell that if the man said one more word, he would learn that she was no common maidservant but that she could hold her own in a brawl. The man took a step forward, with his fellows close behind.

"Come closer and I'll have your eyes out," Martha hissed.

"Will, you've got to get us out of here," I whispered.

Without hesitating, Will stepped forward and drove his fist into our antagonist's stomach. When the man doubled over, gasping for breath, Will shoved him into the crowd, knocking people about as if it were a game of bowls. Will thrust his cane into my hands, grasped Martha and me by our elbows, and led us down Stonegate the way we'd come. Within a few yards, the crowd thinned and we were able to escape the chaos we had helped create.

"I didn't need your help," Martha said in mock anger. "He was a soft one at heart, and once he went down, the rest would run for their lives."

Will laughed. "I was just trying to save him the embarrassment of being thrashed by a woman. It was the Christian thing to do, really."

I could not help smiling, but we all knew that Ward's sermon had lit a fuse. If we did not find Jennet's killer soon, another woman would die.

That night I lay in bed unable to sleep. It wasn't the heat—or at least it wasn't *only* the heat, though it was bad enough. It was the knowledge that at that very moment, Jennet's murderer could be hunting another of the city's whores. I did not put any stock in Silence Ward's claim that God had struck down Jennet for her sins, or that the murderer was doing His work. But if it were true, I hoped that He would treat the killer the same way. Indeed the city was full of dangers: a tile could fall from a roof and dash out the killer's brains; he could fall in the Ouse and drown; he could choke on a meat pie; or tumble down the stairs and break his neck.

But in my heart, I did not believe God would act to stop the murderer. If God truly dispensed justice, where was He now? Perhaps I had spent too much time in Martha's blasphemous company, or had seen too many children buried before their parents. The God I knew was no longer the kind and benevolent figure I'd known in my youth, and He had no interest in worldly justice. He'd taken my husband and my children, loosed war upon England and a murderer upon York. He was a hard God, this one. I could petition, and I could hope, but I had no illusions that He'd listen.

Finally, I climbed out of bed and crept downstairs to get a glass of barley water. I took it to the parlor and sat, gazing out at the darkened street. I must have dozed, for I awoke to see Martha descending the stairs. She, too, went to the kitchen and returned with a glass.

"Martha," I said softly.

"Oh, Christ!" she gasped, nearly dropping her water. "You scared the life out of me." She regained command of herself and joined me in the parlor.

"What has you awake?" I asked.

"I'm worried what the morning will bring," she said, looking out the window at the city. "If the murderer heard that sermon, if he believes that he can turn York into a *city of God*, how could he resist killing another woman? I suppose I am just not one for Ward's charitable hatred."

We sat in silence for a while longer. In so many other situations, I could shape events or force those below me to do my bidding. But as I'd learned at that afternoon's sermon, such was no longer the case even for the city's better sort. Ward had replaced order with disorder, and I could not help seeing the murders as another sign of the chaos he'd wrought. I felt this new powerlessness in my bones and did not relish the sensation. After a few minutes more, as if by silent agreement, Martha and I rose and returned to our beds. I drifted off to sleep sure that the next morning would bring news of another murdered whore.

When I awoke, the sun had just peered over the horizon. From my window I searched the sky for some sign of clouds but found none. I descended the stairs, intending to join Martha and Hannah in the kitchen, but as I passed through the entry hall, I noticed that someone had slipped a sheet of paper under my door. I bent to retrieve it with a sense of dread; if it were from a friend, the messenger surely would have knocked. I opened the letter.

Be warned, vile whore! God will suffer no man to do His prophets wrong: yea, He reproved kings for the sake of His prophets, saying, Touch not mine anointed, and do my prophets no harm! Moreover, he called for a drought upon the land. The Lord will have His revenge on you and yours if you continue in your sinful courses. If you oppose His prophets, He will strike you down, just has He has other whores who have ignored His will!

As I read, I could feel my heart pounding in my chest. Ink stained the page where the author had pressed too hard, and in a few places the tip of the quill had torn through the paper. Whoever had written the letter had done so in high dudgeon, wielding the quill as he would a knife. The letter reeked of violence, both in the words and in the writing.

"Martha, Hannah!" I called out. I could hear a tremor in my voice. When they arrived, I showed them the paper. "I found this under the door—did you notice it when you came down?"

Martha shook her head. "I swept the entry not long ago, and would have seen it then. It must have just arrived." She read the note. "Does the letter draw from the Bible?" she asked.

"Psalms," I said. I knew what she was thinking.

"It's not so different than what the murderer did," she said. "He's using the Bible to threaten murder rather than justify it."

Despite the morning's heat, my skin suddenly felt cold and clammy. In the process of searching for a murderer, had I unwittingly caught his eye? I found myself peering out my front window, as if whoever had left the note might still be there.

"It might not be the murderer," Martha said. "Mr. Ward's followers are fanatic enough that any one of them might have written it."

A note of caution—or was it fear?—had crept into her voice. I could not tell if she truly believed that the murderer might not have sent the letter, or if she merely hoped that he hadn't. She had never been one to frighten easily, and if the note made her nervous, I was all the more concerned. I folded the paper and tucked it into my apron.

"We cannot know," I replied. "We will simply have to be careful." My mind returned to the strange couple I'd seen first at the Castle and then again at the previous day's sermon: the tall, gaunt man and the short, pretty woman. They had witnessed Praise-God's thrashing by Samuel, and Deborah's humiliation at my hands. Might one of them have leaped to the Wards' defense?

A knock at the door made us all jump. Martha peered out the window. "It's a maidservant," she said. "One I know from the market." She opened the door and the servant handed her a note.

"Eleanor Hutchinson began her travail last night," Martha said as she read. "Her time is not yet arrived, but she would like for us to come."

"Good," I said. I think we were both relived that the note heralded a birth rather than another death. Martha and I gathered our tools and departed.

Eleanor Hutchinson lived in St. Michael's parish, not far from the Minster itself. I'd delivered her of two other children, both girls. One had died in her sixth month; the other passed on to God just before she was to reach her second birthday. As we walked, I prayed that this child would avoid the fate of the first two.

When we arrived, the gossips had already filled the room with their chatter, and Eleanor seemed to be doing well. She was relaxed in her shift as she stood with her friends, drinking spiced wine. The women greeted Martha and me and while Martha assembled my birthing stool, I examined Eleanor and the baby. All seemed in order, so we returned to the merry business of gossiping.

Before long the talk turned to Jennet's murder, and it soon became clear that the ghastly details related in Stubb's pamphlet had spread throughout the city. Thankfully, none of the women knew that I had seen the bodies, else I would have been besieged by questions, and Eleanor would have had to deliver the child herself.

"Well, God says that the wages of sin are death," volunteered one woman. "And if we'll not heed God's voice even as the sun burns the city to a cinder, perhaps we'll do so when He drowns us in blood."

She spoke with too much satisfaction for my taste, and I could see Martha's jaw tighten as she worked to hold her tongue. I knew she ached to speak her mind, but as a midwife, she had to keep the peace. Our eyes met, and I nodded my approval at her discretion.

"That's not right, Sairy!" Even though she was in travail, Eleanor would not let such an idea pass unchallenged. "God is not so cruel as to lay the sins of the city on one whore's shoulders. I cannot believe it."

"It is not cruelty," Sairy replied, rising to her feet. "It would be cruel for God to let us continue unchecked in our sinful ways. It would be cruel for God *not* to warn us. While His mercy is without end, His patience is not. If the magistrates are so weak that they will not restrain sin, God will do it for them."

At this, the conversation spread through the room, and the women began to debate questions of God's will, asking whether the terrible summer heat was His doing, and wondering about the duty of magistrates to punish sinners. If Edward were to hear women discussing such weighty issues I felt quite sure he would die of apoplexy. In his mind, such questions were for men to decide.

Even as the women warmed to the topic, another gossip came in with news that changed the conversation to more immediate and bloody matters.

"I heard that there has been another murder," she whispered loudly enough for all to hear. "Another whore," she added, just so there could be no mistake. Martha and I looked at each other warily.

"How do you know?" the other women asked. "Who is it?" God's justice had been forgotten in favor of man's cruelty.

"There was a crowd outside a tenement in St. John-del-Pyke. Your brother-in-law, Mr. Hodgson, was there," she said, looking at me. "He wouldn't say what the matter was. He had that new man with him—the one with three fingers. He tried to chase away all who came, but Mary Marshall heard there were two bodies inside, just like the last time."

Martha and I retreated to the relative privacy of the kitchen.

"What should we do?" she asked.

"I should like to go see what has happened," I said. "If there has been another murder, I want to see the bodies before anyone moves them."

"What about Mrs. Hutchinson?"

"The neck of her womb is still closed," I replied. "The child won't come for hours. I will talk to her." Martha and I returned to the birthing chamber and took Eleanor aside.

"Eleanor," I said. "I am afraid I must go out for a time."

"The murders?" she asked.

I nodded. "I am helping my brother-in-law in his search for the killer, so I must see what has happened."

"But my travail," she said. "What if the child comes while you are gone?"

I put my hand on her arm in an effort to reassure her. "The baby will not be here until the afternoon, so we have plenty of time," I said. "Martha and the other women will stay with you until I return. Martha is an able deputy, and I would happily have her as my own midwife."

"But you *will* return?" Her eyes shifted between me and Martha.

"You will be in travail for many hours yet," I said. "And I'll be just a few minutes' walk away in St. John-del-Pyke. If anything happens, Martha will send for me. It's not far and I'll be able to return in plenty of time."

Martha took Eleanor's hand and looked into her eyes. "Lady Hodgson has taught me well," she said. "I promise that I will not let any misfortune befall you or your baby."

I admired the authority with which Martha spoke. Above all else, a midwife had to comfort the mother, and only a year into her apprenticeship, Martha could do that with ease. Martha's words reassured Eleanor, and she nodded in agreement.

I slipped out of the house and made my way past the Minster, into St. John-del-Pyke. The only saving grace of St. John's was that the overhanging eaves of the parish's tenements kept the full fury of the sun from reaching the cramped and winding streets. It was also small enough that the first shopkeeper I asked had heard rumors of the murders, and pointed me to the right building.

It was not hard to see where the murder had taken place—a crowd had gathered at the entrance to a small courtyard. A member of the town watch stood in the passage, barring all who would enter. I worked my way to the front of the crowd.

"Mr. Hodgson has sent for me," I told the watchman. He nodded and stepped aside. I hoped Edward would not reprimand him too severely; what was the poor man to do, call a gentlewoman a liar?

Edward stood outside the door to a building that even among its poorly wrought neighbors seemed especially close to collapse. As I'd expected, Mark Preston stood at Edward's side. I was surprised, however, to see Stephen, the young man we'd met at Helen Wright's, standing with them. Had the murderer killed another of the whores who worked for Helen? I had only a moment to wonder at that question before Edward saw me. His face clouded, but then he recovered himself and crossed the courtyard to meet me. A slight tremor in his hands told me that this scene would be no less terrible than the last. I readied myself as best I could, and stepped forward to see what our killer had done this time.

Chapter 12

"I'd hoped to keep this secret for a few hours at least," Edward said with a rueful smile. "But hiding secrets from a midwife is a fool's errand."

"What happened?" I asked.

"There are two more bodies," Edward said. "Another man and woman."

"Ah, God," I sighed. "As bad as the last?"

"There's blood enough, I think."

I looked over Edward's shoulder at Mark. If he had been discomposed by the amount of blood or by the fact that two more people had been murdered, he hid it well.

"Do you know who was killed?" I asked. "Was it another whore?"

"Probably," Edward replied. "The man is a carpenter from St. Cuthbert's parish. He had some business before the council last year, and I remember him from that. We've sent for a churchwarden from there who'll know his name."

"And the woman?"

"Another whore, I imagine," Edward said with a shrug, as if her death were of slight interest.

I suppose I should not have been surprised by his callousness, he'd rarely shown himself to be concerned with the fate of the undeserving poor—as he would put it—especially if they were whores. I swallowed my desire to reprimand him for his want of Christian charity, for I knew it would do no good.

"Father! Aunt Bridget!" Will's voice echoed through the court-yard as he tried to shoulder his way past the watchman who held him by the arm. "Get out of my way!" cried.

"Let him through," Edward called. "It is all right."

The guard loosed his grip, and Will crossed the courtyard.

"What is it, Will?" Edward asked.

"I heard about the murders," Will said. "I thought I should come."

I hoped Edward would recognize that Will was simply acting as a dutiful and capable son, and accept the help he had offered.

"Why would the guard not let me through?" Will continued.

I could tell that he took the watchman's effort to keep him out of the courtyard as yet another attack on his wounded pride and that he blamed his father for the insult.

"I told him to keep everyone out," Edward explained. "Your aunt Bridget simply would not be refused."

"What is he doing here?" I inclined my head toward Helen Wright's man.

"That's Stephen Daniels," Edward said. "He discovered the bodies. He says that his mistress owns the building and he is here minding her interests."

I wondered if Edward knew who Stephen's mistress was. I looked over at Stephen, and he shook his head slightly, his eyes begging my connivance. Either he'd lied to Edward or he'd simply failed to mention who owned the building. I had no love for Helen Wright, but something in his look convinced me to let him play his game for a bit longer. I looked at Will, who seemed more than happy to keep his father in the dark.

We crossed to the tenement door. Mark Preston opened it and stepped in. Will started to follow, but Edward held up his hand. "Just Lady Bridget," he said.

"Edward," I said. "He is working with me, and he might see something we miss. Let him in."

Edward thought for a moment and nodded. "Just for a moment," he said, and the three of us stepped into the room.

Upon entering, the first thing I saw was a man's body lying atop the collapsed remains of a rough-hewn table. Like the man at Jennet's, this one had suffered a terrible beating, and once again the killer had left his weapon—this time a heavy iron hammer—next to the body. The left side of the poor man's head was misshapen, leaving no doubt as to which wound had killed him. He seemed to be casting his eyes toward the heavens. Perhaps he'd known that his life had come to an end and he sought God's help; if so, the Lord had ignored the poor man's entreaties. I dwelt a moment too long on the rivulets of blood that flowed from his head and felt my stomach tighten. I turned away, only to have my eyes settle on a second body.

I snapped my eyes shut, but it took only a moment for the violence the murderer had visited upon the whore to engrave itself into my mind. I saw a bloodied face, legs splayed in casual lewdness, an arm bent back at an impossible angle, and, worst of all, a pale neck, stretched and bent, with marks from the murderer's fingers still visible on the skin. I kept my eyes closed as I fought to compose myself. I told myself that this was less gruesome than Jennet's fate, and far less terrible than delivering a child with instruments. I slowly opened my eyes.

The whore lay on the floor next to a low bed, with one leg propped up on the thin mattress. As I gazed at the scene, I began to feel a sense of unease that went beyond the presence of two dead bodies. I crossed the room to look more closely and then I realized what had disturbed me. The whore's clothes were wrong.

"Edward," I said. "This is no whore—look at her dress."

Edward strode over to join me. He'd made his fortune in the cloth trade, so I did not need to point out the quality of the woman's skirts. They were hardly the clothes worn by the kind of whore who would bring a man to a tenement such as this.

"Oh, no," he said. "I didn't notice. Well, who is she then?"

"Give me your handkerchief," I said. A bowl of water sat on a table in the corner. I moistened the cloth, knelt by the woman's body, and began to wipe away the blood. As I did, I noticed that most of it had come from her nose and a cut above her eye, and surmised that the murderer had not used the hammer on her.

"Oh, no," I sighed as a face I recognized came into view. "It's Mary Dodsworth."

Edward gazed at the body in confusion and then looked around the room in search of an explanation for this turn of events.

"What in the world is *she* doing here?" he cried. "She's an honorable woman! What is she doing with . . . whoever *that* was?"

I had no answers either until I remembered that Helen Wright's man stood outside the door, and that Helen would rent rooms to couples who wanted to meet in secret.

"She was an adulteress," I said. "She'd come here to meet in secret with her lover; the dead man must be him."

"Impossible," Edward said. "Her husband is a citizen. He served with me on the common council!"

"You'd be less surprised if you knew how Mr. Dodsworth treated Mary," I replied. "In his eyes, she was no better than a willful child. I can't say I'm surprised that she sought comfort elsewhere, for he offered her none."

"Ah, no," Edward sighed. "Who will tell her husband? He will be in a state when he hears the news."

"Send Will," I suggested. It would not be a pleasant task, but I knew Will would be happy to have the responsibility. Edward considered my suggestion and, to my relief, gave his assent.

"Just tell him there's been an accident and he must come immediately."

Will nodded.

"I must examine her privities," I said. Edward nodded at Mark and Will, and the three men stepped out of the tenement.

Once I was alone, I looked more closely at Mary's body. Her hands were bent into claws, and when I examined them, I found traces of blood beneath her nails. At least she had wounded the killer before she died. I took a deep breath and with no small sense of dread lifted her skirts. I expected that the killer would have mutilated her in the same way he had Jennet, and said a prayer of thanks when I found that she'd not been hurt in this way.

I cast my eyes around the room for anything else that could explain what had happened. Nothing suggested itself. A table, two stools, and a bed—what else did an adulterous couple need? I stepped into the courtyard.

"What did you find?" Edward asked.

"She'd not been cut like Jennet was," I said. "And he hit her with his fists rather than with the hammer."

"That is all?"

"There is blood under her fingernails," I said. "She probably scratched the murderer while she was being choked." I closed my eyes for a moment as an image of Mary's final moments came unbidden to my mind.

"That will help if we find the murderer," Edward observed. "But it's not much help *to* find the murderer." He turned to Will. "Do you know where Mr. Dodsworth lives?"

"Near the Foss Bridge," Will said. "I'll find him."

"I should return to Eleanor Hutchinson," I said. "I left her in travail."

"If you hear anything about . . . this affair, send someone to me," Edward said.

I nodded and turned to Helen Wright's man. "Stephen, would you be willing to walk with me? It isn't far. I should like to learn more of your mistress." He nodded and followed Will and me as we ducked out of the courtyard and back onto the street.

"This is quite a coincidence," Stephen said once we were safely out of Edward's hearing.

"That this week alone four people have been slaughtered in your mistress's tenements?" I asked. "A remarkable coincidence indeed."

"How many people know that your mistress owns those buildings?" Will asked.

"For obvious reasons, Mrs. Wright is as discreet as she can be," Stephen said. "But York's not like London, where you can do as you please and nobody is any the wiser. People talk."

"Am I right in thinking that you've been tasked to investigate the murders?" I asked.

"Mrs. Wright feels an obligation to protect her tenants, just as any landlord would. The city's common women are vulnerable in the best of times, but between the godly meddling and the murderer, things could not be much worse." Stephen paused. "My mistress wonders if it might be possible to make an arrangement." This brought me up short.

"What do you mean?" I asked.

"Mrs. Wright has connections within the city, and knows information that many would prefer to keep secret." A smile crossed his face. "In this, she is not unlike a midwife, I suppose. You both are privy to the city's sins of concupiscence. The difference is that she learns about them nine months before you do."

I did not relish being compared to a bawd, but this did not seem to be the time to complain.

"What does she propose?" I asked.

"Given the circumstances of the murders," Daniels said, "you might find people who refuse to talk to you, particularly when the conversation touches on their illicit activities. If that happens, you tell me."

"Why?" I asked.

"If someone traffics with whores, it is possible—likely, even—that Mrs. Wright has information that they would prefer to keep private. You could use that information as a lever of sorts."

"I am a sworn midwife, not a common tattler." I stood as tall as I could and squared my shoulders. "And you may tell your mistress that I do not traffic in such garbage."

"Mrs. Wright thought you would say that," he said with a satisfied smile. "She said she only traffics in the truth. Besides, you would not be exposing secrets, but offering to conceal them. You would only spread them about if someone refused to help capture a terrible villain. And what kind of man would object to that?"

I saw his point but could not bring myself to relent, not to a bawd.

"Tell her we will find the killer without her help," I said.

"I will do that, my lady," he said with a bow. "But if you change your mind, please do not hesitate to send someone to us. Mrs. Wright is eager to solve these crimes. She used to be one of these women, and feels a certain kinship. Imagine if this man were killing midwives. That is how she feels. Good day." Daniels turned and disappeared into the crowd without a backward look.

"I cannot believe she thought I would resort to extortion," I fumed to Will. "What would that mean for my reputation?"

"Oh, come now, Aunt Bridget," Will said with a laugh. "I will be the first one to say that you are as discreet as any woman in the city. But you must admit that you've acted in exactly that fashion in the past."

"I never have!" I exclaimed.

"Didn't you warn Mr. Hewley that if he did not pay his bastard's school fees you would announce his sins to the entire city? And when Margaret Watkins miscarried, you said it was from too much drink."

"That is not at all the same," I objected. "The boy is bound for Oxford, and Margaret was a sot and a soaker. She's not conceived a single child since that time and it is because of her evil living."

"I know, I know." Will laughed. "I am not saying you are malicious, but you have to admit that you *do* traffic in secrets. And if Helen Wright can help you find the murderer, you ought to let her."

"Perhaps," I said after a moment's thought. We'd arrived at Eleanor's door. "But right now I must attend to Mrs. Hutchinson, and you must find Mr. Dodsworth."

Will nodded soberly. "Thank you for asking my father to send me," he said softly.

"He would have anyway," I replied, and placed my hand on his arm. "He will come around to you."

Will nodded again. "I hope so." We embraced, and Will set off in search of Mary's husband to tell him he'd been widowed.

Inside the house, I found that Eleanor's travail had not yet begun in earnest, and Martha was still in control of the gossips.

"She's at least an hour from needing the stool," Martha reported. I lay Eleanor on the bed and confirmed her condition before taking Martha aside.

"What did you find?" Martha asked.

An image of Mary Dodsworth's battered face and bloodied fingernails leaped into my mind.

"It wasn't a whore this time," I said. "The killer chose adulterers instead. Did you know Mary Dodsworth?" Martha shook her head. "She was killed along with her lover."

"Did the murderer leave any signs?" she asked.

"Nothing of use," I said. "He left the hammer that he used to kill Mary's lover. And she had blood on her fingers, so she likely scratched him. Beyond that, there were only the bodies."

"So if we find marks on John Stubb's face, we'll know that it's him," Martha said.

"Perhaps," I said. "But that would require the devil's own luck. No, I fear that we're still some way from the end of the killings."

Martha and I stood in silence, fearful of what new deaths the future would bring, and despairing at our powerlessness to prevent them.

"Come," Martha said with forced enthusiasm. "We should eat before Eleanor's child arrives."

I nodded. She was right, of course. At that moment, the living needed us more than the dead.

It was not until the early evening that we left Eleanor's side. While the travail had gone well, Martha and I felt half-dead from the day's events. Eleanor's chamber had been pleasant enough in the morning, but by late afternoon we all felt less like her gossips and more like Shadrach, Meshach, and Abednego, cast into Babylon's furnace. Eleanor conducted herself well, and her final travail was blessedly free from excitement—mother and daughter were doing well when Martha and I stepped into the evening shadows and walked home.

Once there, I retired to my chamber so Hannah could help me into a fresh set of clothes and then I joined Martha in the dining room for a late supper. I had just poured a second glass of wine when a rapping came from my front door.

"It's Will," Martha said, recognizing the distinctive sound of his cane. A moment later, he began to pound with his fist.

"Aunt Bridget," he shouted. "Hannah! Martha! Please come!"

I leaped to my feet, my heart suddenly in my throat. What could have gone so wrong? Surely the murderer hadn't killed again, not on the same day. Martha and I hurried to the door, arriving at the same time as Hannah. Will burst in as soon as he heard the latch open.

"They've found another body," he managed at last. "Another whore."

"What?" Martha cried. "So soon?"

"Where is she?" I asked.

"In the southern part of the city this time," Will said. "They found her in a room near Micklegate Bar."

Without a moment's hesitation, Martha and I followed Will

into the night, and we began to wind our way toward Ouse Bridge. Will held a lantern aloft to help us avoid the roughest patches of road, but the broken stones occasionally reached up and grabbed a heel or a toe, nearly sending us sprawling into the gutter.

Despite the lantern—or perhaps because its flickering light made the shadows that much darker—it seemed to me that every alley and alcove could hide an assailant. In the last year, I had been attacked twice under such circumstances, and the threatening note I'd received that morning made the danger seem all the more acute. I felt my body relax when we reached the Ouse Bridge, for one could always find a member of the city watch on duty there.

"Halt!" a voice cried out. "What business do you have at this time of night?" Two men armed with clubs stood in the middle of the bridge. As we approached, one of them recognized me, and bowed. "Good evening, my lady," he said. "You have been called to a birth?"

"Something like that," I replied.

"Enjoy the cool of the evening." The guards laughed and waved us through. Once off the bridge, we entered Micklegate Ward. Here the wider streets allowed us to avoid dark alleyways, and we were able to move forward with more confidence.

"Did your father tell you anything else?" I asked.

"I don't think he knew anything else. An alehouse keeper discovered the body and sent for Joseph around eight o'clock. He called for my father."

"And he brought you along?" I asked. Edward could be so changeable where Will was concerned, I wondered if he had finally decided to treat him and Joseph with an even hand.

"Well, he didn't object when I followed him," Will replied.

I thought I caught a ghost of a smile on his face.

By now we were trotting along Micklegate, and I could not help noticing that it was the same route we'd taken to Helen Wright's. Just before we reached the city gate, Will led us onto a side street. Almost immediately, I caught sight of Edward standing at the center of a group of men who had gathered at a tavern door. Perhaps it was the weak light of the lantern, but I thought he looked more pale than usual. This would be the fifth corpse of the week, so I could hardly blame him for that.

"Lady Bridget," he said when he saw me. "I thought Will might have gone to find you."

I could not judge whether he approved of Will's actions. I imagined he would have sent for me anyway, but I also knew he would have preferred that Will wait for instructions.

"And I am glad he did," I answered. "You found another body?" I peered into the knot of men who had gathered inside the tavern, wondering if Stephen Daniels would make another appearance, but I did not see him.

"Aye," Edward said. "Worse than Mary Dodsworth, I'm afraid. Worse even than the first whore, if you can imagine such a thing. The tavern-keeper found her tonight, but by the look of things, she was killed yesterday. Go up and see for yourselves. I will wait here."

The three of us entered the tavern and, after passing through the main room, climbed the stairs. Lodgers foreign to York would have chosen to stay here for its nearness to the city gate, and it would not be strange for a whore to make her bed here as well. Where there were taverns and travelers, whores would follow.

When we reached the top of the stairs, we found Mark Preston standing, stone-faced, outside one of the rooms. I wondered what he made of his time in Edward's service: no matter how bloody his time in the army, he must have thought he'd left such work behind when he came to York. I marveled once again at his imperviousness to the day's events. Had his time at war so inured him to murder it disturbed him no more than an ill-cooked supper? He bowed slightly as we approached, and opened the door to admit us.

Even before we stepped through the door, a stomach-churning smell assaulted us. I instinctively buried my nose in my elbow, and I could hear Will and Martha coughing and gagging.

"Jesus, what is that?" Martha gasped.

"I should have warned you," Preston said. "He burned her."

"Oh God," I moaned, covering my nose with a handkerchief. I steeled myself for the sight to come, then looked into the room.

The girl lay on her bed, most of her body covered by a rough sheet. Her bare feet stuck out from the bottom of the bed and her hands, both clenched into fists, protruded from the top. A short rope bound her wrists together and then wrapped around the frame of the bed.

"Is this how you found her?" Martha asked. "The murderer covered her?"

"No," Preston said. "I sent for the cover. You'll see why soon enough."

Martha and I crossed the room and together drew back the sheet as far as the girl's waist. Despite the horrid stench, and despite Edward's warning, I still stood amazed at the sight before us. Edward was right. Whoever this poor girl was, she had suffered far worse than Jennet. Somehow the killer had heated an iron and used it to burn her skin. While many of the burns—and there were dozens—obscured each other, my eyes settled on a single mark on her forearm, where the translucent white of her skin had been marred by the perfect outline of a fire poker.

For a few moments, none of us could find words to express the horror that welled up within us. Had I tried to speak, I could only imagine the wail that would have escaped my lips. Her face was twisted into a mask of pain, her teeth bared, her eyes bulging. Scraps of cloth escaped from her mouth. The murderer had stuffed her mouth to silence her screams, just as he had with Jennet.

When we pulled the sheet entirely from the bed, Martha and I cried out in unison. The lower half of the bed was soaked in the girl's blood. The murderer had slashed at the girl's thighs and privities. I could not force myself to look closely, but he must have severed one of her arteries—else there could not be so much blood. This must have been how she died.

I turned my face to the heavens and closed my eyes. Why would God allow such evil to invade and conquer our town? What did He mean by this? I tried to pray that God would turn His hand in some other direction, but could find no words. I felt the sheet being pulled from my hands and opened my eyes to find Will covering the girl. It was only when I exhaled that I realized I'd been holding my breath throughout my feeble prayers. I turned to Will and Martha—they looked much as I felt. The blood had drained from their faces, and they seemed ready to collapse. So much blood; so much pain.

"Where are her clothes?" I asked, trying to find something other than the poor girl's body to study. I spied them in the corner and picked them up.

"There's no blood on them," Will observed. "He ripped them off her before she died."

"No," Martha corrected him. "Look, they were cut."

Sure enough, the cloth had been neatly sliced, and the cord that had bound her bodice had been severed in several places. I folded the clothes as best I could and laid them back on the floor. I cast my eyes about the room, but there was little to see. Except for the bed, the only pieces of furniture were a small table with a lantern on it and a clothes chest. Martha opened the chest—it contained a second shift and a set of skirts, but that was all.

"He used a fire poker to burn her," I said. "Where is it?" It didn't take long to determine that the poker was not in the room— there was nothing under the bed, and no other place to look. At that moment, the room seemed even smaller and more spare.

"He must have brought his own firepot and poker, and took them when he left," Martha said. "He knew what he was going to do to her. He planned it."

I looked again around the room, hoping that it would yield additional secrets. I found nothing.

"There's not much to see," I said. "Let's find out what Edward knows about the girl."

"Wait," Martha said. She crossed to the bed, and gently pulled open the girl's hands. The first was empty, but the second held a small piece of paper.

"Oh God," I moaned. "What now?"

"Revelations, chapter seventeen, verse sixteen," Martha read, and handed me the paper. "The godly are at it again."

"We'll see about that when we find a Bible," I said, and slipped the paper into my apron. "Right now, we'll talk to Edward. Perhaps someone from the tavern saw something."

After we stepped out of the room, Preston closed the door behind us and resumed the grim duty of guarding the dead.

Chapter 13

We found Edward waiting for us at the bottom of the stairs. The same small group of men who had been there when we arrived looked up at us and whispered among themselves. I had no doubt they were speculating about what had happened upstairs and why two women and a young man had been allowed inside. Edward waved us over when he saw us.

"This is Charles MacDonald. He owns the tavern and works the bar," Edward said.

He indicated a small man with a pointed beard and two large, carefully tended mustaches. The poor man daubed at eyes red from weeping. Under ordinary circumstances the mustaches might have provided some amusement, but they seemed out of place on such a sorrowful visage. MacDonald nodded to Will and Martha before bowing to me.

"Did you find the body?" I asked.

"Aye." He spoke with a distinct Scottish accent, but I could understand him. "Betty was late coming down to work. I went up looking for her and found her there, like that."

"She was a whore in the tavern?"

"What?" he cried out, horrified at the suggestion. "Oh, no, my lady! She was a barmaid." I looked at Edward in confusion.

"Mr. MacDonald." Edward sighed heavily. "We know she wasn't *only* a barmaid." MacDonald shook his head, and Edward turned to me. "When she was short of money, she would sometimes go with men as a whore. The constable arrested her last January, and she was warned."

"No," MacDonald said again, as tears filled his eyes. "She wouldn't."

"When did you last see her?" Martha asked, putting a hand on his arm.

MacDonald took her hand and began to weep. I could feel his grief in my own heart, and pitied him, for I too knew the pain of being far from home, destitute of the ones I loved.

"She was here last night," he said. "I left her to clean the kitchen while I went upstairs to secure the money from that night. When I came back, she was gone and the door was locked. I thought she'd gone to her chamber."

"You didn't see her at all today?" I asked.

He shook his head and daubed his eyes with a handkerchief.

"And when she did not come to work tonight, you went upstairs to find her?" Martha asked.

He nodded miserably.

"Mr. MacDonald," I said. "Did you see Betty with any men last night? Did anyone try to . . . win her affection?" Even if he'd closed his eyes to her indecent behavior, surely he could see how a man might make such an offer.

"Not last night," he replied. "None dared look at her after the afternoon's uproar."

"What do you mean?" I asked.

"Oh, the godly were here again, weren't they?" He sighed. "They howled that she was a 'strumpet,' called her a 'whore.' One even screamed at her 'You abominable quean! You'll burn!' It was terrifying."

"What?" I cried. "What happened? When was this?"

"Around four o'clock. Just when people started coming in, three or four of the godly came as well. They stood at my door at first, crying *Sin! Sin!* Some of my customers had just come for their supper! When that wasn't enough, the godly came inside, and one of them stood on a chair and started preaching. Then he started in on poor Betty. One of my servants tried to drive him out, but the big one stopped him, didn't he? More like a mountain than a man, he is. He said he'd thrash anyone who laid a hand on Mr. Ward."

"Mr. Ward was here?" Will asked. "He was the one preaching from the chair?"

"Mr. Ward? Yes, that's what the big one called him," MacDonald said. "I'd never seen him before. He had it in for Betty, though. He's the one who told her she'd burn in hell. He began to lay into her as soon as she came into the room."

"Stubb was here in the afternoon," Will said. "Then he came back and killed her."

"Why would Ward stoop to preaching to a handful of people in an alehouse, when he could gather a crowd on any street corner in the city?" I wondered.

Martha came up with the answer. "Mr. MacDonald, what did Mr. Ward look like?"

"Nothing remarkable," MacDonald said. "Taller than me, but most people are. He had dark hair, and was maybe a bit older than you."

"Could it have been Praise-God?" Martha asked.

"Praise-God," MacDonald said, nodding again. "Yes, that's what the woman called him. It confused me at first, but that was his name."

"Who was with him?" Martha asked. "What did they look like?"

"There was the big man, like I said," replied MacDonald. "Also two women. One was young and pretty with dark hair. The other was old and stout. She seemed a mean one. Then there was another youth, about Mr. Ward's age. He was tall and thin, that one. He was quieter than the others."

"James Hooke," I said.

"It sounds like Stubb's prayer group," Will said, nodding in agreement. "Plus the mother."

"Was there anyone else?" I asked. "You've been very helpful."

"Two more came with them, but they didn't say as much," MacDonald replied. "A man and a woman. An odd pair they were. A tall thin man with a bent and broken nose . . ."

"And a short, pretty woman," I said.

Mr. MacDonald looked at me in amazement. "Yes. How did you know?"

"I've seen them before. They always seem to go together," I said. "How long did they stay?"

"I sent for the beadles, who chased them out, but by then Betty was sobbing in her room. I had a job of it trying to get her to come back out." He gazed at the floor and slowly shook his head. "They were so cruel."

"Mr. MacDonald," I said. "Had you ever seen these people before?"

"I never had," he replied. "And if I never see those devils until the Judgment Day, it will be a day too soon."

"Thank you, Mr. MacDonald," I said. "I am very sorry this

happened." He sniffed loudly by way of response. "Could I trouble you for a bottle of wine?" I continued. "We must discuss these matters, and I think we could all use a glass."

The Scotsman nodded, and while he fetched our wine, Edward, Martha, Will, and I sat together at a small table.

Once we settled into our seats, I asked the question that had been tugging at me for nearly an hour. "The Wards live north of the river. If they wanted to trouble a whore, why did they come all the way to Micklegate? The north has plenty of alehouses and whores."

"Perhaps because it is closer to Helen Wright?" Martha suggested. "Helen Wright connects Jennet and Mary Dodsworth. She could also be connected to Betty."

"Does Helen Wright own this building?" I asked Edward.

He shook his head. "Henry Thompson does. I stood as his surety for the sale." Henry was no less respectable than Edward. We would have to find another connection—if there was one to be found.

When MacDonald returned and filled our glasses, I reached in my apron for a few coins and felt the paper Martha had found in Betty's hand. "Mr. MacDonald," I said. "Do you have a Bible we could borrow?"

"Of course," he said, returning moments later with a leather-bound volume. I looked at the slip and opened the book to Revelations. As I read the passage aloud, I could feel the anger rising from my belly.

"And the ten horns which thou saw upon the Beast, these shall hate the whore, and shall make her desolate, and naked, and shall eat her flesh, and burn her with fire."

"Oh, God, Aunt Bridget," Will breathed. "Do you recognize that verse?"

"Silence Ward quoted it this very morning," Martha replied in my stead. "I told her that God had not killed Jennet, and she started jabbering on about beasts and whores. I took it for godly bible-babble, not some lunatic Biblical prophecy."

"Just because it's misunderstood by the murderer, doesn't make the prophecy lunatic," Edward objected. He did not seem inclined to accept Martha's blasphemy, and I hoped she would have the good sense to hold her peace.

She did not.

"And what meaning could it have that *isn't* mad?" She took the Bible from my hands. "What ten-horned beast is there? And the *horns* hate the whore? How is that anything *but* mad?"

"It is the word of God, and if you persist in your blasphemy, I'll see you in the stocks," Joseph said. I'd not noticed him when he entered the room, but now he loomed over the table. Even as he threatened Martha with public humiliation, he spoke softly, as if he were quoting the price of kersey cloth from Halifax. If he'd raised his voice, I'd have been less worried, but I knew he was deadly serious. This was a side of Joseph I'd never seen, and I hoped Martha would have sense enough to recognize that she'd wandered into dangerous territory. To my relief she did, and quickly fell silent. I reached over and took the Bible from Martha's hands before she could find any more objectionable passages.

"Did you find Mr. Stubb?" Edward asked.

"Aye," Joseph said. "He was already abed, but the beadles have him now. What is it that you've found?"

Edward told him about the verse we'd discovered in Betty's hand.

"And you heard Silence Ward quote the same verse, did you, Martha?" Joseph asked. "You're not much of a Bible-reader, so how can you be sure?"

"I heard the same thing that Martha did," Will said. "Beast and all. It cannot be happenstance."

"Are you saying that *Silence Ward* is the killer?" Edward asked. "A young woman and the daughter of the best-known preacher in the city?" Will considered his response before speaking, for he realized that his father would not accept an accusation against one of the Wards unless it were sound indeed.

"I am telling you what I heard," he said at last. "Silence Ward quoted that passage. It is not some great haphazard." He paused, unsure of how far to go. "You must arrest and question her," he concluded.

"Arrest her?" Edward burst out. "Arrest Silence Ward? Are you mad? You don't arrest Hezekiah Ward's daughter on a whim! The godly would riot!" He stood and looked at Will despairingly. It seemed as if Will's suggestion had disturbed him more than the murdered body upstairs. "Joseph, I must speak to you alone," he said before stalking off, with Joseph close behind.

I reached for Will's hand at the same time Martha did, but he pulled back from both of us.

"Will," I said. "You know you're right."

"Cold comfort that is," he growled. "He'd rather protect godly strangers than the whores of the city. To hell with him. We'll find the murderer on our own."

"Good man," I said with a small smile. "The question is, what do we do now?"

Before anyone could answer, the tavern door opened and John Stubb stepped through, accompanied by two beadles. Once again I marveled that he'd not broken free from the chains he wore on his wrists. "God, why have they brought him here?" I asked.

"He's going to put the whore's body before him to see if she bleeds," Will replied. "If she does, it will prove Stubb's the murderer."

"What?" Martha cried. "Does your father really think bodies will bleed fresh blood just because their murderer is present? I've seen that that's nonsense with my own eyes."

"And I've seen men convicted on such evidence," Will replied.

"Betty's been dead a full day, and from the looks of the bed, she's already been emptied of blood," Martha said. "It's why she's dead, isn't it? She won't bleed for anyone."

"I'll talk to Edward," I said. "Perhaps I can change his mind."

I crossed the room and pulled Edward aside. "Edward, might I speak to you before you take Stubb upstairs?"

He gestured for the beadles to wait.

"How many people have seen the body?" I asked.

"Why do you ask?"

"Please tell me," I replied.

"Mr. MacDonald, of course," he said, counting on his fingers. "Joseph and Mark both entered the room with me, then the three of you. So seven in all. Why do you ask?"

"And you trust our discretion? Each of us?"

"Of course," he said. "Will lacks political sense, but none of you is prone to gossip." I wanted to defend Will, but circumstances required that I ignore the affront.

"We first suspected Stubb because of the pamphlet he wrote about Jennet. He knew too much *not* to have some connection to the murderer." Edward nodded. "This time we know everyone who has seen the body. We should wait to see if Stubb writes another pamphlet. If he writes about Betty, if he knows things that only the killer could know, we'll have more evidence against him. If we are patient, he might well give us the proof that he is the killer."

"A pamphlet would not convince a jury," Edward pointed out.

"Perhaps not, but at the very least we'd have another piece of evidence. Edward, you can't let him see the body."

He thought for a moment before coming to a decision. "The test will prove his guilt or innocence," he replied, pulling his arm from my grasp. "If I can solve the murders tonight, I will. And then we can be done with the foolishness about Mr. Ward's daughter being the murderer." He turned away and motioned for Joseph to take Stubb upstairs.

"Edward, please," I begged, but he followed Joseph without a look back.

Furious, I returned to Martha and Will. "How a man can have such good sense in business yet remain foolish is beyond me," I said as I sat. I explained Edward's decision to test Stubb's guilt.

The three of us sat in silence gazing up at the stairs, awaiting Edward's verdict.

We didn't have to wait long. Not five minutes later, a stone-faced Stubb appeared at the top of the steps, his hands now free of the manacles. Without a word or even a glance in our direction, he descended the stairs and walked out into the night. Moments later, Edward and Joseph came down and joined us.

"I take it she didn't bleed?" I asked Edward.

"No," he said.

I could see Martha fighting to keep a hold on her tongue, so I said what she could not.

"I warned you. We had our chance to connect Stubb to the murders, and you lost it. Now he's free to write his pamphlets, and there'll be nothing we can do."

The corners of Edward's mouth twitched as he considered

my words. He knew he had made a mistake, but he could never admit it, certainly not in front of Will.

"If the Lord had seen fit to expose the murderer on this night, He would have done so," Joseph said. "It was God's will."

Edward nodded in agreement. He was clearly pleased with Joseph's logic. "We'll find the murderer. God will see to it." He turned to Joseph. "Come, you must oversee the whore's burial. Have two beadles dig the grave and find a minister to say the service. There's no sense in waiting until morning." He turned and left the tavern without another word to me or Will.

"Now what do we do?" Martha sighed.

"Somehow Silence Ward *must* be a part of it," Will said. "I don't know how she did it, but we all heard what she said. She had the verse memorized. It is the only explanation."

"Come now, Will," I said as gently as I could. "Your father has gotten much wrong tonight, but how could she have bound and killed Betty? How could she have overcome both Jennet and her man, and then Mary Dodsworth and her lover? She is just one woman."

"Perhaps she and Stubb did it together," Martha said.

The idea gave me pause and I motioned for Martha to continue.

"They're mad enough, that's clear as can be. And you saw her face when she called him *a soldier in the army of the Lord*. If they're as besotted with each other as they are with their God, why couldn't it be both of them?"

"Why not indeed?" I said, warming to the suggestion. "But how can we prove it?"

"We talk to James Hooke," Will said. "He's as infatuated with Silence as she is with Stubb, but far too cowardly to do anything himself. If he knows we're trying to see Stubb arrested, he'll leap at the chance to help."

"But if we're right, he'd be putting the noose around Silence's neck as well," Martha observed. "He'd not want do that."

"We leave that part out," Will replied. "We tell him we think Stubb is guilty, and nothing more."

I wondered what Edward would make of such Machiavellian scheming from his own son.

"But he'll not talk to us, not after last year," I said. "And if Rebecca were to find out that we approached him about *another* murder? I can only imagine her reaction." The previous summer, I had come to suspect both Rebecca and James of murder, and came within an inch of seeing them hanged together.

"Oh, come now, Aunt Bridget," Will teased. "You can't say that you're afraid of that old maul, are you?"

In the past I would not have shied away from angering Rebecca Hooke, but her friendship with the Wards made her much more formidable an enemy, and I was chary of angering her.

"Love will make a wise man play the part of the fool," Will continued. "And James is a fool to begin with. He will turn on Stubb if we give him the chance. If you have any other ideas, Martha and I would love to hear them."

"I'll think about it," I said at last. "If nothing better presents itself, tomorrow we'll try to find him when he's away from his mother. Perhaps he's forgotten her wrath."

Even Will had to smile at the thought; the last time James had angered his mother, she'd broken his nose with a Bible.

The three of us drained our glasses, then started for home. Will returned to his father's house, not far from the tavern, while Martha and I began the much longer walk back to St. Helen's.

Will had loaned us his lantern, but the moon had set, so we had even less light than before.

"God, I could sleep for days," Martha moaned as we neared the Ouse Bridge. "We start the day with a birth, you're interrupted by two murders, and then we are both called to yet another murder in the opposite corner of the city."

"I'm comfortable that the murderer isn't also a midwife," I said with a smile. "She'd not have time to do both."

We lapsed into a comfortable silence as we walked, which was the only reason we heard the footsteps behind us. I froze and glanced at Martha. Even in the lantern's guttering light, I could see she'd heard them as well.

"Are we being followed?" she breathed. "Could it be Stubb?"

"I don't know. I hope not." While Martha could defend herself better than most women, I had little hope that she could hold her own against a giant such as Stubb. In one motion, I pulled her into a darkened doorway and slipped the lantern under my cloak. If we were being stalked, it seemed best to make ourselves as inconspicuous as possible.

We huddled in the shadows, peering back the way we'd come. I could not decide whether to be relieved or worried when nobody appeared.

"I didn't hear a door," Martha whispered. "They're hiding, too."

I nodded. A hundred paces to the north I could see the glow of the lanterns at the guard post on the Ouse Bridge. I considered crying for help, but did not want to provoke our pursuer to violence; if he were close and bent on murder, we would be dead before the watchmen arrived. We would wait—as midwives, we were good at that.

After a few minutes, we heard a shuffling of feet, and two figures stepped out of an alley. They paused and peered in our direction. I heard a whisper, and one of the figures produced a lantern from under *his* coat. They began to walk toward us. I inhaled sharply when I recognized them. The two men following us were Hezekiah and Praise-God Ward.

As they approached, it became clear that they would pass so close to us that we could not hope to stay hidden. I did not think we had much to fear from the Wards—better to be found by them than by Stubb—but I did not relish being discovered skulking in a doorway in the middle of the night. Without warning, I exposed the lantern and stepped into the road.

"Halt!" I demanded. "What business do you have being out at this time?"

Praise-God and Hezekiah nearly leaped out of their boots in surprise, and both men cried out as if I were a knife-wielding highwayman. With a cry of pure terror, Praise-God slung his lantern at me, but it sailed harmlessly over my head and shattered on the street behind me. I fought to control a laugh at my own audacity and Praise-God's panic.

"Well?" I asked again. "Why are you here?"

Praise-God tried to reply, but jabbered like a madman. Hezekiah regained himself more quickly than his son.

"We are visiting one of my flock who is sick to her very soul," he said, as if daring me to challenge him. "The devil's work does not end when the sun goes down, and neither does the Lord's."

"It is true that Satan never rests," Praise-God said, nodding in agreement. Hezekiah gave his son the same withering look that Edward reserved for Will when he came drunk to supper. Praise-God looked more closely at me. "You are the midwife who assaulted my mother," he said, his eyes narrowing. "And my sister."

"Never the mother," I replied.

"And your sister deserved it for her impudence," Martha chimed in. Hezekiah seemed unmoved by the news that I'd attacked his wife and daughter. Indifference to such assaults might seem cruel in some men, but after all he'd suffered at Deborah's hands, I counted the sin as venial.

"You are a midwife?" Hezekiah asked, looking me up and down. "You are attending a woman in travail, I assume?"

I nearly responded that I was—what lie could be more natural?—but something in his voice gave me pause. I realized that I had neither my tools, nor my birthing stool.

"Not tonight," I said with a laugh that sounded forced even to my own ears. My mind raced for some other explanation for our presence on a darkened city street after midnight. "I am not just a midwife, but an herbalist, too," I said at last. "A woman called for me with terrible headaches. I brought some medicines."

Ward's gaze sharpened. I could tell he was suspicious, and I realized that though he had chosen a tyrannical wife, he was no fool.

"We are alike, then," he said. "While you care for the body, I care for the soul." He paused and smiled at me. I found myself strangely charmed; perhaps there was more to this man than a shrewish wife and thundering sermons. "The difference, of course, is that while the body is just so much trash, the soul is immortal."

"But I imagine your wife called on a midwife for her travail," Martha challenged. She was less taken by his smile.

"Of course," he said to Martha. "The midwives of Egypt so feared the Lord they disobeyed Pharaoh and thereby saved Moses. There is no question they can do God's work." He turned back to me. "Now we seem to be without a lantern, my lady. Might I ask you to accompany us back to our inn? We are just across the bridge."

I could not deny his request, of course, and the four of us resumed our journeys home.

When we reached the bridge, the watchmen waved us past without a moment's hesitation, and we soon parted ways. By the time we arrived at my house, Martha and I were both exhausted. As I fell into bed, I said a prayer that the women I served would go for one night at least without a birth, and that the city's whores would go for one night without a death.

The next morning I accompanied Martha as she went to Thursday Market. I'd been searching for a few yards of fine lace, and I hoped one of the merchants might have received a package from France. City residents mingled with country folk as they bought and sold every imaginable good. To serve the needs of buyers and sellers alike, shopkeepers had set up stalls with food and drink, while booksellers advertised their wares by plastering title pages on the fronts of their stalls.

One of these caught my eye: GOD'S TERRIBLE JUDGMENT ON AN UNREPENTANT WHORE it shouted. Below the title lay a rough woodcut showing a half-clothed woman lying on a bed. I looked more closely and confirmed my suspicions: it was a lurid description of poor Betty's final hours.

It seemed that Stubb had used Betty's murder the same way he'd used Jennet's. The only question was whether he'd given us the evidence we'd need to see him hanged.

Chapter 14

I immediately put aside my goal of finding the French lace, and as soon as Martha had purchased the food we needed, we hurried home.

From the pamphlet's opening words, it was clear that Stubb had little new to say. He railed against all manner of vicious acts, and claimed that God would not end the heat afflicting the city until sin had been driven from within its walls. When it came to the murder, it seemed Stubb had written about another woman entirely. In his fevered brain, Betty was not a tavern maid who sometimes resorted to whoredom, but a common streetwalker, selling herself every night to all comers. She seemed a symbol rather than a person.

Stubb inveighed against Betty and other common women for nearly two pages before he turned to the murder itself. He offered a fanciful description of Betty's unrepentant death, and a horrible account of the wounds on her body.

"There's nothing here he didn't see when he was in the room," Martha said in frustration. "We can thank your brother-in-law for that."

"Let's just keep reading," I said, turning the page. Then I caught my breath. "Look—he knows about the papers. *As a sign of God's wrath at her sinful life, the whore held in her hands a trumpet blast from the Lord, holy verses warning her of the fate that awaited all such filthy wretches and beastly sinners.*"

"He couldn't have seen the paper, could he?" Martha asked.

"We found it before he arrived and I put it in my apron," I answered.

"Either he put the verses in Betty's hands himself, or the killer told him about them," Martha said.

"It seems that way," I replied. I could feel my heart racing as I sought a hole in the net we were drawing around Stubb, but I could not find one.

"So at the very least, Stubb knows the killer," Martha said. "And we all heard Silence quote the passage we discovered in Betty's hand. It seems they *are* working together. Will this convince your brother-in-law to question them?"

I shook my head. "It is still too weak. He and Joseph are so close to the Wards that they will not act unless we give them no choice."

I turned to the last page of the pamphlet and let out a small cry, for at the top in large print I saw my name: *BRIDGET HODGSON, a midwife of the city, has been charged with solving this bloody murder, but THE LORD OUR GOD says Touch not mine anointed, and do my prophets no harm! He will not allow His justice to be denied. God will surely stay her hand until His work is complete.*

We sat and stared at the words, unable to speak.

"It's the same language from the note someone slipped under the door," Martha said at last. "*Touch not mine anointed, and do my prophets no harm!* Could Stubb be behind the note as well?"

"And what does he mean that God will stay my hand?" I cried. "How does he think God will do that? Has that cretin threatened my life? Between the note he left and this pamphlet, I'll have him arrested this very day!"

"He'd deny it is a threat," Martha said. "He'll say God will be the one who will strike you down, perhaps with the gout or an ague. His works are a mystery, are they not?"

I tried to calm myself. Martha was right, of course. Stubb had been careful in his choice of words.

We read the pamphlet a second time, searching for any other hints of Stubb's guilt. We found none, and concluded that it would not be enough to see him arrested. It certainly would not convince a jury to hang him. Had we made no progress at all?

A knock at the door pulled me from such melancholy thoughts. I heard Hannah greeting Will and went to meet him.

"Look who's come with me, Aunt Bridget," Will announced. To my surprise, James Hooke—the son of my worst enemy in York—stepped into my home. "I told him we suspected John Stubb is a worse man than he pretends, and he agreed to speak to us."

"Mr. Hooke!" I cried. "It has been too long!"

Even as the words passed my lips, I winced at their absurdity. While it *had* been nearly a year since we'd spoken, it was not mere happenstance. Rather, it was because James knew that if his mother found out he talked to me, she would beat him black and blue. James was not a bright lad, but he knew enough to be afraid of Rebecca. Nevertheless, on this day he had overcome his fear, and I knew I had to take advantage of the fact. I brought him into the parlor and sent Martha for ale.

"Will says you know things about John Stubb," James said even as he sat. "What things?"

I weighed my words before speaking. If he had come in the hope of defeating his rival for Silence Ward's affection, I had to be sure not to impugn her or her family.

"We believe that he is a hypocrite," I said at last. "While he speaks of godliness and of living a holy life among God's chosen ones, in truth he is to be counted not among the sheep but among the goats."

James sat up straight and gazed at me, his eyes alight with anticipation. "What sin is it?" he asked. "Is he a swearer? A drunkard? Silence cannot tolerate a tippler."

"That is what we are trying to discover," Will said. "We have heard rumors, but do not wish to spread them without cause. The Lord does not love a gossip."

"No, no, of course not," James replied. "But if I had some idea, perhaps I could help. What have you heard? I would not tell anyone. Especially not Silence or her parents." In his eagerness to undermine Stubb, James had lost what little artfulness he'd ever had.

"Mr. Hooke," Martha said, handing him a mug of ale. "We think Mr. Stubb might have indulged in his particular sin the night before we saw you at the inn."

"I don't see how," James said, furrowing his brow in confusion. The poor boy was easily fuddled. "We had a young men's meeting in John's room for scripture-reading and prayer. Praise-God prayed for an hour before his mother took him. After he left, John prayed for an hour. Then two or three more of us prayed before we ended. It must have been near eleven before we went home, and John was preparing to sleep."

"But he could have gone out after you left him, couldn't he?" Will asked.

"I suppose he could. What did he do? Did he go a-whoring? The Wards would not approve of that at all!" As pathetic a figure as James cut, I could not help pitying the boy. Even under the best of circumstances, a lad such as he would never go far in our hard world. He was as eager and innocent as a puppy, but surrounded by wolves.

"What about Monday night?" Martha asked. "The day after Mr. Ward preached in the street outside St. Michael's?"

James shook his head. "I don't know where he was on Monday. We had another prayer meeting that afternoon, but it ended before night fell," he said. "What sins do you think John has committed? I've not seen him act sinfully, but perhaps I can join the three of you and help discover them?"

I glanced up at Will and Martha, who both looked aghast at the suggestion that we bring James into our circle.

"We would not want to trouble you," I said. "You have helped us already."

"So you think you'll be able to uncover his sins?" James asked eagerly. "It would be a great service to the city. Mr. Ward says that there can be no goats living among the sheep."

"We shall do our best," I assured him as I walked him to the door.

"I will watch him closely," James said. "If he shows his true colors, I will summon you immediately." I bade him farewell, and rejoined Will and Martha in the parlor.

"What do you think?" I asked.

"I think he's a feather-headed fool," Martha replied. "And the only way James would recognize Stubb's guilt is if Stubb brought him along for the murder."

"But he hardly proved Stubb's innocence," Will said. "Stubb was alone after the prayer meeting, and he could have snuck back out and killed Betty with nobody the wiser."

"Well, it's not much, but we know James will watch Stubb more closely now," I said. "Perhaps he will see something of interest."

"All he sees is that girl's shape," Will said. "*He'd* have killed those women if she asked." He paused. "You don't think James—"

"No, never," I interrupted. "He's a stupid boy, but not a cruel one. We will just have to continue our search.

"If it is Stubb," Will said, "how could we prove such a thing?"

We sat quietly, considering the question. I feared—we all feared—that the murderer would kill again before we found him. "We could set Tree on him," Will said. "It worked before—"

"Absolutely not!" I cried. "I'll not lose—" I started to say *another child* and caught myself before the words escaped me, for Tree was more Samuel's son than mine. "Besides," I said. "The murderer is acting at night. There is little that Tree could discover by following him during the day."

"What then?" Martha asked. We sat in silence. Nobody could answer her. A knock at the door pulled us from our melancholy thoughts.

"Is James back already?" Will asked, going to the door. I heard a woman's voice, and Will returned a moment later. "It's Helen Wright and her man, Stephen," Will said. "She said she's come to talk about the murders."

I told Will and Martha to escort Helen and Stephen to the parlor, and joined them there. Her dress was magnificent: deep blue silk with gold thread woven into the fabric. I could hardly keep from enquiring where she'd obtained such rich cloth, and to my dismay I felt myself growing envious. From the look on her face, I could tell she'd seen my reaction and that she enjoyed it.

"It *is* a glorious color, isn't it?" she asked. "If you'd like, I could send a few yards of the fabric to you. It cost quite a bit, but I have plenty to spare."

While the offer seemed generous, I knew she would enjoy

seeing me wearing her colors, as if I were her liveryman. I let the insult pass.

"What brings you into the city?" I asked. "With the godly in the saddle, it is not a hospitable place for a woman such as yourself." She ignored my affront as I had hers.

"Stephen says you three were at the scene of more murders, two in St. John-del-Pyke and another near Micklegate Bar," she said. "I would like to know what you have discovered." Helen's man leaned against the hearth. He'd removed a piece of wood from his pocket and was carving it with a small knife.

I gazed at Helen while I considered my response. I could not help admiring her audacity in coming to my home uninvited, and liked that she came straight to the point of her visit. Few things would have been more awkward than if she'd pretended that she had come out of friendship.

"We think the killer is one of the troop who came to town with Hezekiah Ward," I said.

"Which one?" she asked. "Stephen has been looking into their affairs as well."

"John Stubb," I said. "And he may have been pushed into it by Silence Ward."

"The minister's daughter?" Helen asked, considering the idea. "I have heard that she's quite the harpy when it comes to women in the trade. But why would she kill the whores? They can't change their ways if they're dead."

"It's not about the whores," Martha said. "It's about the city. They are killing the whores as a warning to the rest of us. The murders are meant as signs of God's wrath, painted in blood."

"That sounds like Ward's gang," Helen said, nodding. "Do you have evidence against Stubb or the girl?"

"Nothing to convince a jury," I admitted. I hesitated, not

wanting to reveal the Bible verses that had connected Ward's party and the murders. It was the only piece of evidence we had, and, as flimsy as it was, I was reluctant to share it too widely.

"If it is Stubb, how is he choosing which women to kill?" she asked.

"He's killing sinners and whores," I said without thinking.

Helen smiled as a schoolmaster might when confronted with an unusually dim child. "Obviously. But the city is full of sinners. Why is he killing *these* sinners in particular? Why Jennet Porter? Why Mary Dodsworth?"

I glanced at Martha, who seemed as taken aback by the question as I felt. We'd never even thought about it.

"We assumed that he killed whoever was at hand," I said.

"Then why would he kill four people in the north of the city, and a fifth in the south?" Helen asked. "They cannot *all* be close at hand. No, I think there's more to it than that. I think he's targeting me."

"What?" Martha and I cried out together.

"Why would you think that?" I asked.

"It is quite obvious," she said. "Jennet had come to me for help, and she died in one of my tenements, as did the two people killed in St. John-del-Pyke."

"And the barmaid?" I asked. "Did you 'help' her in the same way you 'helped' Jennet?"

"I didn't know her," Helen admitted. "But the tavern lies not a hundred yards from my house. He could hardly have found anyone closer."

"But how would he know which whores are in your employ, or which buildings you own?" Martha asked. "You don't make a show of such things, and the Wards are strangers to York."

"There are city officials whom I have trusted with my secrets.

They provide some protection from the law, and I provide them with money and information that would not usually come their way."

"Whom do you mean?" I asked.

"I have reached an agreement with your nephew Joseph," she said. "After the city fell and the constables began to harass the women in my employ, Joseph came to Stephen with a proposal. He said that he could protect me from the rigors of the law if I would pay him a few pounds each month and share with him what I know about his rivals. Soon none in the city will dare oppose him for fear of public humiliation."

Martha, Will, and I sat in stunned silence. From the smile that played across her lips, I could tell that Helen enjoyed delivering this news. Could this be true? Could Joseph be so corrupt as to profess godliness in the light of day, and soil his hands with a bawd's money under cover of the night? I felt my lingering anger at Helen's impudence mixing with my fury at Joseph's hypocrisy. I gazed at Helen's face, hoping for some sign that she was lying to us.

"I cannot believe this," I said. "Joseph would never resort to extortion, and he would never traffic with a common bawd. He has no need."

"Why would I lie?" she asked, still smiling. She seemed quite pleased with my reaction. I could find no answer to her question.

"My brother has been taking money from you?" Will asked through bared teeth. I could see fury growing within him as well. "All this time he's been pretending godliness while taking your money?" His voice rose with each word.

I took his hand, but he shook it off without even glancing at me. Before I could speak, Will leaped to his feet and started for the door. He already held his cane like a sword, and I knew that if he found Joseph while he was in this state, bloodshed would result. I reached for his arm in the hope of stopping him, but he eluded my grasp.

Martha was faster than I and reached the door before Will. "Will, no!" she begged. She took his arms and forced him to look into her eyes. "What are you going to do?"

"I'm going to thrash him within an inch of his life," Will said. "And then I'm going to show my father who his favored son really is."

"You can't," I said. "Not now."

Will ignored me completely, and tried to push past Martha.

"She is right," Martha said, staring imploringly into Will's eyes. "We have to figure out what this means for the murders before we do anything."

Will took a deep breath and worked to regain control of himself.

"There is no profit in confronting Joseph today," Martha said softly. "He will still be there for thrashing tomorrow."

Will nodded, and Martha guided him back to the parlor.

"I seem to have found an open wound," Helen said. "I am sorry."

I studied her face for some sign of insincerity, but her sentiment seemed genuine. Perhaps there was more to her than I'd realized.

"Mrs. Wright," Martha said, hoping to turn the discussion back to the murders. "Why would Joseph help the murderer? If he is so conniving, he'd be better off if he kept the whores alive and mined them for their secrets."

"He wouldn't do it on purpose," she explained. "But to maintain his godly façade, Joseph rails against me both in public and in private. He must have complained of my work to Ward's people, and then this John Stubb used what he'd learned to choose his victims."

"And that's why, out of all the sinners in York, Stubb has killed those closest to you," I said. "Joseph set him on your trail." I could see the logic in her thinking.

Helen nodded. "It is the only explanation. And once Stubb chose me as the enemy in his mad war, he would not have found it difficult to discover which buildings I own. And from there the blood began to flow." She stood and executed a perfect curtsey. "Thank you for your help, Lady Bridget. I am grateful."

"Wait!" I cried. "That is all? What do you intend to do?"

"It is clear that Stubb intends to do me harm. I will defend myself. I have no intention of hiding in my home until he tries to kill me."

"If he is guilty, we will prove it and see him hanged," I said. "You must trust us. It is your only choice."

Once again Helen regarded at me as she would a child. "It is not my only choice," she replied. "I will not take the chance."

"Then what will you do?"

"She means to kill Stubb," Martha said softly.

"What?" I cried. "You can do no such thing!"

"*I* can't, but Stephen certainly can," Helen replied.

I stared at Helen's man. He did not look up from his carving, but a smile flitted across his lips.

"And why shouldn't he?" Helen continued. Her cold-bloodedness sent a chill through me. "If Stubb has already killed five people, and intends to add me to his tally, then no other action makes sense."

"*If* he killed them!" I cried. "*If* he is guilty! If he is innocent, you'll be no different from the murderer himself. You can't kill a man because he *might* be guilty."

"If he were killing your clients, or if he attacked Martha and threatened you, what would you do?" she asked. "Is your love of the law so strong that you would simply stand by and wait for the constables to act?"

"You cannot," I insisted, my voice rising to near a shout. "We have our suspicions but no proof!"

"How long would you have me wait?" she asked, her voice rising along with mine. "How many women have to die before I have your permission? I will not wait until your conscience is satisfied. I will defend the women in my employ, and I will defend myself."

I could not believe what I heard. "You are the one who brought these women into harm's way at the outset! Were it not for you, Jennet would be alive and well."

"There are far worse bawds than me, and were it not for my help, Jennet would be half-starved at the very best. I'll not say that it's good work, but for maids like Jennet it's that or slow death. Which would you have them choose?"

"That does not make what you do right."

"I do my penance," she said. "I pay the fines that the city levies and I've paid the school fees for two lads from my parish. The oldest will start at Cambridge next year, and that'll cost me a tidy sum. Have you given as much to *your* neighbors?"

"Your pennies, pence, and pounds cannot make amends for your sins," I hissed. "Or have you turned Papist and think that good works will save your soul? Perhaps you intend to re-create the stews of Rome here in York."

Helen stood and walked toward me until our faces were mere inches apart.

"I'll not explain myself any further," she said softly. "I will stay my hand for now, but if Stubb attacks another girl, or if I come to fear for my life, he'll not breathe another day. I will see to that." Without waiting for a response, she turned and stalked out of the parlor.

Stephen turned to Martha. "If you learn anything that shows Stubb's innocence," he said, "I suggest you send word immediately." He then handed Martha a carved snake nearly identical to the one he'd given us when we visited Helen and followed his mistress out the door.

Martha looked at the serpent for a moment before slipping it into her apron.

"That . . . that . . . salt bitch!" I fumed once we were alone. "What have *I* given to my neighbors? What *haven't* I given? Peace, comfort, children! Life itself! Who is she to challenge me in such a way?"

Martha knew better than to reply, or even to try soothing my wrath. She slipped from the room and returned with a glass of wine, which I gulped down without tasting it. Once my heart had slowed, I sat and took a deep breath.

Will looked at me out of the corner of his eye, as if afraid I would explode yet again and this time turn my anger in his direction.

"It's all right, Will," I said. "I don't know what it is, but there is something about her that drives me to blind fury." To my surprise, Will laughed.

"You don't know why she angers you, Aunt Bridget? She is your twin and your antipode at the same time!"

"What?" I cried. "She and I have nothing in common!"

"Oh, come now, Aunt Bridget," Will said. "She is wealthy and powerful, and every day she deals in the city's secrets. She keeps them when it suits her, and reveals them when she must. How much of that is not also true of you?"

"It is not at all the same, Will," I protested, but in my mind I struggled to determine just what he'd said that was wrong. "She is a low-born, scandalous woman!"

"And thus your antipode," he said, delighted that I'd followed him so far. "She works in the city's shadows, and you practice in the light. She is an outlaw, and you *are* the law. *Of course* she infuriates you. The strange thing would be if she did not. If you were a bawd or if she were a midwife, you would be good gossips, I think."

I tried to find a suitable answer to Will's charge, but could not. "I take it you'll be staying for supper?" I asked. Will laughed, knowing he'd bested me in our argument.

"Of course."

That evening, Martha, Will, and I drank a bit more wine than usual, and for a time we succeeded in our efforts to talk of something besides the murders. City politics, the latest news of the war between the King and Parliament, even the heat, God help us. But eventually, as we all knew that it would, our talk returned to the killings.

"Time is short," Will said. He gazed out my window into the gathering darkness. "Short for a whore if we do not discover the killer. Short for Stubb if we do not find out that someone else is the killer. It is hard to see how this ends without more blood being shed."

"Perhaps the killer does not do God's work on the Sabbath," Martha offered. "That would give us until Monday, at least." I did not think even she believed it. I felt my spirits sinking as I considered the prospect of finding more and more bodies.

Will stood and made his way unsteadily to the door.

"Stay, Will, won't you?" I asked. "It is late. Stay and come to the Sabbath service with us tomorrow."

"I'll be fine," Will insisted. "I've made it home more cup-shot than this."

"You ought not go," Martha said. "Not like that. The guard on Ouse Bridge will lock you up for the night, won't he? And who knows if the killer will turn from whores to drunkards."

To my surprise, Will relented.

"Perhaps you are right," he said, shrugging off his coat and turning for the stairs. "I'll see you in the morning, Aunt Bridget."

The next day my strange little family went to St. Helen's church for the morning service. Only Hannah did not suffer from too much wine. Will and Martha both drowsed for a time, and I had to bite my cheek to keep from following suit. As the morning's half of the service ended, Mr. Wilson, our longtime parish minister, ascended the pulpit and called for our attention.

"This afternoon's sermon will be delivered by Mr. Hezekiah Ward, a famous preacher newly come to the city."

I looked over at Will and Martha. They both sat straight in their seats, staring at Mr. Wilson. He had their attention now.

"The text for his sermon," Mr. Wilson continued, "will be from Jeremiah, chapter thirteen. *I have seen thy adulteries and the lewdness of thy whoredom, and thy abominations on the hills in the fields: woe unto thee, O Jerusalem, wilt thou not be made clean?*"

"Ah, Christ have mercy," Martha muttered.

I could not have agreed more.

Chapter 15

"How is it that Ward is preaching *here*?" I hissed in the church-warden's ear as we made our way up the aisle and into the blazing heat of the day. The sun seared my eyes, but I would not be stopped. "Have I not made clear my feelings about such fanatics?" As a woman, I could not serve on the parish vestry, of course, but I'd given more than my fair share to the church and the parish poor, so I expected to be heard and heeded on matters such as this.

"I am sorry, Lady Hodgson," the churchwarden stammered. "The vestrymen did not meet to discuss the matter. I only learned of Mr. Wilson's decision this morning." The poor man looked as if he were about to cry. He was the newest vestryman and must have worried I'd drive him from office. I turned him loose, and found Will and Martha.

"Well, that will certainly make it easier to watch the Wards," Will said.

"I'll speak to Mr. Wilson," I said. "This time we may be able to prevent his preaching, or delay the sermon to another Sunday. Once we've caught the murderer, his sermons will be less dangerous."

The three of us waited at the church door for the minister to come out. Mr. Wilson had been vicar of St. Helen's for decades, and while he remained a neutralist in our nation's wars, it was clear to us all that he'd never taken to the ranting style of men like Ward. Despite his aged frame, he walked with the steady gate of a man who knew his place in the community, and felt confident of his own salvation. I could not imagine why he'd ceded his pulpit to Ward.

"Mr. Wilson," I said. "Might I have a word?"

He smiled as he came to greet me. We had dined together on many occasions, and he knew who the parish's benefactors were. The sun accentuated the lines on his face, which had been deepened by the strains of England's war of religion.

"Lady Hodgson, how are you?" he asked with a bow. Somehow, despite the heat and his dark robes, he appeared to be as comfortable as he would have been on a mild spring morning. "I take it you will attend Mrs. Elliott's churching this afternoon?" Jane Elliott had given birth the month before, and this week marked the end of her confinement. I'd had the sad duty of laying out her infant son for burial just two weeks after he was born, so there would be a certain melancholy about the ceremony.

"Of course," I said. "Mr. Elliott has promised to provide ample entertainment afterward. I would not dare miss it!" Mr. Wilson and I talked of parish news a bit longer and then I addressed my real concern. "When did you decide to allow Mr. Ward into your pulpit?"

A pained look crossed Mr. Wilson's face.

"It was not my doing, Lady Hodgson," he said. "You know I do not approve of the hot gospellers, and I would never willingly turn one loose among my flock."

"Then what happened?"

"Your nephew Joseph and the other godly Aldermen happened," he replied with a snort. "It is all that the sober-minded clergy in the city can talk about. Joseph is pushing his ministers into all of York's parishes. If a minister refuses to cooperate, Joseph threatens to eject him from his position. If I refused the 'offer' of Mr. Ward's services, I could be put out of the parish! What would happen to my people then?"

"You know I'd never allow that," I said. "I still have some power in the city."

"Not so much as you might think, my lady." The vicar was old enough to speak frankly, and I did not begrudge him this right. "And if allowing Mr. Ward to preach every now and again is the price for keeping my people safe, then I'll pay it. There is nothing he can say in public that I can't unsay in private. But the sad case is that there is nothing I can do to keep him from preaching."

I could see Mr. Wilson's point, but I nevertheless fretted and fumed all the way back to my house. I was angry not just at the imposition of Ward upon my parish, though that was infuriating enough, but at the role Joseph had played in the invasion.

"Why would Joseph do such a thing?" I asked Will as we walked up Stonegate. "What does he gain by angering me?"

"He's likely aiming at Mr. Wilson," Will replied. "He's sending godly clergy wherever he finds men who prefer ceremony to sermons. If he can't force them out of the city, he'll at least drive them out of the pulpit for the day."

"I knew there was a reason I favored you," I said, taking his arm.

"I know," he replied with a chuckle. "And I, you."

Far sooner than I would have liked, the afternoon bells began to toll, calling the city to the second service of the day. As we walked to the church, I felt dread rising within me both at the thought of what Ward might say and at what the murderer might do in response. We took our places in my pew, and watched the Wards closely as they filed in. Mr. Ward held his Bible before him like a shield, while Deborah followed close behind, her eyes sweeping the church for hidden threats. Praise-God followed along behind her, and then Silence, her head held high, confident in her youth, beauty, and righteousness. The rest of Ward's gang followed close behind, with Stubb bringing up the rear.

The service started peaceably enough, as Mr. Wilson said a few prayers, then called Jane Elliott to the front of the church. Once he'd prayed over her, and she'd given thanks to God for her survival, she returned to her seat. After only the barest of introductions—one that made clear how unwilling he was to give up his place—Mr. Wilson took his seat in the chancel and gestured for Ward to ascend to the pulpit. Once there, Ward raised his Bible high over his head and let out a cry so loud and so full of anguish it startled even the most reluctant members of his audience into attentiveness.

"Why, O Lord, do your people refuse to heed your word?" he called out. "Why do they insist on returning to their sins like dogs to their vomit?"

From there his sermon seemed like the others he had preached. The words differed, but the message was the same. After a few minutes, I paid only scant attention. Rather, I stared at Stubb, James Hooke, and Ward's wife and daughter, who sat together near the front of the church. They, in turn, stared up at Ward as if he were one of the apostles. Could one of them be the killer? Stubb looked the part, of course; what about Silence? She seemed the very soul of godly piety, but I'd been fooled by a murderer before, and knew that the most innocent face could hide the vilest heart. I wondered at man's deceptive nature—how was it that the evil that lay within did not show itself to the world? Ward pulled me back into the present when I heard him cry out Jane Elliott's name.

"What call did the Lord have to strike down Jane Elliott's child?" he asked. "Some will deny that God had a hand in the boy's death. Or they will claim that the Lord's will is unknowable. But God's inscrutability does not relieve us of the duty, yea the *holy obligation*, to seek out His message. Is it mere happenstance that the Lord burned up the child with a fever, even as He burned the city with the sun?"

A few voices cried out *Amen*. Most were from Ward's party, but I could not help noticing a few of my neighbors joining in.

"Just as the city suffers for its sins and must seek out the cause of God's wrath, the mother who has lost a child must search her conscience. She must ask which of her sins caused God to strike such a deadly blow."

Upon hearing these words, my heart rebelled. Could he be blaming Jane for the death of her son? Children died so often and so young that if Ward were right, England's mothers must have been the worst of sinners. How else could we explain the grief that the Lord visited upon them?

I could not tolerate any more. Without a word to Will or Martha, I stepped into the aisle and strode toward the back of the church. My friends and neighbors stared at me as I walked past them. They, of course, knew that my children had suffered the same fate as Jane's, for many of them had been there when I buried both Michael and Birdy. I refused to believe that my sins had somehow brought about their deaths, nor could I bear the thought that my neighbors might believe it. But what if some did?

Ward seemed the devil himself to sow such seeds of discord. As I walked down the aisle, I saw the faces of women whom I'd delivered, women who had lost their own children. Some appeared as furious as I was, some looked stricken at the idea that they were to blame for the deaths of their children. What a monster Ward was, to plant such thoughts!

Thankfully the church door had been left open to allow in some air, and I was able to escape without stopping. I walked home alone, still furious at Ward's words. I slammed the door behind me, and retreated to my chamber for solitary prayer. It seemed the only way to soothe my soul.

I allowed my mind to drift back to the night Birdy died and then further back to Michael's death day. With Martha and Hannah still at the church, I could allow the grief to pour forth from my heart; I sobbed and wailed as I had not done in months. As I cried, I fought to forget Ward's sermon. I forbade myself from asking the Lord what I had done to offend Him so deeply that He would rob me of my beloved children. What sin could merit such a punishment? I asked God for peace, for Him to soothe my soul.

It must have been an hour before I heard the welcome sounds of Hannah, Martha, and Will chattering downstairs. I gathered myself, washed my face in a basin, and went down to join them.

"Oh, my lady, you left before things turned." Hannah laughed. "God, the look on his face!" Martha and Will laughed along with her, and I found myself joining in even before I knew what had taken place.

"It happened about a quarter of an hour after you left," Will explained, wiping a tear from his eye. "Ward asked us, *Is anyone here free from sin? Yea, who carries not the curse of Adam? Speak now!*"

"And then he waited," Martha continued. "Finally, Mrs. Ascough—the baker's wife—stood up and cried out, *I know not who is free from sin, but I do know your sermon sounds like an old dog's fart!*"

At this the four of us fell to laughing, but Martha held up her hand. "Wait, wait, that was not the end of it! When Ward's wife stood to shout her down, Mrs. Ascough would have none of it. *You're as great a whore as any, aren't you? You should leave us alone and trouble yourself more with your daughter. She's a burnt-arsed whore, she is, turning tail to hedge at every opportunity.*"

"And then *she* walked out, as neat as you please, and more than a few followed her!" Will finished. "Oh, Aunt Bridget, the looks on the Wards' faces were worth sitting through the whole wretched sermon."

I sent Martha for a few pots of ale, and when she returned, the four of us retold the story as we drank. As the pain of the afternoon slipped away, I wondered if the Lord might have answered my prayers for peace by giving me this curious family.

"Well, we should go to the Elliotts,'" I said to Martha when we'd finished the ale. "Mrs. Elliott will be quite furious with us if we arrive too late."

"And if we dally, the good wine will be gone," Martha added. Will bade us farewell and left for home, while Martha and I walked toward the Elliotts'.

Some churchings were joyous affairs, celebrating both mother and child. This would be more somber, as we mourned the child even as we gave thanks for Jane's survival. By the time we arrived, two dozen guests had filled the Elliotts' parlors and dining room and were making short work of the wine and food that Mr. Elliott had provided. Martha and I fell in with a group of women, and the talk quickly turned to Mrs. Ascough's eruption against the Wards. Where Martha, Will, and I found jollity, however, some of the women found fault.

"He's not doing any harm," one woman—Mary Good was her name—objected. "He just wants to rid the city of sin, as God intends. Who among us could find fault with that?"

"Do you *really* think that these dog days have been sent by God to punish us?" asked a stout, kind-faced woman.

"God is warning us," Mary Good replied. "He showed us mercy during the siege last year, and we ignored Him. He is merciful to correct us before visiting His wrath upon us in earnest."

"And do you also think that He took Jane's baby as a punishment for her sins?" the stout woman demanded. Her face did not seem so kind anymore.

At this a hush fell over our little group. It was one thing to rail against the sins of an entire city—who could deny them?—but to accuse a woman in the death of her own child was a different matter. Mary started to reply, but her adversary had not finished.

"Do you truly believe that the Lord is so cruel as to avenge Himself on the parents by killing a child? Jane is hardly the worst sinner among us."

"Do we know this?" Mary asked. "And even if Jane is not to blame, who among us knows what sins her husband might be hiding? The heart is a wretched thing, and man is destined to wallow in the filth of sin."

Upon hearing this, I could contain myself no longer.

"Mary Good," I said. "If you are accusing Jane Elliott or her husband of some secret sin, be clear about it. Such hinting and gossiping is cruel sport."

"I know of no sin," she replied. "But the Lord knows all, and he acts to avenge Himself on those who will not walk in His ways. Open your eyes—it is visible in the world around us. When the King turned Papist, God sent Parliament's armies to chasten him. When whoredom spread, He sent this burning summer. If God can raise up armies or drive away the rain, He can take a child into His bosom if it pleases Him. He owes us nothing, and we owe Him all, including the lives of our children."

"And what sin did I commit?" I asked. I could feel anger—the boon companion of that afternoon's grief—coming together in my breast, awaiting the opportunity to burst forth. "What terrible blot is on my soul that would require God to take both my children?"

Mary realized that she'd trod onto dangerous ground, and I could see her trying to find a way to retreat. She might well believe that God had taken Birdy and Michael to punish me for my sins, but she knew better than to say such a thing in my presence.

"The Lord is unknowable," she said at last. "Perhaps the warning is for all of us."

I knew that she spoke out of fear rather than conviction, so forcing her to deny my guilt was a hollow victory. She believed that I—like Jane Elliott—had brought the death of my children upon myself.

"Mary Good, that is such shit!" said a voice from behind me. Martha elbowed her way into the circle of women. The color had risen in her cheeks, and she stared at Mary with a heat akin to the sun's. "If God murders children to correct the parents, He's doing a beggarly job of it. Look at the awful women who've kept all their children." She inclined her head toward a truly poisonous woman who'd borne her husband six children, all hale and healthy. "And who has been a better gossip to her neighbors than Lady Hodgson? Who has done more for the poor of the parish? For its mothers and children? Why should God correct her?"

Mary started to reply, but Martha would not allow it.

"Shut your gob; there's nothing to say. Sometimes children die. Sometimes the sun shines, and sometimes it rains. That's all there is." With that, Martha took my arm and pulled me from that crowd, all the while muttering the vilest oaths.

"Thank you," I mumbled.

"Don't you mind her," Martha replied, leading me toward the door. "There's no need to trouble yourself with such absurd ideas."

We stepped into the street and began walking home. The sun had set an hour before, and I was grateful we hadn't far to go, for the shadows seemed as threatening as ever.

"It's just that sometimes I wonder . . . ," I said.

"Don't even think in that way," Martha said. "God did not take my child because he was born a bastard. Nor did He kill my master because he raped me. Those things just happened. God has no interest in worldly justice."

"No," I said, "That is not what I was going to say."

"What then?"

"I wonder sometimes if God sent you to York when I needed you most."

Martha's laughter echoed through the deserted streets. "Well," she said. "I'd never thought of myself as a divine blessing, but if that's how you see it, I won't deny being one of His angels." She paused and as she thought, her face became more serious. "But it has been a good year, hasn't it?"

"It has."

"Except for the murders, of course," Martha said with a wan smile. "They have certainly complicated things."

This feeble attempt at a joke brought us both back to the possibility that today's sermon would end in death for another of York's whores.

"He'll kill again, won't he?" Martha asked. She spoke so softly I could barely make out her words.

"I don't know why he'd stop now," I said.

"Isn't there anything we can do?" Martha asked. "If

we're right in thinking that Stubb is the killer, there must be something."

"Edward and Joseph won't act," I said. "And in this matter, they are the law."

"We could have Will follow him," Martha suggested. "Or hire a soldier. The town watch helped us last year."

"Will can't just stand out in the street all night, waiting for Stubb to act," I replied. "He'd be taken up by the town watch in no time at all. You know that."

Martha furrowed her brow.

"Wait!" she cried out. I could hear the excitement in her voice. "How is he doing it?"

"What do you mean?" I asked. "Doing what?"

Before she could answer, a woman's scream tore through the night. The sound was human, but barely so, and seemed born of rage rather than terror or pain. We stopped and stared into the shadows.

"What in God's name was that?" Martha asked. My heart thundered so loudly I wondered that I could hear her words.

"Let's get inside," I whispered and we backed toward my door.

Without warning, a woman hurtled out of the doorway across from mine, and once again the street echoed with her screams. She drove her shoulder into Martha's chest, and they both fell to the ground. I heard Martha cursing as she fought to disentangle herself from her assailant.

I threw myself into the fray, grabbing a handful of hair and hauling up and back. Once again the woman's screams rent the night, but this time they were of pain and frustration. Martha leaped to her feet and delivered a ferocious clout to her attacker's face. The stranger fell to her hands and knees, dazed by the blow. I rushed to Martha's side and together we faced our attacker.

When she looked up at us, I recognized the plump and pretty woman from Hezekiah Ward's sermons. Blood dripped from her nose, which appeared to be broken. She stared into my eyes and drew back her lips in a terrible, bloody smile.

"Touch not the Lord's anointed," she hissed. Martha and I backed slowly away. The woman stood and pointed at us. "The Lord will not suffer your sins. He will not." She turned and disappeared into the shadows.

"Inside," I said. "Now."

Martha nodded, and we took the last few steps to my door. Once I locked the door behind us, I felt as if I could breathe again.

"My God, Martha," I said. "Are you all right?"

"My dress is in tatters, but I'm fine. Who in God's name was that?"

"One of Ward's more vicious sheep," I said. "I've seen her at his sermons."

Martha thought for a moment.

"*Touch not the Lord's anointed*," she said. "She must be the one who left the note."

"Or it could be one of the others in that crowd," I said. "Who knows how many fevered brains have joined up with Ward? God, any of them could be the murderer." I dropped onto my couch. How could we sort out the murderous from the mad?

"No, it couldn't be any of them," Martha said. "That's what I was going to say before that demon attacked us."

"What do you mean?"

"If it is Stubb, how is he getting around the city?" she asked. "He's killed five people, all of them at night. And he's done so on both sides of the river. How is he managing to escape the town watch? They stopped us twice on the night we viewed Betty's body, once on the way there and once on the way home. Surely if they found Stubb wandering the street, they'd arrest him."

"If he knew the city well enough, he might be able to slip by on the backstreets." I said.

"But he only just arrived in York," Martha replied. "If he wandered off the main streets at night, he'd walk for hours just trying to find his way home, never mind finding the whore of his choosing. And there are no backstreets that cross the river—just the bridge."

"So how is he doing it?" I asked.

"He has help," Martha said. "It's someone who knows the city, and can talk his way past the town watch. And it is someone who knows Helen Wright's business." She paused, weighing her next words with extreme caution. "It is your nephew Joseph. He's behind the killing."

Chapter 16

"You can't mean that!" I cried. "Joseph? Are you mad?"

"If you consider what we know, it makes sense," Martha insisted. "He'll freely admit that he's part of the godly faction, and you heard him when he thought I'd blasphemed. He threatened to put me in the stocks! He knew Stubb from their time in the army, and he knows the city well enough to guide Stubb through the backstreets. And if they *were* discovered by the city watch, Joseph could simply explain that he is a constable on city business."

"But he would not do such a thing!"

"Why not?" Martha asked. She seemed so sure of herself, she nearly carried me along by the force of her will. "The boy who left for the wars might not be a part of such a scheme, but you've seen how war can change a man. How many men did he kill? Half a dozen in just a few minutes, and who knows how many more before that. What was done to Jennet, Betty, and the others is nothing compared to what he did every day."

"Martha, it cannot be," I said, but with less certainty.

"And Helen Wright said that Joseph knew as much about her

193

business as anyone in the city," Martha continued. "That's why the murderer killed people in her buildings—Joseph led him there!"

"And Betty?" I asked. "She neither worked for Helen nor lived in one of her tenements."

"I don't know," Martha replied, undaunted. "Perhaps they couldn't find the whore they had in mind, or Stubb chose her on his own. But it was with Joseph's connivance. It must have been."

"You can't say anything to Will," I said. "Not until I've had time to consider this."

"Of course not," Martha said. "But if we're going to follow Joseph's trail, we'll have to tell Will sooner rather than later."

"I know," I said. "But not yet."

That night as I lay in bed, I puzzled over Martha's suggestion that Joseph was behind the murders. The more I thought about it, the more plausible the idea became. I recalled my time with Joseph before he'd joined Cromwell's Ironsides. He'd been a nice enough lad, godly in the mold of his father but not a fanatic in any way. We assumed that after he returned from the army, he would marry and then wait patiently for his chance to follow in his father's footsteps. A tolerable life to be sure, and one that many a man—including Will—would envy. There was no place in this future for him to become the executioner of defenseless whores.

But the war had changed him, hadn't it? He'd come back a harder and more ambitious man, one who was willing to do business with a woman like Helen Wright. Joseph was not content to wait for decades until his father's power and money passed into his hands; rather, like the Prodigal Son, he would have his portion now. He had become used to power while in the army, and what greater power could there be than to kill?

But as I drifted toward sleep, it was not Joseph's face that came to mind but Mark Preston's. I thought of the cruelty of his smile, and of his indifference as the bodies piled up. Could *he* be behind the murders? Or could he and Joseph be killing together, as they had on the battlefield? Perhaps this was why Joseph had brought him to York in the first place.

The question of when to alert Will of Martha's suspicions—suspicions I now shared—crept back into my mind. I knew we had to tell him, but could not imagine how to do so, or how he would react. What words would you use to say *I think your brother is a cruel and vicious murderer?* Would Will accept the possibility or turn his anger against us? I also worried that Edward might find out. If Will would be upset at the suggestion, Edward would be furious at me for merely countenancing the thought. And if our suspicions about his son turned out to be true, it would ruin him forever.

The next morning, as the sun rose and began its daily assault on the city, there came a pounding at my door and I felt my stomach sink. The murderer must have killed again. As I'd feared, Will awaited me in the parlor, but his face radiated excitement rather than sorrow. Clearly he brought a different kind of news.

"Aunt Bridget," he said as soon as I came into the room, "the messenger has returned from Manchester."

"From the look on your face, I'd guess that it's good news."

"Nothing that'll see Stubb to the gallows, but it will put another loop in the hangman's knot."

"The constables knew him?" Martha asked as she entered the parlor. She'd been baking, and her hands still were covered with flour.

"They knew the entire mob. All the Wards: Hezekiah, Deborah, Praise-God, and Silence. They knew Stubb, too."

"What did they say?" I asked. "Were there murders there as well?"

"Everything but," Will said. "Mr. Ward preached against whores just as he has here. He ever used the same verses."

"And the rest of it?" Martha asked. "Did they trouble the city's whores?"

"And divided the city against itself," Will replied. "Neighbors nearly came to blows over his sermons, and both Praise-God and Deborah were attacked by one woman's pimp. They escaped a thrashing only because Stubb arrived on the scene."

"Deborah Ward thrashed by a pimp?" Martha cried. "What I'd have given to see that!"

"It says she was the worst of the bunch," Will said. "The constables nearly arrested her for riot."

"How did they escape the city?" I asked.

"Joseph's invitation to York came just in time to save their skins."

At the mention of Joseph's name, Martha and I froze and looked at each other. Will realized he'd said something significant, but had no idea what it was.

"Aunt Bridget? Martha?" he asked, his eyes shifting nervously between us. "What is it?"

"*Joseph* invited the Wards to York?" I asked. "You're sure?"

"It's what the letter says," Will said with a shrug. "The city council summoned Hezekiah Ward to answer for the tumult and divisions he'd sown within the city, and he said he'd been invited to York. Some thought he was lying in order to escape the courts, but he showed them the letter from my brother. What is it?"

Martha and I exchanged another glance. Neither of us wanted to say what we were thinking.

"I suppose now is the time to tell you," I said at last. "Do you think it is possible that Joseph is behind the murders, perhaps with Stubb or Mark Preston as his accomplice?"

"What?" Will cried. "Are you crazed? Joseph?"

"We know how it sounds," I said, taking his arm and turning him away from Martha. I did not want him to think that she had first pointed the finger at his brother. "It seems absurd, but we must consider the evidence before us, and you have added to it. Joseph knew Stubb during the wars, and we know that he's in league with Helen Wright."

Will started to object.

"You must hear me out," I said. "Then he intervened to keep Stubb out of jail after the first murders." Will nodded slowly. His face had grown pale. "And now we find out that it was he who brought the Wards to the city. Joseph is the connection between John Stubb and Helen Wright."

"He wouldn't do such a thing," Will said.

"And whoever the murderer is, he's able to move about the city at night without being taken by the town watch. Joseph could do that. He knows the city as well as you do." I did not mention Joseph's newfound enthusiasm for wild religion—Will knew of that all too well.

"Aunt Bridget, it is impossible," Will said, but I could tell he was considering the possibility even as he spoke. "What would he gain by this?"

"Power to reform the city," Martha said. "The knowledge that he is doing God's work. Would that not be enough?"

"He would never," Will said, but with less certainty than before. "Yes, he's changed, but not into a murderer. My brother is not a murderer."

"We hope not," I said. "But if Stubb is the killer, he must have help from someone who knows the city. And someone who knows Helen Wright." Will stared out the window for a time, not saying anything. At last he came to a decision.

"I think you are wrong," he said. "But it is something we need to consider. Aunt Bridget, you mustn't tell my father—not until we have something more than mere suspicion. It would destroy him entirely."

"Of course," I said. There was nothing to be gained from upsetting Edward.

"What do we do now?" Will asked. "I can't interrupt dinner to ask Joseph if he's schemed to murder five people in the hope of ending whoredom."

"You could search his chamber," Martha suggested.

"He's not fool enough to be caught that way," Will said. "And if Stubb is doing the killing there would be no evidence to find."

"Have you noticed him coming and going at night?" Martha asked.

Will shook his head. "The house is big enough that he can do what he pleases and nobody is the wiser. And even if I did, such is the life of a constable, especially one who hopes to drive sin from the city. He's fond of telling me, *the Lord did not rest in the nighttime*. Bloody fool."

"For now, you can watch him," I said. "Offer to accompany him if he goes out at night. Tell him you want to learn more about the duties of a constable."

"I don't think that will work," Will snorted. "He talks to me like my father used to. *With your foot, you'll never keep up*. Or if he's feeling sorry for me it will be even worse: *A constable must be of sound mind and body, Will. I'm sorry*. No, I'll have to find another way."

Will gazed out the window. The pain on his face could not have been clearer, and I put my arm around him. I marveled that any man could reject his own brother for nothing more than a malformed foot, but knew that the fault lay with Edward. He taught Joseph such lessons, both by his refusal to groom Will for government and through his daily condescension.

At my invitation, Will joined us for breakfast, and we talked more of the murders and of what we should do next.

"Perhaps Mark Preston is the one behind the murders," Will suggested hopefully. "He's a born killer to be sure."

"I considered that," I said. "Even though he is in your father's house, he still is subject to the town watch. They would take him as quickly as they would Stubb. No, somehow the killer has convinced the town watch to let him travel around the city at night."

"What do you propose we do?" Martha asked.

I considered the question, but had no good answers. If we were right about Joseph, how would we prove it?

"Why don't we go back to the harlots?" I suggested at last.

"What do you mean?" Will asked.

"We should find the women we talked to before, Barbara Rearsby and Isabel Dalton," I said. "Perhaps they've seen or heard something since we last spoke to them."

"We could ask them if they have seen Joseph and Mark lurking about," Martha added.

"They might not have mentioned it before," Will said, nodding. "They'd hardly bother to mention a constable chasing whores."

"Who should we visit first?" Martha asked.

I thought of Isabel Dalton and Elizabeth, her red-haired daughter.

"Let us start with Isabel," I said. "She seemed most likely to notice if something were out of the ordinary."

We wound our way through Hungate parish, this time avoiding the wrong turns we'd taken the previous week. When we neared Isabel's house, we saw two women standing at her door. As we approached, one of them started toward us at a dead run. It was Barbara Rearsby, the whore we'd talked to in the Castle.

"Lady Hodgson, thank God you're here!" she cried. The poor girl's eyes were red from crying and even now she fought to control her sobs. She fell to her knees when she reached us, and broke down in tears.

"Barbara, what is it? What has happened?" Martha asked.

"It's Isabel," she said at last. "She's been murdered."

Martha and I looked at each other in horror.

"Ah, God," I said. The news pierced my heart like an arrow, and my mind immediately leaped to Elizabeth. "What about her daughter? Where is Elizabeth?"

"One of the other women had her last night while Isabel worked. She's safe, but hasn't stopped crying."

I said a prayer of thanks for this small mercy.

"Is Isabel's body inside?" I asked. Barbara nodded and led us to the door. Even from a distance, I could see that the second woman was with child, and very near her travail.

Barbara explained who I was, and that I was trying to find whoever had been murdering the city's whores. The pregnant woman curtsied before looking at Will with ill-disguised suspicion.

"He is not with the city," I said. "He is with me."

"He can stay, but he'll not go in," she replied. "Men have uncovered her enough, I think."

"And who are you?" I asked. I was not accustomed to other women deciding such matters on my behalf.

"Sarah Briggs," she said. "I worked with Isabel until my condition forced me to stop. Now I help the others as best I can until I am delivered."

I thought I could probably force my will, but did not see the benefit. I nodded to Will and he took a step backward, relinquishing his place. Sarah opened the door so we could enter, and my eyes were drawn immediately to Isabel's body where it lay next to the bed. Someone had put a cloak over her, but her bare legs splayed crazily out from underneath as if she'd been captured in the midst of some wild dance.

Martha and I drew back the cloak. Though I had prepared myself for a terrible sight, I still gasped at her blood-covered face. Rather than killing her in fulfillment of some obscure verse from the Bible, the murderer had chosen to stave in her head and leave it at that. I looked around the room for a weapon—perhaps a fire poker again?—but found none.

After a moment I realized that once the initial shock of seeing Isabel's face had passed, I felt only the barest sense of terror and revulsion and this troubled me. I had seen so much death that Isabel's corpse contained no new horrors. *Yes, a whore died here today,* my heart told me. *What of it?* Is this what had happened to Joseph? Did death no longer matter to him?

"We should look in her hands," I said. Martha knelt to open one of Isabel's hands, and I the other. They were both empty.

"Why no verses?" Martha asked.

Without answering, I lifted Isabel's skirts to examine her privities. A piece of paper that had been hidden in the folds of cloth fluttered into the air before settling on her bosom.

Martha picked it up. "Isaiah, chapter one, verse twenty-one," she said. I picked through the skirts and found a second piece of paper. *Revelations 19:2,* it read.

"He just dropped them on top of her?" Martha wondered. "Why the change?"

"I don't know," I said. I knelt and looked at Isabel's legs. While the murderer had slashed at Jennet's and Betty's thighs, Isabel's were bare and bruised but otherwise unharmed.

"This time he didn't cut her," I said. "Why not? He seemed set in his ways."

Martha and I looked around, as if the room would offer some explanation. It yielded none. We stepped outside to find Will, Barbara Rearsby, and Sarah Briggs waiting for us.

"Who found her?" I asked.

"I did," Sarah replied. "I was minding Elizabeth for the night. When Isabel had not come back by morning, I left Elizabeth with a neighbor and went in search of her."

"Did you put the cloak on her?" Martha asked.

The whore nodded but said nothing, and I found myself at a loss. I gazed up and down the street, as if the murderer might have left some clue outside. From the corner of my eye, I saw a curtain in the window across the street fall back in place. Someone inside had been watching us. I crossed to the door and knocked.

The door opened to reveal an elderly woman with clothes as shabby as the tenement in which she lived.

"Good woman," I said. "May I speak with you?"

The woman looked me up and down.

"Yes, my lady?" she replied.

"Were you in your home last night?"

She furrowed her brow for a moment and I wondered if old age had begun its terrible work on her mind as well as on her body.

"Why no, my lady," she said at last. "The Lord Mayor sent his carriage for me. He said he desired my company for the evening, so I went. He read me poetry until midnight."

I felt my face redden, and Martha hid a smile behind her

hand. Before I could react, Sarah stepped forward and took the old woman by the arm.

"Now, there's no call for that, Mrs. Cowper," she said. "Lady Hodgson is a friend." The old woman squinted at me as if to say *I'll decide that*, but apparently concluded that I could indeed be trusted.

"I was here last night," Mrs. Cowper said. "I expect you're here about the row they had."

"You heard something?" asked Martha.

"Aye, even with my bad ears I heard the shouting. A more terrible clamoring I've not heard in years. I came out and yelled that I had sent my boy to summon the beadle, and that seemed to quiet them down."

"And did the beadle come?" Martha asked.

"No, and I don't have a boy to send." The woman laughed. "My threat had no more teeth than I do." She drew back her lips to reveal an unbroken set of gums.

"Did you see who was making the noise?" I felt a flicker of hope that the old woman had witnessed the murderer fleeing the scene. Even in the dark of night, she'd have known Stubb if she saw him.

"When I looked out the window, I saw one of them," she said. "But he wasn't alone. As he hurried off, he kept calling out *Wait, wait!* as if he feared being left behind."

Martha and I exchanged glances.

"There were two men here last night?" I asked. It seemed that we'd found another clue that Joseph and Stubb were working together.

"Aye," she replied. "I only saw one of them, but unless he was shouting at himself, there must have been a second. What happened in there, anyway? One of the doxies run off with a gentleman's purse?"

Sarah took the woman's arm again. "Isabel died last night," she said. "Lady Hodgson is a midwife, and she's hunting for the man responsible."

The old woman grimaced and moaned softly.

"Ah, poor girl," she said. "And you think the man I saw killed her? I wish I'd gotten a better look, then. Not too many around here put out lanterns at night, no matter what the Lord Mayor says. The wax is too dear."

"Can you say anything more about him?" Martha asked. "Was he tall? Short?"

"He wore a dark coat," she said. "Wasn't big or small, either, just the same as everyone. He had the collar up to hide his face, but I thought it was because he had been robbed by a whore. I took him for a fool and nothing worse."

I felt the little bit of hope I'd had disappear. If Mrs. Cowper had been a few years younger or if the streets had been a bit brighter, we might know who the murderer was, but in the end we'd learned little of use except that the murderer did not kill alone.

"Will, you'll have to send for a constable," I said. "Your father will want to hear of this murder, too." He nodded solemnly. I bade the old woman good day as Sarah gave a cry and her knees buckled as if a great weight had been dropped on her shoulders.

"What is it?" Barbara asked, catching her by the arm. "The baby?"

"Aye," she hissed through clenched teeth. "My waters have broken."

"Well, God is smiling on you today," Mrs. Cowper said. "You don't even need to send for a midwife." She turned to me. "You all might as well come inside. I don't think it's what you're used to, my lady, but it'll do at a pinch."

Martha and Barbara took Sarah by the arms and helped her into Mrs. Cowper's home. I rolled up my sleeves and followed them in.

Chapter 17

In keeping with her station, Mrs. Cowper's tenement was small and spare, but she kept it as clean as one could want. Sarah's labor pang had passed, and except for the drops of sweat rolling down her face, you'd never know she was in travail. We followed the old woman to the back of her home, where I laid Sarah on the bed and examined her.

"Everything is in order," I told her as she sat up, "and you are still some hours from delivery." We returned to the room that served as Mrs. Cowper's parlor and kitchen, where the rest of our company waited.

"Barbara," Sarah said, "will you fetch the gossips?"

"Of course. I'll be back shortly," she replied, and dashed off in search of Sarah's friends. By then Mrs. Cowper had busied herself in her small kitchen, stoking the fire to heat a pot of water.

"Ordinarily, I'd use this water for the herbs in my garden," she said. "But this seems more urgent."

"You've kept your herbs alive though the heat?" I asked. I'd thought I'd have to send Martha back to my house for my valise, but with a little luck, perhaps not.

"I have everything you'll need, including an eaglestone," she said. "It's been years since I delivered a child, but I still love tending my herbs."

"You were a midwife?" I asked and the old woman nodded. After a week of terrible fortune, I said a prayer of thanks for this unexpected stroke of luck. We heard a knock at the door and Will poked his head in.

"Aunt Bridget," Will said. "There is some other business we must see to." He inclined his head toward the tenement across the street. I realized he meant Isabel's body. "We must summon the constable."

Obviously he was right—we couldn't bury Isabel ourselves, and sooner or later we would have to tell city officials about her murder.

"There is a beadle living above the White Cross," Mrs. Cowper said, referring to a nearby alehouse. "He's a good man and will come readily enough."

"And why don't you summon Joseph as well," Martha suggested. "Tell him you'll guide him to the body. Then you can watch his reaction to things."

Will considered Martha's suggestion before responding.

"All right," he said. "He'll not betray anything, but I'll try." Will slipped out, leaving us women alone.

"How is it that you are hunting a murderer?" Mrs. Cowper asked. "Isn't that a job for the Justices and constables?"

"How long were you a midwife?" I asked by way of a reply.

"Years," she said. "From the birth of my last child until the arthritis took my hands from me. But that was fifteen years ago, at least. I knew your mother-in-law passably well. She lived across the river, so we did not meet often, but we helped each other from time to time."

The mention of Phineas's mother surprised me. She'd trained me in the mysteries of midwifery after I'd come to York to marry her son. She'd been under no illusions about his nature, and I think she wanted to make sure I had a life of my own.

"I am helping the city in the search," I said. "It is not so uncommon."

The old woman laughed at this.

"Not uncommon if they're hunting a bastard's father, but a murderer? I'm neither so young nor so old to believe everything I hear."

"It is unusual," I admitted. "But we live in unusual times."

"That we do." Mrs. Cowper nodded.

"Mrs. Cowper," Martha said. "Do you have a Bible?"

"It's been some years since I could read it, but I should, somewhere." She shuffled into the back room, and returned a moment later with a well-worn book. "Are you with the Puritans, then?" she asked.

Martha looked at me, unsure how much to share with the old woman.

"It's related to Isabel's murder," I answered. "We think she was killed by the same man who killed the other whores."

"And what's the Bible got to do with it?"

There seemed no way to avoid telling her the truth now.

"I need you to be discreet," I said.

"I am still enough of a midwife for that," she replied.

"And Sarah, you must promise not to tell anyone either," I said. "If the information escapes, it could help the killer cover his trail."

"I won't say anything," she said.

I nodded. "The murderer has been leaving Biblical verses in his victims' hands. He seems to believe that he has a divine warrant for his actions."

Mrs. Cowper shook her head in wonder. "There are those who say the end of days is at hand. Sometimes I think they may be right." She handed the book to Martha, who began to search for the passages.

"Here's Isaiah," she said. "*How is the faithful city become a harlot! It was full of judgment; righteousness lodged in it; but now murderers inhabit it.*" She read the passage again, this time to herself. "Damn him! Does he not see that this passage condemns *him*, not the whores?"

"He is using whatever text he can, however he can," I replied. "If he's made his peace with butchering women, he'll not worry overmuch about mangling the Bible. What is the other verse?"

Martha turned to the end of the book and found the passage from Revelations.

"*For true and righteous are His judgments. He hath judged the great whore who corrupted the earth with her fornication, and He hath avenged the blood of His servants at her hand.*"

"Well, that's a better choice," said Mrs. Cowper. "But I don't see how it helps you find the killer."

I had to admit that I didn't know either.

"Why weren't the verses in Isabel's hands?" Martha asked. "All the others—save the adulterers—had the papers in their hands."

I puzzled at this for a time. It seemed that for everything the murders had in common, there also was a difference. "There's no rhyme to any of it." I said. "Some women had their privities cut, some did not; some were connected to Helen Wright, but Betty was not; some women had verses in their hands, some had them lying on their bodies, and some had no verses at all."

"What do you mean, *Some suffered when their privities were cut?*" Mrs. Cowper gasped. "Are you hunting a man or a monster?" Her shock at the murderer's brutality reminded me how hardened I'd become to the horrors he had visited upon his victims. When had I learned to speak so loosely of such terrible events?

"In some cases, the murderer cut at the whores' privities and legs until he hit an artery," I said. "That's how they died. But he didn't do that to Isabel."

"Or Mary Dodsworth," Martha reminded me.

"But she wasn't a whore," I said. "Merely an adulteress."

"He's killing adulteresses, too?" Sarah asked.

"So it seems," Martha replied. "And he killed her lover, as well."

"The sins of the flesh seem to be the ones he hates the most," Mrs. Cowper observed. "Why is that?"

"We don't know," admitted Martha. "Nor do we know why Isabel escaped the abuse suffered by Jennet and Betty. And why wasn't she bound up the way the others were? The murderer simply struck her and then ran."

And then I knew the answer. "That's exactly it," I said. "When Mrs. Cowper shouted that she had summoned the beadle, the murderer dropped the papers and fled. He had no way of knowing it was a ruse."

"And that's why Mrs. Cowper heard the man cry after his comrade," Martha finished. "If he'd been found wandering about the parish covered in blood, they'd have taken him straight to the gallows."

While we could not be sure if the story we'd woven approached the truth, it did fit what we knew, and in light of the mean progress we'd made up to that point, solving any part of the puzzled offered us some comfort.

With Sarah's final travail still some hours away, we women

settled in and talked of the news of the town and of ourselves, and eventually Mrs. Cowper and I fell to talking about midwifery. I asked how she had come into the practice, for every woman had a different story and I loved to hear them all. While some women followed their mothers or—like me—their mothers-in-law into the profession, most came to it on their own.

"It was entirely by chance," Mrs. Cowper explained. "I started as a gossip, no different than any of the other women in the neighborhood. Soon I started assisting midwives with little tasks like making the caudle. Eventually I found myself serving as a midwife when one could not be found or arrived too late.

"Around the time the German wars started, a midwife asked me to be her deputy, and five years later I had a license of my own," Mrs. Cowper concluded. "That was nearly thirty years ago."

There could be no mistaking the note of sadness that had crept into her voice. I could not imagine my own life without my mothers and babies, and my heart ached for her plight. I understood why she still kept her herb garden.

"Have you no children?" I asked.

"I have three daughters," she replied. "All gone to London. They send me letters sometimes, but they have lives and husbands, and children of their own now." We lapsed into silence, and I could not help wondering if that was the future that lay before me as well. Would I lose my work and grow old, with none but my maidservants as companions?

Suddenly, the front door flew open and four women burst into the house, laughing and full of good cheer. Sarah pulled herself to her feet to embrace her gossips, and from that moment all ill thoughts were banished from my mind. In addition to the happy conversation, the women had brought baskets of food, a pot of ale, and several bottles of wine.

"Martha," I called. "Get some wine before it's drunk and make Sarah's caudle." With such a merry crowd, I did not think the wine would last for long.

"In my house, we use my caudle," Mrs. Cowper responded. She snatched a bottle from one of the gossips and busied herself heating the wine and adding the herbs and spices. When I tasted it, I had to admit it rivaled my own. She must have been a fine midwife in her time. Naturally enough, the talk soon turned to Isabel's murder, and it became the strangest gossiping I'd ever heard, as the women both celebrated the birth of Sarah's child and mourned the loss of their friend.

"What will happen to her daughter?" Martha asked. "Has she family in the city?"

"No, none," replied one of the gossips. "The churchwardens probably will put her with a widow." While some orphans lived with more distant kin, newcomers to the city often had none. When that happened, the parish paid a poor woman to care for the child. Some of these women loved the children they received, but even the luckiest child grew up in poverty. Bad luck could mean a bad caretaker and a horrible fate.

"Oh, you'll never guess what I heard this morning!" a gossip named Alice cried. No doubt she sought to turn the conversation away from such a dismal topic. "You know that one-eyed preacher? His son came around the Black Swan again last night."

Martha and I looked at each other uncertainly as the women burst into laughter.

"Praise-God Ward?" Martha asked in disbelief. "Hezekiah Ward's son?"

"Aye," replied the gossip. "It's hard to forget that name, especially when it's hung on a man in search of a whore. And I'd have gone with him, too, but I came to the tavern a few minutes too late. It was a shame—they say that he pays well."

"Praise-God Ward comes around looking for whores?" I said dumbly. "He hires you?"

"Well, not me," Alice said. "But others. I saw him go off with Isabel on Saturday."

"I wonder if hearing all his father's sermons has shrunk his yard," one of the other women said, holding her thumb and forefinger just a few inches apart. The gossips roared with laughter and fell to mocking the godly for all their pretensions and hypocrisies. Martha and I slipped into Mrs. Cowper's chamber, where we could talk in private.

"What do you make of that?" I asked. "Praise-God going with whores?"

"Including Isabel, the night before she was murdered," I replied. "It cannot be happenstance."

"Could *he* be the one killing the women? Could he have bought Isabel on Saturday, and killed her on Sunday?" Martha asked.

"But why?" I asked. "He is godly enough, but he seems more mouse than murderer."

"He *seems* a mouse, but we've been wrong about murderers before," she pointed out. She was right, of course. Could there be more viciousness and violence in Praise-God than we had seen? Could he be cruel enough to burn Betty in such a heartless fashion?

"Remember that whoever killed Isabel was not alone," I said. "Mrs. Cowper heard the murderer calling after his companion. Praise-God might not be so murderous, but what if his comrade is? Whom was he following?" I asked. "John Stubb? Mark Preston? Joseph?"

"It could be any of them," she said, shaking her head in frustration. "They are all men of blood."

A knock came from the front door, followed immediately by the sound of the gossips roaring at Will when he tried to enter the parlor. He protested valiantly, but within moments they had driven him back outside. Martha and I returned to the parlor, and found the women in high spirits.

"*I need to speak to Lady Hodgson,*" Alice mocked. "*Please!*"

I could not help smiling at their antics. It was rare that such women could mock a man so openly, and I would not begrudge them this opportunity. Martha and I found Will standing outside, still shocked by his rough treatment at the gossips' hands.

"'Tis merry when gossips meet," Martha teased. "Is it not?"

"If there is a more terrifying sound than that, I have no desire to hear it," Will replied before turning to more serious business. "I brought Joseph to the body," he said. "I watched him closely, but could see no sign that he knew of the murder, or where the body was. I pretended to lose my way in the hope that he'd correct me, but he never did."

Martha did not even try to hide her disappointment. "That does not mean anything," she said. "If he is the killer, he'll not be trapped so easily."

"Perhaps not," replied Will. "But I still don't believe that he is involved. He is my brother. There would be some sign, and I would recognize it."

"We may find our answer sooner than we thought," I said. "Sarah's gossips say that Praise-God has been coming to the whores of late."

"What, hectoring them as he did Betty?" Will asked.

"Not that," Martha replied. "The only talking he did was to negotiate a price."

"Really?" Will said, his brow arched in surprise. "The Puritan's son is also a whoremonger." He considered the news for a moment. "Do you think he is also the killer?"

"He came to Isabel on Saturday, and she died on Sunday," I replied.

"He could be the one Mrs. Cowper saw fleeing from Isabel's room," Martha added.

Will frowned as he thought. "*Could be* is hardly enough to see him hanged. We cannot even prove it was him. And even if it was, we have to find out who he was with."

"But how?" I asked.

"We ask," Martha replied.

"What do you mean?" I said. "Surely he'll deny everything."

"We start with what we learned from the whores," Martha said. "He's a fornicator, a liar, and a hypocrite. We threaten to tell his father about the entire business. That will throw him on his heels, and then we'll press him about the murders."

"That might well work," Will said. "My father may not approve of me, but his scorn at my drinking would be nothing compared to Hezekiah Ward's wrath when he finds out his son's a whoremonger. Even if Praise-God doesn't fear the gallows, he'll fear his father."

"And once he's scared enough, he'll confess?" I asked. "It seems a bit far-fetched."

"It seems that way because you're not frightened of your father," Will replied. "Look at Praise-God's life. He trails his father around England, meek and mild. He wants to be a minister, but he knows he'll never compare to Hezekiah. He'll do anything to keep his whoring a secret. Perhaps that's why he wanted to kill them."

"What if he denies it?" I asked. "We have no proof."

215

"If we delay until we have proof, it will put another whore's life in danger," Martha said. "We cannot wait another day. We must act now."

In the distance, the Minster bells began to toll, and I looked up at the sun as it hung in the midmorning sky. We were still several hours from noon, and already it seemed as hot as we could bear. I also recognized that the setting sun would bring with it the threat of another murder. If we waited to confront Praise-God, and he proved to be the killer, we would be complicit in that death.

"I should think Sarah will be delivered by dinner. We'll find Praise-God right after."

"I'll fetch Tree and search out Praise-God at the inn," Will said. I started to object, but he interrupted. "I'll keep him safe, Aunt Bridget. But I'll need someone to bring you a message if Praise-God leaves the inn. Don't worry. Praise-God will never even see the boy." I nodded. Tree would be safe enough.

Martha and I bade Will farewell, and returned to Sarah and the gossips.

A few hours later, Sarah gave birth to a girl who came into the world squalling with admirable strength, surrounded by her mother's friends. I said a prayer that she would not follow her mother into whoredom, but I knew it happened far too often to hold out much hope. Once Sarah was comfortably settled, I gave Mrs. Cowper three shillings for her trouble and a few more to help pay for Sarah's lying-in. Martha and I dined on bread and cheese that the gossips had brought, then we set out to find Will.

As we neared the Three Crowns, I heard Tree's voice calling out to us from an alley. I turned and saw that he'd tucked himself onto a windowsill, almost invisible unless you knew to look for him. His position offered a perfect view of the door to the Three Crowns. Will was nowhere in sight.

"If Will has left you here by yourself, I'll have his head," I swore. "Climb down from there, Tree. You'd best be going home."

"It's all right, my lady," Tree chirped from his perch. "Will paid a lad to ask if the Wards were in their rooms. When he found out they weren't, he decided to search the rooms himself."

"Will's inside?" I asked, dumbfounded. "What happened to our plan?"

"He didn't say anything about a plan." Tree shrugged. "He said I'm to throw a stone at the window if I see any of them, especially that big one."

I looked over at Martha, unsure what we should do next.

"Let's go in," she said. "We're doing no good waiting out here, and we might find something he'd miss."

I nodded in agreement.

"Tree," I said. "We're going in as well. If you see any of the Wards coming, do as Will told you so we can escape. If anyone sees you, turn and run, do you understand?" The boy nodded, and Martha and I crossed the street toward the inn. I said a prayer that the Lord would help me bring an end to the slaughter that had lately come to York.

As we climbed the stairs, I felt the sweat born of the day's heat change into one born of fear. If we were right, Praise-God had a hand in a half-dozen murders: If he were he to find us in his room, would Will's sword be enough to protect us? What if his comrade were with him? Martha stopped outside Praise-God's room and knocked.

"Will, are you in there?" she whispered. The door opened and Will gestured for us to enter. He looked up and down the hall before closing the door behind us and securing the latch.

"I grew tired of waiting," he said before I could reprimand

him for abandoning our plan. "I thought I might find something to use when we question him."

I could tell from his voice that he had indeed uncovered something of interest.

"What did you find?" I asked.

Will held up a large black book. "His Bible. Praise-God is mad as can be and he hates whores worse than the devil himself."

Chapter 18

Martha took the book from Will and began to leaf through it. "God, he's written on nearly every page."

"Aye," Will said. "But look for the verses you discovered on the bodies." Martha retrieved the papers we'd found in Isabel's room from her apron, and turned to the first passage.

"Jesus," Martha said. She handed the book to me and pointed at the passage, but it would have been impossible to miss.

While Praise-God had lightly underlined many verses, the passage from Revelations had received special attention. Using heavy black ink, Praise-God had drawn a star in the margin, and the word *whore* had been blackened out completely, as if he'd hoped to scrape the word from the page. I turned to the passage from Isaiah and found that it had received the same rough treatment.

"Are they all like this?" I asked Will.

"I couldn't remember all of the verses, but once you start looking, they are not hard to find. Anything to do with whore-dom, fornication, or adultery is marked that way."

As I flipped through the book, a passage near the beginning

caught my eye. I turned back and found it in Exodus. Praise-God had drawn black brackets around *Honor thy father and thy mother.* Next to the brackets he'd written, *What does this mean? How might I do this?* I showed the passage to Martha and Will.

"Surely he's not questioning the commandment," Will said. "He seems dutiful enough." Martha just shook her head.

I continued to turn the pages, now with Will and Martha peering over my shoulder. In Genesis, I found that he'd drawn similar brackets at the beginning and end of the passage in which God ordered Abraham to sacrifice his son Isaac. In the margins he'd written, *What if God had not stayed Abraham's hand?*

"Not a bad question," Will said grimly.

"I wonder what Praise-God thinks of murder?" I asked, and turned to the account of Cain and Abel. I found it odd that he'd given that event no more attention than any other.

"Did you find anything else?" I asked, looking about the room.

"He's got a little chest," Will said, pointing. "But it's locked." He looked over at Martha, who smiled slightly. She knelt before the chest and examined the lock.

"I won't even need my tools for this," she said dismissively. She removed a pin from her apron and cast her eyes around the room. She spied a nail that had fallen into the groove between two floorboards, and with just those tools went to work on the lock. In a few moments we heard a *click.*

"Always spend more on a lock than you think is necessary," she said as she opened the chest. She poked through the contents, doing her best not to disturb the order. She carefully lifted the sleeve of a linen shirt and held it for us to see. On the end of the sleeve—at the very point at which it would extend past the jacket cuff—was a stain that looked for all the world like blood. Martha looked more closely.

"He tried to wash it out but couldn't. He just spread it out," she said. "Too bad he never spent time in service. I'd have it out in an hour."

"So it seems he's our murderer," I said. "With help or without, he killed six people." Martha and Will nodded. For some reason this moment felt less like the triumphant completion of a Herculean task than the final steps of a long and difficult march. The dead were still dead, and the fact that we'd found the murderer would not change that. We were startled from our thoughts by the *plink* of a stone against the window.

"Someone's coming," Will said. "We must go."

Martha laid down the bloody sleeve, closed the chest, and snapped the lock shut. Martha and I followed Will out of the room. Will opened the door across the hall and led us in before closing it behind us. The room we'd entered was a mirror image of the one we'd just searched. It had the same low bed and dull white walls. The only difference was that its windows overlooked a courtyard rather than the street.

"Before I came up, I asked for this room in particular," Will explained, a hint of pride creeping into his voice. "I thought I might need a place to go if Tree saw someone coming." He stayed close to the door, listening for footsteps. When he heard the door across the hall open, he cracked our door and peered out.

"It's Praise-God," he whispered after closing the door. "And he's alone. We should talk to him now." Will and Martha looked at me, clearly waiting for my approval.

I hesitated.

"You want to summon the constable," Will said.

"We ought to," I replied.

"But we have Praise-God now!" he cried.

"No," I said. "Not yet."

"You're afraid to confront him?" Martha asked.

"I'd be a fool if I weren't," I replied. "And you would be, too. He's killed six people—there's no reason to think he wouldn't kill us just because we're not whores or adulterers."

I turned to Will. "Go get a constable, anyone but your brother. And hurry. We'll wait here."

Will looked like he wanted to argue, but he nevertheless dashed off. We heard him thundering down the stairs, and could feel the crash of the front door as he threw it open.

Martha and I had not waited more than a few minutes when she looked up at me, a light dancing in her eyes. I recognized the look on her face, and my heart sank.

"No," I said. "You're staying here."

"You are the one who said he's more mouse than murderer," she said. "He fled Isabel's murder bleating like a sheep that had lost his shepherd. By himself he's no danger, but if we wait until his comrade arrives, then we *will* be in danger. We must confront him when he is alone."

"Martha, no," I said, though I knew she would not listen. "Wait for the constable. He won't be long."

Without a word, or even a look in my direction, Martha stepped past me, opened the door, and crossed the hall. She turned the handle and pushed on Praise-God's door. When it didn't yield, she took a step back and drove her shoulder into it. The door burst open, and over Martha's shoulder I could see Praise-God whirl around to face her, a look of shock on his face. I had no choice but to follow her into Praise-God's room, and I shut the door behind me.

"Wh-wh-what are you doing?" he managed at last.

"We know your secrets," Martha said. She crossed the small room and stood with the tip of her nose just inches from his.

"We know what you've done." Although he was taller than Martha, there could be no question which of them was the mouse.

"What do you mean?" Praise-God asked, his voice shaking. "There are no secrets before the Lord. He will reveal all that is hid."

"Before He reveals anything, we will do it for Him," Martha replied. "And we'll do it in public, too."

"I have no secrets. I stand blameless before the Lord." If I'd not seen the evidence myself, I would have believed the lad. Either he genuinely thought he'd done no wrong, or he was the most accomplished liar I'd seen in some time. I stood back and let Martha play the hand.

"We know you went with whores," she said. "We know and we'll tell everyone. Then they'll see that you're naught but a rank hypocrite."

"I never did!" he cried. "We preached to them; we tried to save their souls." He paused for a moment and regained himself. "But the mouths of the reprobate are filled with lies, and the mouths of whores even more so. None will believe you."

"It's not the preaching I mean," Martha said. "We know about what you did *after*. I've spoken to them myself. They said that on Saturday you came and hired a woman named Isabel, and took her away with you."

"I—I—I don't know anyone named Isabel," he stuttered. I could not help feeling we were near a confession. "They are liars. That is all."

"The first person we'll tell is your father," Martha said. "I cannot imagine what he would say if he learned that his son resorted to whores most nights of the week."

A shadow flitted across Praise-God's face at this threat; we were closer still to the truth.

"My father, like my God, knows that I am innocent."

"The whores laughed at you," Martha said viciously. "They said you have the smallest prick they'd ever seen. Oh, how they laughed."

Curiously, this insult drew a smile from Praise-God, and the tension left his body.

"Now *you* are the liars," he said. "I don't know what you are hoping to achieve by this assault, but you should leave me in peace."

The fear I'd heard in his voice had vanished. Even Martha seemed surprised by this exchange and for the first time she seemed more uncertain than Praise-God. Something had gone wrong, but I could not tell what. I knew I had to do something or else we'd lose control of the situation for good.

"Give me your Bible," I said.

"What?" he said. From the look on his face, I knew I'd cut near to the bone. "Why? No, I won't."

I reached past him, picked the book up off the bed, and opened it to Revelations. I found one of the passages where he'd attempted to scratch the word *whore* from the page.

"What is this?" I demanded. "Is this what you do to the women after you've finished with them? Destroy them?"

"Whores are not beloved by God," Praise-God explained. "He will destroy them and all those who traffic with them. He has sent this heat as a warning, but the city will not heed it. He will have His revenge."

"And you think that by slaughtering them you are doing God's work?" demanded Martha, following my lead.

"I did not kill them," Praise-God replied. If the accusation of murder surprised him, he hid it well. "Those who hate sin are beloved by the Lord," he said, gesturing at the Bible. "God *demands* that we hate whoredom."

From the corner of my eye, I saw the lock from Praise-God's

chest lying on his bed. He must have opened it as soon as he returned to his room. I stepped around him, opened the chest, and with a flourish pulled out the shirt that Martha had found. I intended to confront him with the bloody sleeve, for what could he say to that?

But when the shirt came out, a crowbar that had been wrapped inside slipped out and fell to the floor; Isabel's blood still covered one end of the weapon. The three of us stared at the bloody bar, only slowly realizing what it was. For a moment I feared that Praise-God might seize the weapon and use it on us, but he showed no interest in escape.

"You used this to kill Isabel," Martha said, picking up the bar. Praise-God sat on the bed and put his hands on his knees. He seemed unsurprised by this turn of events, and was far more composed than he had been when we accused him of procuring whores.

"If that was her name, then yes I did." He looked at the crowbar. "I didn't even realize it was still in my hand until I got back here. Then I didn't know what to do with it. I couldn't think."

"And you killed Betty," I said.

He shrugged. "I didn't ask their names. They didn't matter." I could not tell if he meant that the women he'd killed didn't matter or their names didn't. Each was horrible enough.

"Who was with you?" I asked. "Who helped you do it? John Stubb? Joseph Hodgson? Your own father?"

With that question, Praise-God seemed on the verge of panic.

"What? Nobody!" he cried. "I killed them by myself. All of them."

"We know that's not true," I said. "And the Lord hates a liar."

"Did John Stubb help you?" Martha asked. "He must have killed many men in the wars, so it would be no great feat on his part."

"I killed them myself," Praise-God repeated. Before we could ask any further questions, we heard the pounding of feet on the stairs, and the door burst open. My nephew Joseph stood in the door, a sword in his hand. Several beadles stood behind him.

"Aunt Bridget," Joseph said. "Are you all right?"

"Mr. Hodgson," Praise-God said before I could answer. "You should arrest me. I murdered the whores."

"What?" Joseph cried out. "*You* murdered them?"

"Yes," Praise-God said. He stood and crossed the room. "I killed all of them. Last night I killed one of them with the crowbar that maid is holding. And I killed a whoremonger, too. He was the first."

Joseph grasped Praise-God by the arm and pulled him toward the door.

"Take him to the Castle," he said to one of the beadles. "Tell the jailor to put him in double irons." The beadles dragged Praise-God down the hall.

Joseph turned back to us. "You are lucky I arrived," he said. "God was with you today."

"Joseph," I said. "He is lying."

"What do you mean?" he asked, surprise clear on his face. "Why would he lie about murdering the whores? And if he is lying, where did he get the weapon?"

"He did not do it by himself," I said. "He had help, or he helped someone else do it." As soon as I said the words, I knew I had made a mistake. If Joseph were Praise-God's comrade, I'd just alerted him to our suspicions.

My fears became more real when Joseph's face hardened and he gazed at me through half-closed eyes. With menacing deliberation, he reached over and took the crowbar from Martha's hand.

"Why would you say that? Did he say something before we arrived?" he asked.

I cursed myself for my stupidity. I could tell from Martha's face that she recognized the seriousness of the situation.

"No, nothing," I said. "He seems like such a gentle boy; we could not believe he'd do such a thing."

Joseph regarded us a bit longer. I felt like nothing so much as a lamb alone before a wolf.

"I'll interrogate him further," he said at last. "If anyone helped him, I will find out."

We heard the sound of someone rushing up the stairs. The uneven gait signaled Will's return.

"Aunt Bridget!" he cried before he appeared in the doorway. He was sweating profusely and out of breath. When he saw Joseph, he stopped midsentence. Joseph turned to face his brother.

"There you are. Thank you for the warning about Mr. Ward. The beadles have taken him to the Castle. I'm sure our father will be very proud of you when I tell him."

Will's face twitched, and I could tell he resented Joseph's condescension, but he said nothing. Joseph turned back to me.

"Do not worry any more about Mr. Ward," he said. "You are to be commended for catching such a beast, and the city thanks you for your service, but the hunt is over. I will go to the Castle and finish the interrogation." He nodded at Will, then disappeared down the stairs.

"Oh God, Aunt Bridget, I'm sorry!" Will cried. "I found another constable, but as we made our way here, Joseph saw us and sent him away. It was the devil's luck. Then Joseph ran ahead, and I could not keep up." He looked disdainfully at his cane.

"There was no harm done," I said. "Any other constable would have done the same thing. There is nothing left to do here. We should go." The three of us descended the stairs and stepped into the afternoon sun, which struck with such force that it robbed me of my breath.

"If God is pleased that we've captured a murderer, he's not showing it," Martha said. "It's hotter than ever." None too soon, we reached my home and found refuge in the parlor. While Martha filled three glasses with small beer, I told Will what had happened at the inn after he left.

"And you still think Joseph might be Praise-God's comrade?"

"We must consider the possibility. He made it very clear that we are not to pursue the matter any further."

"But we must do something," Martha said as she entered the room. "There is still a killer out there."

I had no ready answer, and from the look on Will's face, neither did he. It seemed possible—likely, even—that for the second time in a year, a murderer would slip through my fingers. We talked over the matter for a time, but none of us had a solution. Will went home, and Martha and I retired to our chambers. That night as I prayed, I asked God what he meant by such events, and prayed that I would see justice done.

The next morning, Will appeared at my door, his face grave.

"What is it? There can't have been another murder." I said.

"Joseph convinced my father to try Praise-God last night," Will said. "And *he* convinced the Lord Mayor."

"What?" I cried.

"My father was willing to wait until we could find a judge, but Joseph argued against it. He said that since Praise-God had confessed, there was no reason to wait. They called it a 'special assize'."

"Did he learn nothing the last time he hurried through a trial?" I asked.

Will offered a slight smile. "I asked him that. He thought that because you and Martha were the ones who caught Praise-God, you wouldn't object."

"And the jury convicted him?" I knew the answer, of course.

"He is to be hanged as soon as an executioner arrives from Hull. If one lived here in the city, he'd be dead already. Joseph said we could manage without one, but for once my father stood firm."

"Joseph is in a rush to see Praise-God dead, isn't he?"

"Aye," Will said. I could tell he wanted to say more but could not find the words. I put my hand on his arm.

"You're worried that Joseph might be the one who helped Praise-God," I said. "And the reason he sought a hasty trial was to make sure Praise-God is hanged before he tells anyone else."

Will nodded, but refused to meet my eyes. My heart ached for him. Whatever their disagreements, and despite Joseph's late cruelties, Will loved his brother, he did not want to accept his guilt. I had no remedy to offer, so I sat with him in silence and did my best to comfort him. When Will left, our parting was melancholy.

Not an hour later, I was at prayer when Martha knocked on my door. "What is it?" I demanded. I knew Martha took some perverse pleasure in interrupting my prayers, and I usually tolerated it, but the murders had set me on edge, and I had sought solace in the Lord.

"Mrs. Cowper is here," Martha replied. "She says she learned something that might help us find Isabel's murderers. Both of them."

Chapter 19

I clattered down the stairs, eager to hear what Mrs. Cowper had to say.

"She brought a girl with her—I think she's another whore," Martha said. "And she has Isabel's daughter with her as well."

"Elizabeth?" I asked, thinking of the way the girl's red hair had blazed in the sunlight and of the life she faced now that she had been orphaned. "Why?"

"I don't know."

"Does Mrs. Cowper know that Praise-God has been convicted?" I asked. "Another witness against him is of no use."

"She didn't say. She and the girl wanted to see you before they said anything more."

I hastened to the parlor and found Mrs. Cowper and a young woman waiting there. Elizabeth stood in the corner, gazing at the shelf on which I kept my mementos. She looked up when I came in.

"Is this your daughter?" she asked. She pointed at a small portrait I'd had made of Birdy when she turned six.

"Aye," I said. "Her name was Bridget, but we called her Birdy."
The girl nodded. "And she died?"

"Yes." I did not tell her about Michael.

"How old was she?" The death of a child did not frighten her. I supposed her mother's murder might have pushed her beyond ordinary fears.

"She was eight."

"I'll be eight next Michaelmas," the girl replied, clearly pleased to have something in common with Birdy. "My mother died, too," she added.

"I know," I said. "I'm sorry that she did."

Elizabeth nodded. "I'm sorry Birdy died. She looks nice. Were these her checkstones?" She picked up a wooden box on the shelf. I said they were. "Can I play with them?"

Although the sight of the game usually brought me to tears, I could not help smiling at the light in Elizabeth's eyes when she asked. Birdy and I had played every Sunday afternoon from when she was just five. We'd last played the week she died.

"I must speak with Mrs. Cowper, but why don't you take them to the kitchen and ask my servant to play with you? Her name is Hannah, and she is very kind."

Elizabeth smiled and—checkstones in hand—walked toward the kitchen. The sunlight through the dining room window transformed her hair from red to a burning gold. While not in the least similar to Birdy in appearance, she was a beautiful child, and it seemed to me that she had some of Birdy's audacity.

I turned back to Mrs. Cowper and the whore who had accompanied her. I did not know the lass's name, but thought I'd seen her at the Quarter Sessions, accused of fornication. She was still young, but soon she would begin the swift descent into a whore's old age. In the dim light of a tavern, a man might be able to ignore the deepening lines on her face, but that would not remain true for much longer. All too soon some young country girl would replace her, and she would wander into oblivion.

"Martha says you've learned something of the murders," I said. They both nodded. "I should tell you that the city arrested a man yesterday—probably the one you saw fleeing Isabel's murder."

"We heard that," Mrs. Cowper replied. "And the city is better for it. But I've got other news. After you left, I started asking around about the boy who was taken for the murders. Jane here knows him, too."

"You knew Praise-God?" I asked. The girl nodded earnestly. "Did he hire you?"

"Aye, he did, but not for himself."

"What do you mean?" I asked. "He procured you for someone else?"

"Yes," she said, and looked at Mrs. Cowper. "I won't get in trouble for this? I don't need any more trouble."

"I told her that once she talked to you, she would be done with the business, and none would trouble her again," Mrs. Cowper explained.

"And that I'd get a sixpence," the girl added.

I looked at Mrs. Cowper, who had turned quite pale.

"I'll not pay a whore for lies," I said, standing up. "You should take her back before I summon the beadle."

Mrs. Cowper and the girl leapt to their feet, clamoring for me to stay.

"Lady Hodgson," Mrs. Cowper said. "It is not like that at all. She told me the truth before I mentioned the money. But she did not want to venture so far, or risk being punished, without the prospect of a reward."

"Tell me what you have to say," I demanded. "I make no promises."

Mrs. Cowper nodded to the girl.

"Last week the preacher's son came to the alehouse I frequent, twice in the same day," she said.

"He came to you twice? What do you mean?" I asked.

"In the afternoon he brought others with him. They preached and cried against us, told us we were damned." I looked at Martha, and she nodded. It sounded like the same thing that had happened before Betty died.

"And then he came back?" I asked.

The girl nodded. "That night. I thought he'd come to do more preaching, but he kept his head down and his collar high, as if he didn't want anyone to see him. A lot of the men do that, so I knew why he'd come. I didn't recognize him until I sat down. I said I wanted to use the room upstairs, but he said he'd give me an extra penny if I came with him. I made him give it to me first."

"Where did he take you?" Martha asked.

"I don't know exactly," the girl said. "A room in All Saints in the Pavement, I think. It had its own door so nobody would see us go in or out."

"And?" I asked.

"He'd brought me to be with that preacher," she said. "The one with one good eye."

Martha and I stared at the girl for what seemed an eternity.

"He brought you to Hezekiah Ward," Martha said at last.

"The one-eyed preacher," the girl repeated. "I didn't know his name, and he didn't tell me. And it wasn't just me, either. Me and Jennet Porter—the girl who was murdered?—we were gossips. "Right before she died, the lad took her to the preacher, too."

"Why did he send for you?" I asked, though I felt stupid doing so. "Did he preach to you?"

"No," the girl said with a smirk at my naïveté. "He used me as a man does. But he was very kind. He told me I was good, and that he loved me just as God does. He paid me twice what I usually get, too."

Martha and I looked at each other, trying to absorb this news. I turned back to the girl.

"Do you know who I am?"

"Yes, my lady. I knew even before Mrs. Cowper came to me."

"Good. Then you know that you should not lie. If you do, I will see that the beadles and constables hound you so far from the city that the next whoremonger you find will be an Indian. If you are spinning a tale, you must tell me now. I will let you go in peace. If I find out later that you are lying, you are finished." I did not relish threatening such a poor creature, but I had to know that she was telling the truth.

"I would not lie, my lady," she said, before realizing the absurdity of such a statement coming from a whore. "I am not lying," she said. "The preacher's son brought me to his father. I swear."

I looked again at Martha, who nodded. She agreed that the girl was telling the truth.

"How is it that you have Elizabeth?" I asked Mrs. Cowper.

"The parish needed a place for her, and it was the least I could do for Isabel." I knew taking on Elizabeth would add a considerable burden to Mrs. Cowper's life, but I could not help thinking that Elizabeth could have done much worse.

"How is she?"

"Well enough for a whore's orphan. She is a good girl." As

234

she prepared to leave I gave Mrs. Cowper a shilling to share with the whore, and then two more.

"If you need anything for Elizabeth, you must tell me," I said.

She nodded her thanks, and called into the kitchen for Elizabeth. When the girl arrived, she took Mrs. Cowper's hand and handed me the box of checkstones.

"Thank you, my lady," she said as we walked to the door. "I had fun."

"I'm glad," I said. "Tell Mrs. Cowper that you are welcome to come here any time you wish to play at checkstones."

The girl smiled and then the three of them disappeared toward Stonegate. As I watched them go, I said a prayer. It was a hard world, and harder still for women who were old, alone, or orphaned. Once they'd gone, I joined Martha in the parlor.

"Do you believe her?" I asked. "With her promise of a sixpence, Mrs. Cowper gave her ample reason to lie."

"If she had been lying, you would have scared her out of it, I think. There's no sense in risking the city's wrath for a mere sixpence. Even she would see that. But how does this help us find Praise-God's associate?" She paused. "You don't think it could be Hezekiah, do you?"

"I don't know, but it does complicate things," I said. "He preaches against whores during the day and turns into a whoremaster at night?"

"So it seems," Martha said. "But hypocrisy is no new thing for their kind."

I considered this and in a blinding moment worthy of the Apostle himself, I realized what had happened.

"No, that's not it at all," I said.

"What do you mean?"

"Hezekiah Ward's not a hypocrite," I replied.

"Of course he is!" Martha cried. "With one breath he damns whores to hell, and with the next he whistles for them? It's the worst kind of hypocrisy!"

"I don't think it is," I replied. "*Joseph* is a hypocrite—he condemns whoredom, but then accepts Helen Wright's money. He does not care about the sin.

"But Hezekiah Ward is different," I continued. "He genuinely believes that whoredom is a sin, even as he practices it."

"And that is why he is so frantic against the whores in his sermons," Martha said. "He hopes he can make up for his own sinful deeds."

"Aye," I replied. "I think that he *wants* to resist the temptation of the flesh, but there are times when he cannot. That's when he sends Praise-God to bring him a doxy."

"It makes sense," Martha said. "But he's gone beyond the preaching, hasn't he?"

"Preaching was enough when he was in Manchester," I said. "But not anymore. Now he sends Praise-God once so he can lie with them. And then a second time—"

"So he can kill them," Martha finished.

"This also explains how they escaped the city watch," I said. "What guardsman is brave enough to arrest a preacher on his way to offer solace to the sick or dying? They wouldn't even need to know the smaller streets—they could walk down the pavement bold as brass. We saw it with our own eyes the night we found Betty's body down in Micklegate."

"It is a fine theory," Martha said, nodding. "But Joseph still could be the one directing Praise-God. He would have a different motive for the same crimes."

I considered this for a moment, and realized that she could be right, for it would explain why Joseph was so eager to see Praise-God hanged. Hezekiah *or* Joseph could be behind the murders.

"Only Praise-God knows for sure," I said. "And he is to hang the day after tomorrow."

"Then we'd better find the truth soon," Martha said.

"Edward is our best hope for stopping the execution," I said. "We must speak to him as soon as possible."

"Why would he help us?" Martha asked. "If you are right that Hezekiah Ward is behind the killing, a godly minister will be hanged, and your brother's entire party will be humiliated. If I am right, Joseph will be hanged."

"He is still interested in justice," I said. "And we'll not mention our suspicions about Joseph."

We arrived at Edward's house in good time, and Mark Preston met us at the door.

"What business do you have with Mr. Hodgson?" he asked.

I looked closely at his face, wondering once again if *he* might be somehow connected to the murders. Would it be too much to think that he'd connived with Joseph *and* Praise-God?

"It is none of your concern," I replied. "But I am sure he will see us."

Mark gave me a mirthless smile and bowed. "I am sure he will," he said, and led us to Edward's study.

We found Edward behind his desk studying a large sheet of figures, and when we entered, he came around to embrace me. Martha, Edward, and I settled in large, opulently covered chairs, while Mark hovered behind his master.

"Joseph told me about your role in finding the man who's been murdering York's whores. The city is very grateful."

I glanced at Martha, unsure of how to broach the matter that had brought us to his house. I was especially wary of doing so in Mark's presence, but I saw no option other than forging ahead.

"Actually, that is why we are here," I said. "I would like you to postpone Praise-God's execution."

"Whatever for?" he asked. "You found the evidence yourself, and even heard him confess. Why should we wait?"

"We don't think he was the only one who killed the women," I said.

"Of course he was," Edward said. "You found the crowbar in his room. You found the blood on his shirt. He confessed in your presence."

"He was there and he deserves to hang," I said. "Of that there is no doubt. But someone else was with him when he killed those people." I looked up at Mark, but his face remained impassive.

"Why do you think this?" Edward asked.

"A woman saw *two* people fleeing Isabel Dalton's home," I said. "She recognized Praise-God, but not the other." The lie escaped my lips even before I knew it had formed on my tongue. Mrs. Cowper had seen only one man and hadn't been able to say who he was. I had not come to Edward's intending to deceive him, but now it was too late.

"What is more, you have met Praise-God," Martha volunteered. "Do you believe that he has the stomach for such violence?"

Edward considered the question.

"From what we've seen of him," I added, "he's more likely to have observed the crimes than committed them himself."

At last Edward nodded. "You may be right," he said. "But Joseph interrogated Praise-God, so we should speak with him as well."

I felt my heart sink. Joseph would never countenance the

postponement of Praise-God's execution, not if he were guilty as well.

Preston disappeared and a few moments later returned with Joseph. A look of surprise—or was it fear?—flitted across Joseph's face when he saw me and Martha, but he quickly regained himself.

"Your aunt wants to delay the execution of Praise-God Ward," Edward said. "She says that someone helped him kill the women."

"Really?" he asked. His surprise seemed genuine. "I questioned him myself, and he says he was alone when he killed them. He was very clear on that point."

"But a witness saw two people at the site of the last murder," Edward said. "Isn't that right, Lady Bridget? Who is the witness? Perhaps we should speak to him."

I hesitated. If Joseph and Edward questioned Mrs. Cowper about what she'd seen, the truth would come out.

"I was not clear," I said. "Mrs. Cowper did not see two people. She saw Praise-God calling after another as he hurried from the tenement. But she was sure there were two people."

Joseph's eyes shone as he pounced. "I know Mrs. Cowper. She is quite aged. I am surprised she could recognize Praise-God at night."

I felt myself losing control of the situation as Joseph picked at the small lies I'd told. Someday he would make a fine Justice of the Peace.

"She saw a man fleeing the tenement," I said. "As he fled, he called on someone else to wait. There had to be two people."

"So she didn't even recognize Praise-God?" Joseph asked. "I am not saying he is innocent—he is not—but it does not sound like Mrs. Cowper saw anything at all."

"She says there were two people," I insisted. "One must have been Praise-God, and we should discover who the other was."

"Or," Joseph said, "she saw one person who was mad. Given all that he's done, Praise-God could have been calling to Satan, the Holy Spirit, or nobody at all. While I will grant that Mrs. Cowper saw Praise-God, that is all we can be sure of."

"Why don't you ask him again?" Edward asked.

"Father, we should not trouble an already troubled mind," Joseph said. "If we open this door, who knows what will step through? He might say anything to delay his hanging. He could accuse *anyone* of helping him in his crimes." Joseph seemed so sure, so believable, that I knew what Edward would decide before he spoke the words.

"I appreciate your concern, Lady Bridget," Edward said. "And I am not unmindful that the last time we had a conversation such as this, you were right and I was wrong. But the lad admits that he killed the whores and insists that he was alone. Delaying his hanging would simply give him hope where there is none, and offer him the opportunity for more mischief. Praise-God will hang on Thursday, when the executioner arrives from Hull."

When Martha and I left Edward's study, we found Will waiting for us.

"I heard you'd come to see my father," he said. "What about?"

"Not here," I said softly. "Come with us."

Once we were safely outside, I told him what we'd learned about Hezekiah Ward from Mrs. Cowper and the whore.

"Hezekiah Ward resorts to whores?" he said. "That is certainly a surprise. And you thought my father should know?"

"Well, no, not exactly," I said. I explained my theory that Hezekiah rather than Joseph had been Praise-God's comrade.

"But here Lady Hodgson and I part ways," Martha interjected. "I admit that Hezekiah Ward is a fool and a fornicator, but I still suspect your brother. He is far too intent on hanging

Praise-God. He is hiding something." She looked up at Will as if to gage his reaction.

Will nodded. "I know it might be him. I pray it is not, but . . ." His voice trailed off.

"Whatever the case, only Praise-God knows the truth," I said. "We'd hoped your father would delay his hanging so he could be questioned further."

"And Joseph convinced him otherwise?" Will asked. I nodded.

The three of us trudged back across the river, our spirits low and sinking.

"If Joseph is behind the murders, he's well on his way to covering his tracks," Will observed. "That was neatly done indeed." I could not recall ever hearing him sound so morose.

"We still don't know if he's guilty," I insisted. "Hezekiah could be the one."

"Why don't we talk to James Hooke again?" Will said. "If anyone has seen the Wards' comings and goings, it's him. Perhaps he will remember whom Praise-God went with the night Isabel died, whether Joseph or Hezekiah. Whoever it was is likely the killer."

Martha and I looked at each other. She nodded.

"It couldn't hurt to talk to him," I said. "Find him and bring him to me."

Two hours later, Will arrived at my door with James Hooke in tow. He sent James into the parlor and pulled me and Martha aside. To my surprise, Will had the smell of liquor on him. I opened my mouth to reprimand him, but Martha spoke first.

"I told you what would happen if you went back to drinking, didn't I?" She spoke through clenched teeth. "Did you think I spoke in jest?" Her anger was clear to see, and I was surprised by her intensity.

"I know, I know," Will said, putting up his hands in a futile attempt to ward her off her fury. "But I found him in an alehouse, well on his way to drunk. What was I to do—sit there and ask for barley water?"

Even in her state, Martha recognized the logic behind Will's argument.

"James is back to his old habits?" I asked. While James had haunted York's alehouses in his youth, he'd stopped the previous winter after he joined in with the godly.

"Silence Ward refuses to speak to him," Will said. "She's mourning what happened to Praise-God, and won't see anyone except her mother. He's trying to drink away her memory."

"Well, you can hardly blame her for wanting to be alone," Martha said. "Her brother's going to hang for murder. He should let her grieve."

"James thinks he could comfort her," Will said. "He may be a fool, but he's a loyal one."

"How did you convince him to come here?" I asked.

"Ah, that," Will said. "I told him that we think Praise-God is innocent."

"You did what?" Martha and I said together.

"It seemed the best way to get him off the alehouse bench. I convinced him that if we can prove Praise-God is innocent, Silence will speak to him again. And if he is the instrument of Praise-God's release, she'll be grateful to him."

"But we know he's guilty!" Martha cried. "For God's sake, we *proved* he's guilty."

"Yes, but he doesn't know that. Just talk to him. Pretend you're trying to prove that Praise-God *couldn't* have committed the murders."

I considered this for a moment and saw how his plan could work.

"We say we want to prove that Praise-God was with his father when the murders took place," I said.

"Or with Joseph," Martha suggested. "And that he couldn't have done it."

"Exactly," I said. "If we find out who he was with when the murders took place, we'll know who our second murderer is."

Martha and I joined James in the parlor. In the time we'd been talking to Will, James had given in to the alcohol and drowsed. Martha shook his knee, and he woke with a start.

"Hullo, I'm awake," he said, pulling himself upright. The smell of liquor was overpowering, and he appeared to have poured quite a bit down the front of his shirt.

"How are you, James?" I asked.

"I talked to Will," James replied. "He said that you could prove that Silence's brother didn't kill those whores. Is that true?"

"We don't think he killed the whores," Martha said. "It is just a matter of proving he was somewhere else when they died." She was far more adept than I at the art of deception, so I let her continue. "We want to find out who he was with, and we think you might be able to help us."

"What do you mean? How can I help?"

"Were you with Praise-God on Sunday night? It was the night of the last murder."

James nodded enthusiastically. "Mr. Ward had many people to the inn for bread, beer, and broth."

"Did Praise-God leave before you did?" Martha asked. At this, the lad's face fell.

"Everyone was there when I left." He shook his head in despair.

"What about before Sunday?" Martha asked. "Did Praise-God ever go off with someone at night? With Joseph Hodgson, perhaps?"

"No, only his parents," James said. "Sometimes Mr. Ward took him. Sometimes Mrs. Ward did." At the mention of Hezekiah Ward, I smiled slightly at Martha. My suspicions seemed on the verge of being proven correct.

"Where did Mr. Ward take him?" I asked. "Did he ever talk about it?"

"The two of them went to preach together," James said. "Mr. Ward said the city was filled with lost sheep. He would be their shepherd no matter the time of day."

"Do you know where they went?" Martha asked.

"It doesn't matter," James said, and tears began to course down his cheeks. "It won't save Praise-God. He is a good man. He and his father tried to save the whores, the two of them. And for their trouble Praise-God will hang. He will hang, then Silence will flee the city with her mother and John Stubb, and I'll never see her again."

"You knew that Hezekiah and Praise-God went to the whores together, just the two of them?" I asked. I had assumed that they would keep these visits a secret.

James nodded. "The two of them preached against the whores, and afterward they went to offer solace. They told the whores that if they repented, they could be saved."

"Do you remember the last time the two of them went to a whore?" I asked.

"Aye," James said. "Do you know the whore who died Sunday night?" He meant Isabel. "Mr. Ward and Praise-God preached to her the day before she was killed."

"They preached to Isabel on *Saturday?*" Martha asked. "Not on Sunday? Are you sure?"

James nodded enthusiastically. "I remember because I'd gone to court Silence. I was there when Mrs. Ward found out that Mr. Ward had gone to the whores."

"James, you must be clear," I said. "Mrs. Ward *knew* that her husband had gone to the whores?" If this were true, it would change everything.

"Well, not like that," James said. "I told you: Mr. Ward only wanted to save them. It nearly drove Mrs. Ward mad, though. Her fury reminded me of my mother's."

Martha and I looked at each other, and I could see that neither of us believed Deborah Ward could be fooled by so transparent a lie. The pieces of the puzzle had just shifted.

James saw the look and once again leaped to Hezekiah Ward's defense. "It is not how it sounds," James insisted. "He didn't go to use them as most men would. He and Praise-God were preaching to them."

"Yes, of course they were," I said. "And when Mrs. Ward found out that Mr. Ward was preaching to the whores, what did she say? What were her words?"

"She said she'd not live with a man who did such things, which seems uncharitable to me. She said she wondered that he never learned the price of his sins." James shook his head in wonder. "Her anger was something to behold." He paused and furrowed his brow in thought. "But how does this help free Praise-God? Mr. Ward and Praise-God went to Isabel on Saturday and the murder wasn't until Sunday."

I took his arm and led him to the door. "We have more to learn, James, but you have helped us enormously," I said. "We will tell you when Praise-God goes free."

He opened his mouth to speak but I closed the door before he could and returned to the parlor.

"It wasn't Hezekiah Ward *or* Joseph who was with Praise-God," I said. "It was Deborah Ward. *She* is the one who killed the whores."

Chapter 20

"Mrs. Ward?" Martha cried. "A moment ago we were sure it was Hezekiah."

"And before that you thought it was John Stubb," Will added.

"We should have seen it, shouldn't we?" I continued. "We know how she hates whores, and if she discoverd that her husband frequents them it is no wonder. How could that not drive her to madness?"

"How is she getting around York at night, then?" Martha asked. "The guards will let a minister or an Alderman pass, but they would certainly stop an old woman and her son."

"I don't know," I said after a pause. "Perhaps she said she was visiting a dying friend, or going to comfort a soul-sick member of her husband's congregation. You've seen her. If she set her mind and her tongue to it, the sheep on the night watch would run to get out of her way."

"Even if you're right," Will said. "How can we prove it? If Praise-God wouldn't confess to Joseph before, why would he confess to us now?"

"We have to try," I said. "Or else he'll hang and his accomplice will escape."

They couldn't argue with that.

"We'll go to the Castle and talk to Samuel," I said. "Perhaps he can help us."

The moment we stepped into the street, late afternoon sun assaulted us, as if it were bent on doing us harm. The oppressive heat did much to thin the crowds on the streets as the city's residents sought refuge indoors until evening offered some scant relief. As we crossed the bridge into the Castle, we saw a soldier standing over a draught horse that had died while still in the harness. The Castle yard seemed a little desert sent straight from Araby and even the slightest wind drew up sand and dust. We found the door to Samuel's tower wide open and walked in. Tree sat at a small table watching closely as Samuel showed him a new trick at cards.

"What, he's not yet taken enough of my money?" Will cried when he recognized the nature of the lesson.

"Hullo, Will," Tree replied. "Samuel is showing me how to deal myself the ace when I need it most."

"A useful skill, I'm sure," I replied, staring at Samuel. "But is it one for a boy to learn?"

"Oh yes," Tree replied with boundless enthusiasm. "It's the best card in the deck, and if your opponent has it, you could lose all your pennies. So it is better to be sure that it is in your hand. When I have learned how to deal it, I'll show you."

I could not help smiling at the boy's guilelessness.

"Samuel," I said. "We need your help with an important matter."

Samuel's face lit up—he was never one to miss the opportunity to make a few pence, and a gentlewoman in need of a favor offered just such an occasion.

"Do you know where they are keeping Praise-God Ward?" I asked.

"You need to see him?" Samuel asked. "It will not be cheap. Each of you will have to pay his keeper at least two shillings."

"That's outrageous!" Will cried.

"Well, you could wait a few days and the price will go down," Samuel said. "Of course, he'll be less talkative then, having been hanged."

I balked at the outrageous sum, but we had no choice.

"It is important," I said.

"Well, I won't tell his keeper *that*," Samuel said. "Or the price will go even higher. If he thinks you're just curious, he won't try to overcharge you. But I will need the money now."

I handed him the coins and he disappeared into the Castle yard. While we waited, Tree set about showing us the various cheats that Samuel had taught him.

Samuel returned a few minutes later. "You can go over there now, but his keeper says you'll have a devil of a time talking to him."

"What do you mean?" I asked. "Is he ill?" The low dungeons were famously noxious, but I would not have thought he'd succumb so quickly.

"Not that," Samuel said. "He won't stop talking long enough for anyone to get a word in. He's been crying and praying since he was sentenced and won't stop for nobody. The Lord Mayor's tried, your brother-in-law has tried—even his father got no response. He'll not stop praying for anyone. He stops when he sleeps, but that's all. He won't even eat the food his sister brings him."

"Which means there's more for us," Tree chirped.

"What do we do?" Martha asked.

"Well, your money's spent, so you might as well see him," Samuel said.

There was no denying that, so Samuel led the three of us across the Castle yard to another of the towers built into the wall. Samuel banged on the door, and it opened to reveal that tower's keeper. He was a tall man with a thin, rat-like face and eyes that bulged when he spoke. He wore the same heavy leather belt as Samuel, complete with a cudgel and a large ring of keys.

"Welcome, welcome!" the keeper cried as we entered. "More visitors for young Mr. Ward, more coins for old Mr. Hopkins! Since the poor lad arrived, I've had a procession like none I've seen since the King's men marched out of the city."

"Lady Hodgson," Samuel said. "As you have guessed, this is Praise-God's gaoler, Eli Hopkins."

"A pleasure, my lady," he said with an ostentatious bow. Payment of six shillings for simply unlocking a door seemed to put him in a good mood.

"Samuel told us that your prisoner is not entirely well," I said.

"That's fair to say," Hopkins replied. "The only peace I get is when he falls asleep, and that's never for more than a few minutes at a time. He quieted down just before you came."

As if this was Praise-God's cue, a heartrending wail echoed up the tower stairs.

"Father, though I am a wretch, worse than a wretch, worse than a worm, I beg You to forgive me for what I have done!" Praise-God's voice trailed off into a miserable cry that bespoke a soul irredeemably lost.

Samuel and Will looked around nervously, and whatever good

250

cheer my money had brought to Mr. Hopkins evaporated in an instant; even Martha had gone pale.

"Will you take us to him?" I asked Hopkins.

He nodded, lit a small lantern, and led us down a spiral staircase to the lowest cell in the tower. The door creaked open to reveal a room lit by a window so small that it needed just a single bar to prevent escape. On the outside, the window would have been at ground level—were the Ouse to rise, Praise-God's cell would be the first to flood. Despite the heat, water seeped in from the river and ran down the walls, which the feeble sunlight showed to be green with slime. The rushes on the floor had turned black from the damp. I did not know if his family had refused to pay for less pestiferous accommodations or if the city had refused to provide them, but were it not the height of summer, Praise-God would be hard pressed to live until Thursday. He knelt at the side of his bed with his back to us. He glanced over his shoulder when we entered but quickly returned to his prayers, whispering feverishly in a voice audible only to him and his God.

"I'll leave you," Hopkins said, handing the lantern to Will. "He's still in double irons, so you should be safe."

We crept across the room, none of us wishing to be the one to interrupt his prayers. When he showed no signs of acknowledging our presence, I coughed softly.

"Praise-God," I said. He continued to pray as if I'd said nothing at all. "Praise-God."

He still did not respond.

"We came about your mother," Martha said.

For the first time, I detected a break in his prayers. He looked over his shoulder at Martha, his mouth still moving. Their eyes locked and he stopped praying long enough to lick his lips.

"Who are you?" he asked, though he'd seen us just the day before.

"I am Martha Hawkins. This is Will Hodgson, and Lady Bridget Hodgson. We were the ones looking for whoever killed the city's whores."

"I did," he replied. "I told them that." He turned away and began to pray again.

I feared we'd lost him, but he turned back to Martha as if he'd just remembered something.

"You came about my mother?" he asked. "Has she sent word to me? I should like to see her before I hang."

Martha opened her mouth to reply and stopped. One wrong word would surely send him back into his world of prayer and wailing. In an instant, I realized that a simple lie would clear the path ahead—but only if Deborah Ward was guilty. If she was innocent, Praise-God would never utter another word in our presence.

"Praise-God," I said. "Your mother is dead."

I heard Will cough behind me, and a look of surprise flashed across Martha's face, but she quickly recovered herself.

"We came to tell you this, and offer you what comfort we could," I continued. Even in the paltry light of the cell, I could see the muscles in Praise-God's face working as he fought to maintain control of himself. His eyes slammed shut before opening just as quickly, his mouth stretched into a ghastly smile, and tears began to run from the corners of his eyes.

"Dead?" he asked, his voice that of a man on the edge of lunacy. "How? What happened?"

"A whore named Elizabeth killed her with a knife," I said. "She says your mother attacked her."

Praise-God broke down and began to sob, his entire body shaking with each heaving breath. Without warning, he turned and lunged in my direction. With a shout, Will drew his sword and leaped forward, but he was too late. Praise-God seized my shoulders, and I felt his chains digging into my chest. For a moment I thought he meant me harm, but then he buried his face in my neck and wailed as if the world had come to an end. Will realized I'd been embraced rather than attacked and stepped back.

As gently as I could, I loosened Praise-God's grip, and then I wrapped my arms around him and let him cry. While he sobbed, Martha and Will slowly withdrew into the shadows. They did not know what I had planned—even I was not entirely sure—but it seemed clear that they could do little to help. Eventually, Praise-God's sobs turned to quiet weeping. How long he cried I could not say. He rested his head on my breast while I stroked his hair.

"I was afraid this would happen without my help," he said at last. "I should have been there."

"You helped your father to the whores?" I murmured. "And then you helped your mother kill the same ones."

"Yes," he whispered. "My father demanded it, and I could not deny him. I knew helping him was a sin, but so too is disobedience."

"Your mother demanded your help, too?"

"She tried to chase them away, and to get him to stop, but he kept up the pursuit. She warned him that her patience had reached an end, and that he must reform himself. When he ignored her loving remonstrance, she took up the sword. I had to tell her which whores my father used. She said that they drew him onto Satan's path, and God demanded that they be punished."

"Why did you listen?" I asked. "You could have refused her."

"Disobedience was the first sin, the sin of Adam and Eve, was it not? I had already sinned by bringing the whores to my father. I thought I could cleanse myself of that sin if I drove them away.

And I wondered if my mother was right. Perhaps if I drove the whores away, my father would not be able to sin. I thought I could save his soul."

Drove them away? I thought, fury rising in my throat. *You slaughtered them!* Instead I simply said, "The first woman's name was Jennet. Tell me what happened."

"My mother said we were only going to threaten her. I thought we'd warn her away from my father, she would tell the others, and all would be well. I thought we might not even hurt her."

"But something went wrong."

"At the time, I thought it was a mistake, but now I don't know," he said. "I took my mother to the tenement, and knocked on the door. A man answered and my mother told him to move aside. He refused and my mother tried to push past him. He grabbed her arm and shouted that he'd paid his money and would have his whore."

"And she struck him?"

"I did. He was shouting the most terrible oaths. He said if we didn't leave, he'd dash our brains out. I picked up the fire iron and hit him. I just wanted him to stop. He started to stand up, so I hit him again. And again. Then the whore—"

"Jennet," I said.

"—came in. My mother pushed her back into her chamber and onto the bed. Then she made me bind her fast."

Praise-God had clamped his eyes shut, as if he could keep the memories of all he'd done from flooding into his mind. His body convulsed in one more sob.

"She brought the rope with her?" I asked.

Praise-God moaned and tightened his hold on me, his embrace nearly driving my breath from my lungs.

"It was in her apron," he said at last. He knew what this meant, but did not want to say it aloud.

"She planned to kill Jennet from the start," I said for him. "She never did intend to warn her off."

At this he looked up at me. "But she did!" he said. "She told the whore of her wicked ways, read to her from scripture. But she would not listen."

I waited, for I knew what had happened next.

"And then my mother lifted her skirts. I did not know what she was doing. Suddenly she had a knife and there was blood, so much blood." He sat in silence, his eyes open, staring into nothingness. After a time he breathed deeply, then went on. "My mother had some papers with her. She said they had scripture on them. She thought they might serve as a warning to the other whores in the city. She put them in the whore's hands so there could be no mistake."

As if the memory of Jennet's murder had been a boil in need of lancing, Praise-God seemed at peace. He looked around his cell as if seeing it for the first time.

"You have to tell me the rest," I said.

"I know." He nodded. "Is there any food?" I gestured to Martha, who dashed upstairs and returned a moment later with a small loaf of bread and a pot of ale. Praise-God tore into the bread with the ferocity of a wolf savaging a lamb.

While I knew that the boy was a murderer, I stood awestruck by the parents who had made him such. How could they have done this to their own son? I would give ten thousand worlds to hold my Birdy and my Michael one more time, and these two had transformed their son into a monster. God help us all.

When he'd finished the bread and ale, Praise-God continued his story. "I met the second one when we went to preach against whoredom across the river."

"Betty was her name."

Again, he continued as if I'd not spoken.

"It was worse than the first. I first took her to my father one day, and then my mother. This time she brought a pot of coals so she could burn the whore as God would. She left the scriptures again. I hoped it would be the last one, that the scriptures, or John Stubb's pamphlets, or my father's sermons, would bring an end to whoredom in the city. They did not."

"It was you who told Stubb what to put in the pamphlets?" I asked. Who else could it have been?

"Me?" Praise-God asked. "No, that wasn't me. My mother was terrified when the pamphlets came out. She feared it would bring you to our doorstep. And I suppose it did." He paused for a moment. "No, it was one of Mr. Hodgson's men who did that. Mr. Hodgson always took him along to the murders. He saw the bodies and told John all about them."

"Mark Preston," I said. "The man with the missing fingers."

"Yes, that was him," Praise-God said.

"Praise-God," I said. "How did you get past the town watch? They stand sentry on the bridge every night."

"This was my mother's idea," he said with a slight smile. "She told them she was a midwife from Manchester, and she'd been summoned to a birth. They even offered to accompany us if we needed a guide. We never had any problems."

"What happened then?" I asked.

"Next was the whore who had the little girl," he said. "That one broke my heart—I had no desire to make the girl an orphan, but my mother insisted that God would be avenged. It was when we got to her that things began to go awry."

"What do you mean?"

"As soon as my mother came in, the whore started to scream

Murder! Murder! Somehow she knew why we'd come. A neighbor-woman yelled out at us, so I hit the whore. I had to quiet her."

"That's why you fled," I said.

"My mother didn't even have time to show the whore the nature of her sins. She just dropped the scriptures and hurried off."

"What about Mary Dodsworth and the other man?" I asked. "You forgot them."

"Who?" he asked. "What man do you mean? We killed one man and three whores, four people in all."

"On the same night your mother burned Betty," I said. "She killed an adulteress and her lover in the north of the city."

"No," Praise-God said, shaking his head. "She never did. She had no love for adulterers, but she only killed whores."

"Praise-God, you must tell me the truth."

"I am," he insisted. "She went to three whores, and killed them. But that is all."

"Praise-God," I said again. "There is no reason for you to lie now. Your mother is dead and your fate is sealed."

My words disquieted him and he rose to his feet. His shirt hung open, and the lantern illuminated his bare chest. I could nearly see his ribs beneath his alabaster skin. From the corner of my eye, I saw Will edging forward in case Praise-God attacked me.

"You killed two men and four women," I continued. "There is no sense in denying it."

"The only man I killed was the first one," he said. "And I had to kill him for my mother's sake." He looked me in the face, his eyes sharp. "I am not a liar. God does not love a liar. Do not ask again."

I nodded, and he sat down on his bed. I did not know what this meant, but I knew not to push him.

"You will have to tell this to the judges," I said. "They must know the entire truth."

"I will tell them about the murders, but not about my father," he said softly. "It would ruin him, and he is a good man."

Praise-God lowered himself to his knees, turned back to his bed, and began to pray again. Will, Martha, and I crept to the door, unwilling to disturb his prayers.

"Will you come back?" he asked when he heard the door open.

"I will," I said. *And I will bring Edward, who will see your mother hanged.* I could hear Praise-God's whispered prayers until the door slammed shut.

"Praise-God didn't kill Mary Dodsworth," Martha said as we crossed the Castle yard.

"We don't know that," Will said. "If he's willing to kill, he's willing to lie."

"No, she's right," I said. "Even if he would lie, he isn't lying about that. There was blood on Mary's hands and flesh beneath her fingernails. But there are no scratches on Praise-God's face or chest. Someone else killed Mary and her lover, and I know who."

Chapter 21

"Aunt Bridget," Will protested as we hurried across the yard toward Samuel's tower. "Why would you believe him? Perhaps the scratches healed, or she scratched the mother."

"It's not just that," I said. "There were no scriptures left with Mary Dodsworth's body. How could I have been so blind? The Wards always left scriptures. It was nearly as important as the murders themselves. Even when Isabel screamed out and Praise-God and his mother had to flee, they threw the papers on the body."

"Nor was she cut," Martha added. "God, what fools we were. The murders were nothing alike!"

"If it wasn't Praise-God and Deborah Ward, who was it?" Will asked. "You've spent days hunting whoever was killing the whores. How can you have discovered another murderer in mere minutes?"

"It can only be her husband," Martha answered for me. "And if it weren't for the other murders, we would have seen it right away."

"Aye," I said. "Who does such violence to a woman? Either

someone who hates her or loves her. She was rumored to have taken a lover. She *must* have been killed by her husband."

When we arrived in Samuel's tower, I sat down to write a letter to Edward. We would have to hurry, but if all went well, two more murderers would be in gaol by sundown. I finished the letter and gave it to Tree.

"Deliver this to Mr. *Edward* Hodgson," I said. "If anyone tries to take it from you, whether his son, his manservant, or the devil himself, you *must* refuse. If this letter miscarries, all our plans will be for naught."

"Yes, my lady," Tree said, nodding solemnly before dashing into the Castle yard. I turned to Samuel, for I would need his help as well.

"I need two guards," I said. "I'll pay them twopence apiece, and they won't have to do much."

"I've got no prisoners to mind," Samuel replied with a laugh. "And twopence happens to be what I charge for not doing very much."

"Of course," I said. "And usually I would come to you first. But on this occasion I need guards who can frighten a man, and—"

"And you don't think a dwarf is up to the job?" he asked with mock outrage. "You *were* there when I overcame Praise-God with just one blow, weren't you? He's a murderer, many times over, and I bested him!"

"Except that my hope is to frighten someone," I explained. "And while you are many things, intimidating is not one of them."

"Fair enough," he said. "I'll find you your boys. They'll be big enough for you. Where do you need them?"

I told him I'd meet them at the bridge into the Castle, and as Will and Martha followed me there, I explained my plan to them. We had to wait only a few minutes before two of the Castle guards approached. Even from a distance, I knew they would serve my needs. They both stood at least a half head taller than Will, and must have outweighed him by three stone each.

"Lady Hodgson?" one of the men asked. "I am Corporal Matthews. Samuel said you needed help."

"Just for a bit," I said. "We're not going far." I explained my plan as quickly as I could, and the five of us trooped across the Castle bridge.

The Dodsworths' home lay near Fossgate Bridge in the eastern reaches of the city. Three-story buildings crowded the narrow cobbled street; after the heat of the Castle yard, the shadows of Fossgate felt especially welcome. The Dodsworths lived on one of the main roads into York, so whatever happened next soon would be known throughout the city. When we arrived, I nodded at the corporal, who stepped forward and pounded on the door.

"Open up," he bellowed.

We heard the scurrying of footsteps inside, and a moment later the door opened, revealing the Dodsworths' maidservant. She was perhaps twenty years old, with thin blond hair hanging down around her carrion-lean face.

"What is it?" she asked. "Mr. Dodsworth is occupied with important matters and does not wish to be disturbed."

I stepped forward and looked the girl in the eye. She held my gaze for a moment, and then bowed her head.

"Is that how you address a gentlewoman?" I demanded. "I know that your mistress taught you better manners than that."

"Yes, my lady," she said with a deep curtsy. "I am sorry."

"Much better," I said. "Mr. Dodsworth's wishes are not of our concern. Tell him if he does not come down immediately, these men will fetch him out."

The girl's eyes widened at my threat, no doubt imagining her master's wrath if his household were invaded by strangers. She started to close the door, but I pushed back against her.

"Leave the door and summon your master," I said. She nodded and dashed up the stairs.

Jonathan Dodsworth appeared at the top of the stairs, simultaneously trying to tuck in his shirt and lace his breeches, and doing a bad job of both. He clattered down the stairs, and when he arrived at the door, he drew himself up as if he were cock of all men. I judged that in a proper state he would be quite handsome, but he'd not shaved or even washed in some time, and even from the doorstep I could smell the liquor on his breath.

"What is the meaning of this?" he demanded. "Why are you troubling me when I have so recently buried my wife?"

I did not reply, but waited as his eyes took in the scene before him and his fuddled mind tried to figure out why we had come.

"Lady Hodgson?" he asked, momentarily puzzled. Then he looked at the guards standing behind me, and he realized what had happened. In that instant, his face fell and the air of bellicosity he'd brought with him vanished.

"You knew we would be here eventually," I said.

"I thought it would be sooner," he replied. His body seemed to shrink with every word. "Every time someone knocked at the door to offer condolence, I thought it would be the beadles come to take me away. Why did you wait so long?"

"Open your shirt," I said. He untied his shirt and bared his trunk. Angry red wounds crossed his chest and neck.

"Do you see what she did to me?" he asked softly. "She called me a beast, but it was she who savaged me. First by her whoredom and then with her claws, she savaged me through and through." By the time he finished speaking, his voice had fallen to a whisper.

"So you killed her," I replied.

"It's not why I went there," he said, sounding more like a boy than a man. "I knew she had a secret, so I followed her. When I saw where she'd gone, when I looked through the window and saw what they were doing..." His face twitched as he fought to keep control of himself, but after a few seconds he lost the battle. He clapped his hands over his face, but they could not muffle the sobs that sounded as if they had been torn from his chest.

I marveled that the same man who had murdered his own wife now could grieve for her. I stepped aside, and the guards moved forward, taking Dodsworth by his arms. He offered no resistance as they led him back to the Castle.

By now it seemed all the neighborhood had come out to see Dodsworth's fate. I recognized one of the women and called her over. "Their maidservant is still inside," I said. "Tell her what has happened. If you can, find her a kind mistress." The woman nodded, and Martha, Will, and I set out for the Castle and what I hoped would be the final act of the bloody play in which we'd found ourselves.

As we passed through the Castle gate, I could see the guards leading Jonathan Dodsworth into the same tower where Praise-God was being kept. I sought out the Castle's commanding officer, and told him what had happened. I waited while his clerk wrote up a letter to the Lord Mayor explaining the case and the need for a trial. Though there would not be the same rush to execute Dodsworth as there had been to hang Praise-God, I doubted he would see another Sabbath. Good riddance. Now I could turn my attention to the Wards.

"I asked your father to be here at four," I said to Will. I glanced at the sun, to gage the time. Was it was my imagination, or did it burn less fiercely? "He should be here soon." We walked to Samuel's tower where we found him and Tree sitting down to a dinner of bread, fish, and cheese, along with ale for Samuel and a small beer for Tree.

"Ah, good!" Tree cried. "I hoped you'd be back, so I got some extra." He dashed to the cupboard and produced a loaf of bread and a large piece of cheese. We found places to sit as best we could—Martha and Will sat together on the stairs leading to the upper cells—and had a more enjoyable meal than we'd had all summer. Whether it was the arrests of Praise-God and Jonathan Dodsworth or the hope that we'd soon have Deborah Ward in prison, the tide seemed to have turned in our favor; soon all the guilty would be punished and life could return to normal.

When we'd eaten I went into the yard to wait for Edward, who arrived at four o'clock, just as I'd asked him to. My mood soured somewhat when I saw he was accompanied by both his son Joseph and Mark Preston. The next hour would be a difficult one, and their presence would not make it any easier.

"Why so secretive, Lady Bridget?" Edward asked as we approached each other. "If you want me to interrogate Praise-God Ward again, you've wasted both my time and yours."

"It's not an interrogation," I said. "More like a complete confession. But he is in a very delicate state, and if he is overtaxed, he could return to his prayers and then we would hear nothing more from him. I should like the two of us to see him alone."

"Father, I really should be there," Joseph objected. "I sent him here, and helped to try him. If there is more to his story, I want to hear it." To my dismay, Edward nodded.

"Joseph will accompany us," Edward declared. "But Lady Bridget will do the talking. You will remain silent."

Joseph looked none too pleased, but he nodded in assent. The guard gave Edward a lantern and led the three of us down the stairs.

"I'll go in first," I murmured. "We do not want to startle him." Joseph and Edward nodded, and I entered Praise-God's cell, closing the door behind me. He was kneeling at the side of his bed, precisely where he had been when we left. Only his whispered prayers distinguished him from a statue.

"Praise-God, I have come back," I said.

"I heard you come in," he replied. He stood and faced me. "You have brought men for me to tell?"

"Aye," I said. "They need the truth to put the matter to rest."

The lad nodded. "They can come in." I opened the door for Joseph and Edward, and they slipped in as if they were housebreakers rather than city officials.

"Tell me again about the murders," I said to Praise-God. "Start with the first."

In a calm, quiet voice, Praise-God and I talked through each of the murders. While he described his mother's actions in terrible detail, he kept his promise not to mention his father. I did not demand it for fear of losing his trust. When he finished, I turned to Edward.

"Have you heard enough?" I asked.

He nodded. "He will have to say as much to the jury, but I will order the arrest of Mrs. Ward."

As soon as the words passed Edward's lips, my stomach lurched, for I knew what chaos would ensue. Praise-God gasped and I turned to face him. His eyes had become impossibly wide, and he'd drawn his lips back, baring his teeth. He looked as if he meant to rip out my throat.

"Arrest my mother?" he hissed. "She is alive? You lying whore! You told me she had been killed!"

Even before he lunged, I ducked my head and darted for the cell door. If the situation had not been so dire, the astonished looks on Joseph's and Edward's faces would have moved me to laughter. But at that moment I wanted nothing more than to escape from Praise-God before he got his chains around my neck. As I pulled open the cell door, Joseph cried out in alarm. I heard the sound of a fist striking flesh, and a body crashed to the floor.

Joseph and Edward followed me out the door, and secured it behind them. Inside, Praise-God began to howl anew, and I knew that if he saw me again, he'd try to kill me. Praise-God's curses—the foulest imaginable—chased us up the stairs. I found Martha and Will at the top. They stared at me in confusion, wondering what had gone wrong.

"What in God's name happened down there?" Joseph shouted at me. "You told him his mother was dead?"

"I told him that a whore killed her," I replied.

Joseph's eyes bulged and he opened his mouth to protest.

"Hear me out," I said. "You saw what he was like before. He was so lost in prayer that he wouldn't speak to anyone. I convinced him to tell the truth. Will and Martha can attest that it was the only way to find out what happened."

Both nodded in agreement, but Joseph would not be mollified.

"And how did you think he would react when he learned that it was all a ruse? Did you consider that?"

Joseph had taken the same tone with me that he would with an incompetent servant. Whatever the merits of his complaint, and I *had* made a mistake, I felt my anger rising. I would not be harangued by my own nephew.

"You are in no position to give lectures," I replied. "Were it not for me, you would have hanged him in on the morrow, and the truth would have died alongside him. Now we know that his mother is no less guilty than he is, a fact you had no interest in discovering."

"I did nothing untoward," Joseph replied, barely containing his fury. "And I'll not stand for such sauciness, even from you."

"Aye, you will, boy," I said. "So long as I live, I'll speak my mind as I see fit."

Joseph stepped toward me—I cannot imagine what he intended—and Will moved to meet him. Edward intervened before the brothers came to blows.

"All of you, stop," he commanded. "What's done is done. Joseph should have been more diligent in seeking the truth, and Lady Bridget should have found another route to it. But now we have it, and that is what matters."

Joseph started at me with ill-disguised anger, and I am sure that my face reflected the contempt I felt at that moment.

"Joseph," Edward continued, "take some men and arrest Mrs. Ward. I will assemble a jury and arrange for a trial in the morning."

"Yes, Father," Joseph growled. He cast one more poisonous look in my direction before disappearing into the Castle yard.

"Lady Bridget," Edward said, "you must forgive Joseph. He made a terrible mistake, and his reputation will suffer. He will be removed as constable at the very least." He paused, shaking his head in disbelief. "I cannot imagine the scandal that will come from this business—the son *and* wife of a godly minister both hanged for murder? The reputations of godly men throughout England will suffer terribly. This is a dark day indeed. But do not worry, Lady Bridget. I do not hold you responsible for what has happened."

I opened my mouth to defend myself, but before I could, Edward followed Joseph into the Castle yard.

"Well, that must be a relief," Will teased. "To think that he might have blamed you for what people will say about the Wards!"

I shook my head in disbelief. I loved Edward deeply, but at times his blindness seemed willful.

"The matter is finished," I said. "And that's what is important. As for consequences, I will take what comes. Will, would you join us for a glass of Canary sack at the Angel? I hear they have received new bottles."

Will smiled, and with Praise-God's shouts fading behind us, we started back toward the city.

Before we reached the end of Castlegate, however, it became clear that our journey would not be so smooth. A crowd blocked the street, and even from a distance, we could hear the now-familiar cries of Hezekiah Ward. He stood on the back of a cart, surrounded as usual by Silence, Deborah, and John Stubb. Deborah clearly had no idea that she would soon be taken for murder.

"My God, he never stops, does he?" Martha sighed. "If he is preaching against whores, I'll pull him down myself."

But when we came close enough to hear his words, it became clear that York's whores were no longer on his mind.

"Is not the example of my own iniquitous son enough to prove that wickedness lies in every man's heart? Was not Adam, the father of all men, also the father of the murderer Cain? What man knows the sinful hearts of their children? Tomorrow my son will be hanged, and God's justice will be done, for the land doth indeed cry out for blood. And we should take his death as a warning against following in his footsteps, for in our hearts we are all base murderers, just as he is, and we all deserve eternal damnation!"

"I do wish Joseph would hurry," Will said. "I would give my last penny to see Ward's face when his wife is arrested."

"Oh, my people, my beloved flock," Ward continued. "On this day, I have terrible, heart breaking news. Tomorrow I will preach on the occasion of my son's hanging, and then I will bid you farewell."

Martha, Will, and I looked at each other. He would preach at his own son's execution?

"I have received a call to London, that den of depravity and sin, a place whose brothels are rivaled only by Rome's, a place where evil carriage is complimented rather than condemned. The Lord demands that I seek out sin, and there is no place else where the need for godly preaching is so great. So farewell, my people, farewell!" When Ward stepped down from the cart, the crowd surged forward, crying *No! No! You must stay!*

"God help us," Martha said. "Now I surely need that drink." The three of us edged around the crowd, and made our way to the Angel. The innkeeper offered us a table by the window, and brought us a bottle to share. We'd just poured our drinks when Will pointed out the window and smiled.

"Here he comes," he said.

A moment later, Joseph marched by, followed closely by a half-dozen beadles.

"He's not taking any chances, even when he arrests a woman," Martha said.

As Joseph and his troop disappeared in the direction of the Three Crowns, we drank to their success and to ours. After we'd finished, Will went south to his father's house, while Martha and I returned to mine. That night I gave thanks to God for bringing two murderers to the scaffold and allowing me to take an instrumental role in it.

• • •

Early the next morning Will arrived, overflowing with fury and taking it out on my door. "What on earth is it?" Martha cried as she let him in.

"Praise-God is dead," Will announced. "And my father refuses to try Deborah Ward without him. She is to be released from gaol this morning."

Chapter 22

"What has happened?" I cried, trying to make sense of this news. "He seemed well enough when we left him."

Will shook his head in despair. "A messenger came from the Castle. He meant to tell only my father, but word spread throughout the house soon enough. If you'd heard my father raging, you would have thought the world had come to an end."

"Will!" I demanded. "Tell me what happened!"

"I don't know. Nobody does. When the turnkey brought Praise-God his breakfast, the door was jammed shut from the inside, and even two stout guards could not open it."

"Then how do they know he hasn't just barricaded the door?" Martha asked. "He might not want to be hanged."

"The gaoler went around the outside, so he could look in the window. I don't know what he saw, but it was enough for him to send word that Praise-God was dead."

"Come," I said. "We must hurry to the Castle. You can tell us the rest on the way."

That morning the sun blazed down upon the city with renewed

fury, mocking us for thinking that God's anger had been assuaged by the mere capture of a murderer.

"Why is it that your father intends to free Deborah Ward?" I asked as we walked east on Castlegate. We shaded our eyes against the sun, but it did little good.

"He is loath to try her without Praise-God," Will said. "You and he could appear before the jury, but in the end it would be the word of a dead lunatic against the wife of a godly minister. He has no wish to be humiliated in such a public way."

"God's blood," I muttered. How had things gone so wrong so quickly? When we crossed the bridge into the Castle, we saw a crowd outside the tower where Praise-God had been kept.

"Lady Hodgson," a voice called. The two guards who had helped to arrest Jonathan Dodsworth approached us carrying a timber large enough to frame a house. Despite their size, the two men struggled under their load.

"Corporal Matthews, how are you?" I asked. "And what in heaven are you doing?"

Grateful for the chance to rest, the guards stopped and set the beam on its end. The corporal mopped his brow with his sleeve. He was so thoroughly covered in dust, he appeared more Saracen than Christian.

"You've heard the news?" he asked as he caught his breath.

"That Praise-God Ward is dead?" I asked. For a moment I worried that something else had happened that morning, but he nodded.

"Aye, and they can't get his door open. We're to bring this over to knock it down." He patted the beam. "It should do the trick."

When the men hoisted the beam back on their shoulders, Will, Martha, and I fell in behind them. As the guards approached the tower, Corporal Matthews bellowed a warning and the crowd parted like the Red Sea itself. We took advantage of the path, and followed the guards down to Praise-God's door. The landing-place at the bottom of the stairs was thronged with Castle officers and city officials, and they stumbled over each other to avoid being caught between the battering ram and the door.

"Finally!" Joseph cried. "Now don't just stand there—get this door open!" The two guards, and two others who'd been waiting for them, held the beam to their waists and hugged it tight.

"One, two, three!" Corporal Matthews cried.

The squad took four rapid steps toward the cell door. The ram struck with a thundering crash and the door flew open. When the guards backed up and tried to turn around, the beam trapped Joseph and the other officials against the wall, giving us a momentary advantage. Martha, Will, and I were the first into the cell.

The room seemed unchanged from our last visit, except that Praise-God appeared to be standing by the window, gazing at the sky. We crossed to the window and found that he was neither standing nor staring. He had somehow freed his right hand from his manacles, and secured the chain to the bar in his window. He had then wrapped the other end of the chain—with his hand still in it—around his neck and strangled himself. His sightless, bloodshot eyes bulged, and his tongue protruded horribly between his teeth. In his final moments, he had bitten partly through it, and black blood ran down his chin and over his neck.

"Ah, God," I heard myself mutter. "He chose to strangle himself over a proper hanging?"

"He chose death over betraying his mother," Martha replied as she gazed at his face.

By now guards, Aldermen, and constables had pushed their way into the room, and their cries of horror and despair filled the air. Joseph made his way to the front of the crowd, and found himself next to me. He glanced in my direction, but did not acknowledge my presence.

"Help me get him down," he called out. One of the other constables came forward, and together they lifted Praise-God's body and unwrapped the chain from his neck. The other end fell from the bar and landed on the stone floor with loud *clank*. They carried the body over to the bed and laid it flat.

"I've seen enough," I said. We pushed our way out of the cell and climbed the stairs. Hopkins, Praise-God's gaoler, sat by himself, his head in his hands. I motioned for Will and Martha to wait outside while I crossed over and sat on the chair next to him.

"What happened?" I asked. When he recognized me, he started to stand, but I bade him to remain seated.

"I swear I don't know, my lady," he said. "He screamed in fury for nearly an hour after you left. I've never heard such terrible oaths, and that's no mean feat. He wished every plague upon you and your descendants. It was a marvel to hear."

"He stopped after an hour?" I asked.

"That was when young Mr. Hodgson came to see him."

"Joseph Hodgson visited Praise-God after we left?" I asked. I felt horror creeping up within my guts.

"Aye, he went down and spoke to Mr. Ward for some time. After he left, Praise-God was quiet as could be, and I was grateful for the peace."

"But he was dead," I said.

Hopkins shrugged miserably. "I can't say when he died, but the officers are in a fury."

"How did he free his hand from his fetters?" I asked.

"I don't know," the gaoler moaned again. "I set them myself. Mr. Hodgson said that I must have done a poor job of it, else this would not have happened." He paused and looked up at me, his eyes plaintive. "But I didn't, my lady, I swear. I've put irons on hundreds of prisoners, and never had one break free. He could never have freed himself. I'll lose my place for this."

He buried his face in his hands again. I placed a hand on his shoulder, though I knew it would do little to console him. After a moment I joined Will and Martha in the Castle yard.

"What happened?" Will asked as soon as I emerged. "What did he say?"

"Not here," I replied. "There are too many ears about. Let us go to Samuel's."

We crossed the Castle yard to Samuel's tower, only to find a crowd had gathered there as well. To my dismay, I recognized many of them as Hezekiah Ward's followers. The women and even some of the men were weeping, presumably at the news of Praise-God's death. John Stubb towered over the group, and I saw the woman who had attacked me and Martha. I considered summoning a bailiff and having her arrested, but she seemed so wasted and forlorn I could not do it.

"Let us wait," I said. "Once they have gone, we will have some privacy." We crossed the yard and stood next to the tower adjacent to Samuel's. As we waited, a door opened behind us, and Hezekiah Ward stepped out, inadvertently joining our little circle. We locked eyes for a moment, and then he looked at the ground.

"I was meeting with the Castle warden," he said. Even from a few feet away, I could scarcely make out his voice. "I have to make arrangements for Praise-God's burial." His voice cracked when he said his son's name, and to my surprise, compassion welled up within me.

I looked more closely at him, expecting—no, wanting—to

see the whoremaster and the hypocrite, but all I saw was a father faced with the horrible task of burying his son. The lines on his face had become so deep that he resembled an ageing mariner rather than a middle-aged preacher, and the whites of his eyes—even the dead one—had turned red from hours of weeping. Even as he stood there, tears began to flow, and his face seemed to crumple in upon itself. Memories of the days I had lost my children poured over me and I put my hand on his arm, offering what little comfort I could to such a flawed and sinful man. Ward took one last hitching sob, then walked alone toward the Castle gate.

"God," Martha said after a moment. "I never thought I'd feel pity for a man such as that." Will and I nodded in agreement.

We stood in silence for several minutes, watching Samuel's tower. Eventually the door opened, and Edward appeared, followed by Deborah Ward. I stared in amazement as she stepped forward. She had caused the death of her own son, and should have been in the depths of hell, but she held her head high and her shoulders back, the very picture of stiff-necked pride. How was it that Hezekiah mourned so deeply for his son, but this harridan carried on as if his death were unworthy of her attention?

I strode across the Castle yard toward her. I did not know what I intended to do when I reached her, but fury had burned away whatever compassion I felt for Hezekiah. As I approached, our eyes met and her face hardened into a terrible iron mask.

"You are the one who murdered my son," she declared, her voice rising in anger. "Have you come here to lord it over me, you reprobate slut? Have you not done enough to my family?"

I hesitated for the barest moment and considered retreating. Nothing could be gained from confronting her under such circumstances. But I caught sight of a face peering down from the narrow window of one of Samuel's upper cells—it was Jennet's friend Barbara Rearsby. The constables must have taken her yet again. In her pale face and sad eyes, I saw all the women who had died at Deborah Ward's hands: Jennet, Betty, and Isabel. I saw their wrecked and bloody bodies and I heard their final terrified cries as death overtook them. Fury roiled up in me and I found I could not simply turn my back on the woman who had tortured them so.

"Reprobate?" I cried. "You dare call *me* reprobate? You dare ask what *I* did to your family?" I strode toward her, shrugging off Will's and Martha's hands as they tried to restrain me. "Your husband is a whoremonger; your son was a pimp and a murderer," I hissed. "And you? I don't have the words to describe what you are. Beast, blue devil, foul spirit, fiend of hell—none of these capture your evil ways!"

Deborah raised her hand to strike me, and I hurled myself forward, ready, even eager, to join in the fight. It is probably for the best that Edward and others stepped in. Edward threw himself between us, absorbing a vicious blow from Deborah in the process. In that moment, Martha got a firm grasp of me and pulled me back, my arms and legs flailing, and Will wrapped his arms around me, lifting me up and away from the skirmish. Deborah and her people scurried off toward the Castle gate, with Edward close behind, urging them on.

Once they were safely away, Will put me back on the ground and released his grip on my waist. I turned to face him, furious that he'd interfered. Blood flowed freely from his nose, and dripped onto his shirt.

"Oh, God, Will, did I do that?" I cried. In the midst of the scuffle I must have struck him with an elbow.

He pulled a handkerchief from his pocket and did his best to stanch the bleeding. In that moment, the rage that had flared up inside me burned itself out.

"No, Aunt Bridget," he mumbled through the blood. "When you flew at Mrs. Ward, I decided to bloody my own nose."

I had to laugh at this, and I embraced him. "Thank you," I said. "And I'm sorry." When I stepped back, I saw that we both were covered in his blood, making Martha the only one of us still fit to appear in public.

"Don't worry," he said. "The blood will wash out. Now tell us what Praise-God's gaoler said." The Castle yard had emptied, so I could now speak freely.

"Your brother was the last one to see Praise-God," I said. "The gaoler says that before Joseph's visit, Praise-God was the very picture of bedlam, crying and cursing without pause. But after Joseph left, he heard nothing."

"Joseph came back?" Martha asked.

"Aunt Bridget," Will protested. "Surely you don't think that Joseph did this! First you accused him of murdering the whores and now you accuse him of killing Praise-God?"

I did not reply because in truth I did not know what I thought.

"*Do* you think that I killed him, Aunt Bridget?" Joseph's voice nearly made me leap from my skin. He stood at the entrance to Samuel's tower, leaning against the doorpost. He could not have been more at ease. He walked toward me, his obsidian eyes gleaming. "You thought that I killed those whores, and now you accuse me of murdering a man even as he is in fetters? Do you truly believe that I could be so evil?"

"Then tell me what happened," I demanded. I felt a tremor in my voice and could only hope that Joseph did not hear it.

Joseph allowed himself a mirthless smile before answering.

"It is true that I saw him last night. I told him that his mother had been arrested for murdering the whores and that he would be the most important witness against her. I said that if the jury did not believe him, she would go free, so he should compose himself as best he could. But he was alive and in chains when I left him."

Despite the heat of the day, the cruelty of Joseph's smile chilled me to the marrow. I realized then that I had been wrong about how the war had changed him. He was not an earnest magistrate with fond dreams of building a city on a hill, but a hard and ruthless villain, bent on seizing power for its own sake.

"Then how did he escape his fetters?" I asked.

"That *is* a mystery," Joseph replied. "But you cannot say justice has not been done. He was to hang anyway, and by the look on his face, this death was far more horrible than the one the hangman would have brought to him."

"You know he did not kill the whores by himself," I said. "How is justice done when Deborah Ward goes free?"

"God will have His justice in His time," Joseph said. "But can you envision the scandal if Praise-God had not died when he did? Hezekiah Ward is the most renowned minister of the gospel in these parts. Mrs. Ward's trial would have been famous throughout the nation. And if we executed her and Praise-God together? The spectacle would be unmatched in memory. It truly beggars the imagination."

"You wanted this to happen," I said. "You connived at Praise-God's death."

"And what would the King's pamphleteers say?" Joseph continued as if I had not spoken. "Our enemies would write about the case for years. Pamphlets about the murders, poems about the trial, songs about the executions. *See!* they would cry. *See what hypocrites the godly are?* We would lose all authority, and as Mr. Ward would say, the people would run back to their sins as a dog returns to his vomit. No, the Wards will leave the city, and take their troubles with them. It truly was best that Praise-God died, and I would not regret it if I'd had a hand in his death."

I looked at Will to see how he was taking all this. He stared wide-eyed at his brother, as if seeing him for the first time. He had forgotten about the blood running from his nose to his chin.

"What is it, brother?" Joseph asked, a ghost of a smile on his lips. "I told you I did no wrong." He turned on his heel, and ambled across the Castle yard, every inch the image of a man enjoying a job well done. Before Joseph reached the gate, Edward met him. The two men embraced and then talked for a time.

"I don't imagine he's confessing to Praise-God's murder," Will said.

I put my arm around his shoulders. I could only imagine what he felt at that moment. What did it mean when your father rejected you in favor of a cold-blooded murderer? After a few minutes, Joseph disappeared through the Castle gate, and Edward crossed the yard toward us. I imagined he would have harsh words for me over the row with Deborah Ward, and the prospect soured me even further. I was in no humor to accept his reproofs.

"Lady Bridget," he said as he approached. "Might I speak with you? Alone?"

"No, Edward," I said. "You may not. Not unless you've come to tell me that you will question the gaoler to find out how Praise-God died."

"Question the gaoler?" Edward barked, caught somewhere between laughter and anger. "Are you mad? He'll be whipped, not questioned."

"Does it matter that Joseph visited Praise-God just before he died?" Will asked. If Will had hoped to turn his father more to anger, he could not have found better words. Edward's face hardened into stone and he turned his gaze on his son.

"Joseph left him alive and well," Edward replied. "And if you say otherwise, if you *think* otherwise, I'll see you whipped alongside the gaoler. Whether you are my son or not, you'll suffer. Praise-God is a suicide and that is the end of it."

"And Deborah Ward?" I asked, eager to deflect Edward's wrath away from Will. "Why won't you try her for murdering the whores? You heard what Praise-God said with your own ears."

"I did," he replied. "And we cannot credit the word of such a man."

"You credited it enough to arrest her yesterday," I said.

"And today her accuser showed himself to be capable of self-murder."

"You know that she is guilty," I pleaded. "You must put her before a jury."

Edward's features softened for a moment.

"Lady Bridget," he said. "There is nothing I can do. If I thought Deborah Ward was guilty, *and* that I could prove it, I would put her on trial. But I don't and I can't. Can you imagine the chaos that would come with a trial, whatever the verdict? No, the Wards will leave for London on the morrow, and we will be well shut of them." He scowled at Will before turning toward the gate and walking away without a backward look.

As Edward receded into the distance and disappeared through the gate, I feared that despair would overcome me. Could it be that earthly justice never would be done? Were Jennet, Betty, and Isabel so low, so inconsequential, that the law would never avenge their murders? My mind raced as I tried to find a solution, but I could not. In this place and on this day, Edward *was* the law, and he had made it clear that the Wards mattered and the murdered women did not. He had decided that maintaining the power and the prestige of the godly magistrate counted for more than justice. And what of Praise-God? I doubted we would ever know the truth of what had happened in that cell. If Joseph had strangled Praise-God, he had chosen the perfect victim. A man as frenzied as that would certainly have resorted to self-murder, and none would dare say otherwise.

"Come," I said at last. "We should go home."

"No," Martha replied. "I won't."

I looked at her in shock.

"What do you mean?" I asked. While we'd had our disagreements, she'd never refused me so bluntly.

"I won't just go home and let her escape!" she cried. "She killed three women, and if she is set loose in London, she'll kill more there."

"There is nothing we can do," Will said.

"Yes there is," she said, and started off on her own. "I will return before supper."

That afternoon, the sun persisted in its efforts to desiccate the city. I heard that a neighbor's cow fell dead in the fields outside the city, and the apple blossoms browned and blew away. Martha came home just as she promised and went about her work. Despite my earnest entreaties, she refused to tell me where she had been or what she had done.

"I do not know what may fall," she said. "Perhaps nothing, perhaps something."

I questioned her more, but she maintained the same steadfastness and discretion that served her so well as my deputy; she would not say another word.

I rose early the next morning and with Martha in tow set out for Edward's. I was still troubled by our argument at the Castle, and wanted to make amends as best I could. Our route to the Ouse

Bridge would take us past the Three Crowns, and I wondered whether we would catch sight of the Wards on their way out of the city. I hoped not, but when we reached the inn, we found that a large crowd had gathered outside.

"Ah, no," I sighed. "I do not think that I can hear another of Mr. Ward's sermons." I was considering what other route to take to the Bridge when I heard a voice shouting my name.

"Lady Bridget, Lady Bridget!" Tree weaved through the crowd, more excited than I'd seen him in some time. "Have you already heard? Is that why you're come?"

"Have I heard what?" I asked. "We are trying to get to Micklegate."

"If you are going to find Mr. Hodgson, he is already on his way," Tree replied. "Wait, and he'll meet you here." He seemed pleased at my good fortune, but by now, he had completely befuddled me.

"Tree, what are you doing here?" I asked.

"Samuel had sent me into the city for ale," he said. "I was here when I heard they found the bodies."

"Tree, what is going on?" Martha demanded. "What bodies?"

"The people from the inn said that the murders have not yet stopped," Tree replied. "They discovered two more corpses this morning."

Chapter 23

"Oh God!" I cried. "How so? Could she not leave the city without spilling more blood?"

"There are bodies inside?" Martha asked.

Tree nodded. "That's why Mr. Hodgson is coming."

I was suddenly sure that Martha knew more about what was happening than I did. I looked at her closely, but her face remained a mask.

"Come on," Tree said.

He grasped my hand and began to pull me through the crowd. When we reached the front of the inn, we found a beadle standing at the door and trying his best to ignore the shouts of those around him. Some wanted to know what had happened; others asked if yet another whore had died. More than a few men stood in their shifts; they must have been cast out of their rooms by the beadles. When the beadle saw me, relief flooded his face.

"Lady Hodgson!" he cried. "What am I to do?"

In truth, I had no idea, for I did not know what was happening.

"Keep them out until help arrives," I said. "I'll go in and see what is going on."

"Yes, my lady," he said. "They are up on the third floor."

I glanced again at Martha, sure that she knew who "they" were, but she remained silent. We climbed the stairs to the top floor of the inn, and found another beadle standing outside one of the rooms. His face was as pale as a new-washed shirt, and he seemed no less happy to see me than his comrade downstairs. Without a word, he opened the door to the room and ushered us in. Even before we entered, the smell of excrement assaulted us. Inside, the smell was much worse, and I cried out in horror at the gruesome scene.

A man and a woman hung from the room's center rafter. They both had sacks on their heads, and their hands had been bound in front of them. The ropes around their necks had been tied off at the center post of the window. I did not need to remove their masks to know who they were. I looked at Martha, wondering if she somehow had a hand in this, but she seemed as shaken as I felt. Neither of us spoke as we gazed at the bodies. Through the open window, I could hear the crowd outside the inn. The only noise from the room itself was the uneven creak of the rope as the bodies swung slowly back and forth. I was pulled from my terrible reverie by the sound of men climbing the stairs. Edward had arrived, I guessed. I stepped into the hallway to meet him.

Edward, Joseph, and a squad of constables and beadles appeared at the top of the steps and hurried toward me.

"What in the devil are you doing here?" Joseph snarled.

Edward raised his hand to silence his son.

"He asks a fair question," Edward said. "And we will pursue it later. But now is not the time."

Martha and I stepped aside so the men could enter the Wards' room.

"Ah, blood of Christ," Edward moaned when he saw the bodies. Martha and I slipped in behind him. Joseph crossed to the window and pulled ineffectually at the knot.

"Someone give me a knife," he demanded. One of the beadles obliged, and together they cut the rope and lowered the woman's body. A constable caught her, and laid her on the floor. Edward knelt and removed the sack from her head. Deborah Ward's eyes had rolled up, so that she'd died gazing at the heavens. Her tongue, swollen with blood, protruded from her mouth and—like Praise-God—she'd nearly bitten through it.

"Ah, Jesus," Joseph moaned when he saw her face.

"Come on, let's get the other one down," Edward commanded. Joseph and the beadle obeyed and a few moments later, Hezekiah lay next to his wife.

"My God!" cried Will as he came in to the room. Joseph gave Will a baleful look before turning back to the bodies.

I cast my eyes about the room, hoping to find some sign of what had happened. Two clothes chests sat against one wall of the room. The first had been closed and locked, but the other stood open. Inside I could see a fine wool jacket lying atop several linen shirts. I caught a glimpse of something peeking out from the jacket's sleeve and bent down for a closer look. When I saw what it was—what I *thought* it was—I gasped and reached for it.

Martha proved more dexterous than I, and she snatched it up. She glanced at me as she slipped it into the folds of her apron. I started to protest, but she shook her head slightly, her eyes deadly serious. Now was not the time.

"What is it?" Edward asked. "Did you find something?"

"No, sir," Martha said without a moment's hesitation. "Lady Hodgson is merely overcome by the terrible sight."

I could not tell if Edward believed her, but he returned his attention to the more urgent matter of the bodies before him. I ached to ask Martha what she had found, but knew that I could not do so until we were away from Edward and Joseph. I inclined my head to the door, and Martha nodded. We tried to slip out without attracting any attention, but failed miserably.

"Beadle," Joseph ordered. "Make sure that Lady Hodgson and her girl are comfortable in one of the other rooms. Take my brother in there, too. I will speak to them in a moment."

The beadle nodded and led the three of us across the hall. I did not relish the conversation that would follow when Joseph joined us, but saw no way to avoid it. Like the Wards' room, the one across the hall had a large, comfortable bed—no straw mattresses here—and two fine wood chests against the wall.

The beadle remained with us, so we waited in uneasy silence for what seemed an eternity. I searched Martha's face for some sign of her thoughts, but she seemed unaffected by the course of events.

While we waited, more men went in and out of the Wards' room. The beadles brought two large canvases in which they wrapped the corpses, then they carried the bodies down the stairs. They dropped one, and we heard cries of horror and a voice roaring, "Well, wrap her back up!" I hid a smile behind my hand, and I thought I saw the corners of Martha's mouth twitch ever so slightly upward.

I could hear Edward, Joseph, and others searching the Wards' room. Men grunted as they moved the bed, and I heard a crash as they broke the lock off Mrs. Ward's clothes chest. By now they certainly would have found whatever Martha had hidden in her apron. After they finished the search, Joseph came into the room where we waited.

"What happened in there?" Joseph hissed. His voice had a steel edge to it, and I knew that we would have to choose our words carefully if we were to escape the room unscathed.

"I don't know what you mean, sir," Martha replied with such exaggerated innocence that what followed surprised no one.

"You'll speak when I speak to you, drab," Joseph snarled, his fists clenched. Will stepped forward, but a withering glance from his brother froze him on the spot.

"Lady Bridget," said Joseph, barely controlling his fury. "Tell me what happened here."

"Joseph," I said. "I will tell you this once. I had nothing to do with the Wards' deaths. How could any woman have bound and hung two people?"

A muscle in Joseph's cheek twitched repeatedly as he worked to contain himself. I could not help noticing that he'd dropped one hand to the pommel of his sword, as if he longed to draw it and put us in our places.

"If I knew how you'd done it, you'd already be in the Castle," Joseph replied. "And not in the care of your dwarf friend, either."

"If you know I am innocent, nephew, why do you interrogate me?"

"I did not say you are innocent. I said I did not know how you killed them."

"Be careful what you say, Joseph," I said. "And remember to whom you speak. You are a constable, for a year perhaps. I am a gentlewoman by blood and tradition. Do not forget that." I did not know how hard I could push back at Joseph, but I also could not allow him to batter us into submission.

"Given your fondness for justice and the law, I find that argument puzzling," Joseph replied. "The law would insist on hanging a gentlewoman *or* her servant if she were guilty of murder." He stared at Martha in order to make clear the nature of his threat. "Before you leave this room, you will tell me what happened. You might not have hanged them yourself, but I know you had a hand in it."

"What do you mean?" Edward asked as he entered the room. "Are you accusing Lady Bridget of killing the Wards?"

If Joseph had been in control of himself, he would have recognized his father's incredulity, but anger overruled common sense.

"Who else?" Joseph barked. "You saw her anger when we released Mrs. Ward. You know she is willing to sacrifice good order on the altar of her own idea of justice."

I started to object, but Joseph pushed ahead.

"Did you think I would not discover Sarah Briggs, the whore you delivered of a bastard? Why didn't you report her to the city, Lady Bridget? Why did you keep the news to yourself? What about your oath? What about the law? Oughtn't she be whipped?"

Edward looked at me in surprise, hoping—I think—for a denial of some sort. I sought an explanation but found none. My mouth flapped open and closed, but I could find no words.

"Do you see?" Joseph asked. "The scene across the hall was how she dispenses justice. She has no concern for the law and none for order."

"And you would prefer the tyranny of law without justice," I replied at last. I'd had enough of Joseph's panting after power.

"I'll hear no more lectures from you," Joseph spat. "I do not know what your role was in murdering these two, but I will not rest until I discover it and see you hanged, and if your slatternly maid was a part of it, I'll see her on the gibbet beside you."

I think that even Edward felt that Joseph had gone too far, but it was Martha who came forward first.

"So long as you're talking of murderers, you should look to yourself, shouldn't you?" Martha cried. "We may never see you hanged, but we will see you cast down from the power you love so much, and brought at low as Praise-God Ward. You're no better a man than he was."

With horrifying speed, Joseph drew his sword and slashed it across Martha's face. She clapped her hand to her cheek and fell to the floor with a cry. Will roared, drew his sword from his cane, and charged at Joseph. He drove the crown of his head into his brother's face. Joseph's nose broke with a sickening *crack*. Blood spattered across both their faces, and Edward's, too.

Joseph stumbled back, shaking his head to clear the blood from his eyes and screaming in anger. Edward cried out for them to stop, but neither would leave off the fight until the other lay dead. Joseph lunged at Will, his sword carving an arc toward his brother's neck. Will deflected the blow and ducked under it, then swung his fist at Joseph's wrecked nose. Joseph fell back on to the bed, spitting blood.

Edward hurled himself between his sons, but one of them—I could not tell which—knocked him back and to the ground. Now it was Will's turn to attack. His sword swung wide of Joseph's throat, but not by more than an inch. Joseph avoided another killing blow when he lashed out with his feet, kicking Will's legs from under him.

Will stumbled back, his arms reeling madly as he tried to keep his balance. The tip of his sword clipped the floor and flew from his hand. As Will scrambled to find the handle of his sword, Joseph rolled off the bed and leaped to his feet. While the brothers regained themselves, I grasped Martha's arm and pulled her to the side.

Will and Joseph rejoined the battle with a ferocity seen only in civil wars, swords and blood flying, the small wounds they inflicted on each other multiplying. I looked for Edward, but could not find him in the melee. At some point Will suffered a grievous cut on his crippled leg, and within moments he seemed to be wearing parti-colored trousers, half crimson, half tan. Despite this wound, Will lunged forward and cut open Joseph's shoulder, and soon his arm hung by his side, useless.

It seemed an eternity before a small army of beadles crashed into the room, knocking the door clear from its hinges. They threw themselves at Will and Joseph both. Thoroughly exhausted by their fight, both men went down without a struggle.

I helped Martha to her feet, and as gently as I could, prised her hand from her cheek. A horrific welt stood out on her fair skin and blood oozed from the top edge, but the wound seemed far milder than the blow. Mercifully, Joseph's goal had been to humiliate and disfigure, not to kill. He had struck her with the flat edge of his sword.

"Come," I said. "We will find some water." She nodded but said nothing.

By now the beadles had disarmed Joseph and Will and hauled them to their feet. Their wounds would need to be bound, but if they could avoid infection, neither would suffer more pain than he deserved.

"Oh, Christ!" one of the beadles shouted. "Jesus Christ! Murder! Murder!"

We all turned to see what the matter was. Only then did we notice a pair of legs sticking out from behind the bed. I cried out in horror when I saw what had happened. In the distance, I could hear Will's and Joseph's screams mixing with my own. Edward—my brother-in-law, protector, and benefactor—lay slumped against the wall, his eyes staring sightlessly at the ceiling above.

My memories of the hours that followed are indistinct at best. I remember seeing the front of Edward's shirt saturated with blood. I saw that he died clutching his own neck, trying in vain to slow the flow of blood from the fatal wound. When they saw their father's body, Will and Joseph cried out in unison, their bloody quarrel forgotten. They fell to their knees before their father and begged that their eyes might be deceiving them. They screamed even as the bailiffs dragged them to the Castle.

With both Will and Joseph in jail, it fell to me to care for Edward's body. Martha and I laid him out on the bed and washed the blood from his neck and chest. So much blood. Someone, I know not who, brought us a woolen shroud and helped us to wrap him.

A while later—minutes? hours?—Mark Preston arrived with three other servants and they carried Edward's body across the river to his church. They would bury him in the chancel the next morning.

Martha and I leaned on each other as we walked home. Hannah had heard the news, and she met us at the door. She helped us both from our blood-spattered clothes, brought us wine, and saw us to bed.

The next morning, Hannah, Martha, and I donned our mourning clothes and crossed the bridge to Micklegate Ward. Between his friends, colleagues, and representatives from the city's most important guilds, Edward's mourners numbered in the hundreds and his black-clad pallbearers included the Lord Mayor, Aldermen, and Members of Parliament. Nobody mentioned Will's and

Joseph's absence, of course, but it could not have been far from anyone's mind. Save Will and Joseph, I was Edward's closest living relative, so I was given pride of place in the church. I sat in Edward's pew, staring at the stained glass and trying to open my soul to the beauty of holiness. I imagine the minister preached, but cannot say that I heard a word of his sermon. Rather, I wondered what the Lord meant by all this, and what the future would bring.

As the service went on around me, I thought of the grief that fathers and sons brought upon each other. Though he did not mean for it to happen, Hezekiah Ward's actions led to his son's death. And I supposed that even from the grave, Praise-God had a hand in his father's murder. For his part, by favoring Joseph over Will, Edward had stoked the rivalry between his boys. Obviously he never imagined it would lead to murder, especially his own, but it is a rare life that goes as planned.

After Edward's burial, city officials summoned a jury to investigate his death. The Lord Mayor and jurors questioned both Will and Joseph, of course, but not for very long; it seemed unlikely that either of them would confess to murdering their father. But they kept Martha and me for hours. An Alderman had died, and the thought that his killer might escape justice drove the Lord Mayor quite mad.

The problem was that neither of us had seen who struck the blow that ended Edward's life. I relived the afternoon's events countless times, but could not see the moment when the blood began to flow in earnest. I had been too worried for Will to see my brother-in-law's life pouring out between his fingers. His last sight had been his sons trying to kill each other. In the end, everyone agreed that either Will or Joseph had killed their father, but no one could say which of them struck the fatal blow. The Lord Mayor retired to consider whether the city would hang both or neither.

After the inquest, Martha and I returned home and I retired to my chamber for prayer. To the surprise of some within the city, the summer's heat had continued with undiminished fury. The ministers continued to beg God for mercy and redoubled their calls for repentance and reform.

For my part, I asked God to find a just solution to Will's situation, and to soothe the wounds of those who had suffered so much during that terrible week. As I meditated upon all who had died, an image leaped into my mind—I saw Martha reaching into Hezekiah Ward's clothes chest and snatching something away before I could see what it was. I ended my prayers as quickly as I could without giving offense to God and sought out Martha. I found her and Hannah in the courtyard doing laundry. I sent Hannah inside and turned to Martha.

"What did you find in Mr. Ward's chest?"

She stopped washing and stood. I waited while she dried her hands and considered her response.

"If I tell you, it will make you a part of what happened," she said. "And your knowledge will change nothing, for you can do nothing with it. Do you still want to know?"

I nodded.

"It's inside."

We went into the kitchen and Martha ducked through the low door into the buttery. She returned a moment later. She held out her hand and opened it. Sitting in her palm was an intricately carved wooden serpent, a twin to the one that Stephen Daniels had given her the week before.

Chapter 24

"You found that in Hezekiah Ward's chest?" I asked.

"Tucked into the sleeve of his coat," she replied. I knew what it meant, of course, but my mind whirled as I sought another explanation, one that would not make my deputy a murderess.

"Tell me what happened," I said finally.

"When we left the Castle after Praise-God died, I went to Helen Wright's." Martha looked everywhere in the kitchen save into my eyes. "I did not know what else to do. I could not simply shrug my shoulders, and walk away from the murders. Those poor women . . ." Her voice trailed off and she took a deep breath before continuing. "Where else was I to go? To another constable? A Justice of the Peace? A maidservant—even your maidservant— would not carry much weight with such men. And even if I convinced him to examine the murder, what good would that have done? Praise-God was dead, and Joseph and Edward had decided to end the case there."

"What did you tell Helen Wright?" I asked.

"The truth." Martha looked at me for the first time when she said it. "Only the truth. I told her that Deborah Ward and Praise-God had killed all those women. That they had left Elizabeth an orphan. I told her that Hezekiah Ward was a whoremonger and a hypocrite. And that justice would never be done, that the dead would never be avenged . . . that those with power would not suffer for their ill deeds."

For a moment I thought of Martha's master, who had met his own bloody end after he had raped Martha. I pushed that image away and brought myself back to the present.

"Helen Wright did this," I said. "She sent her man to kill the Wards." Martha looked down at the miniature viper in her hand but did not respond. Nor did she protest when I took the snake from her. "Finish the washing," I said. I did not ask Martha if Helen had told her what she intended. I told myself that it did not matter, but in truth I did not want to know the answer.

After Martha had gone, I stared at the wooden figure for a time. I could not say her decision to go to Helen Wright surprised me: Martha had less faith in the law than I, and fewer misgivings about acting outside of it. I also felt that by taking the serpent, I had assumed a portion of Martha's guilt; now I had to decide what to do with that burden.

But what could I do? The little viper did not prove who had killed the Wards, and it would not convince a jury to hang Stephen Daniels. Nor could I say that I would want that to happen. Martha had gone to Helen Wright in the hope of obtaining a measure of justice, and Helen had provided it.

I opened the oven door and tossed the viper on top of the embers. It took only a moment for the figure to blacken and then burst into flame with a small puff of smoke.

• • •

The next morning, before the sun had begun to hammer the city, I slipped out of my house and made my way south toward Micklegate. I gazed at Edward's house with its black banners draped over the windows and doors before continuing through the gate and out of the city. When I reached my destination, I climbed the stone steps and pounded on the door.

Stephen Daniels smiled when he saw me, and ushered me into the parlor. "Mrs. Wright will be with you in a moment," he said. "She has been expecting you. You may sit if you wish."

I nodded my thanks and he left me alone.

A few minutes later, Helen swept into the parlor, Stephen close behind her. As always, she had chosen a dress made from the finest silk decorated with the richest and most delicate needlework.

"Lady Hodgson," she said. "It is a pleasant surprise to see you again."

"Your man told me that you've been expecting me," I replied, unwilling to give even an inch.

"And so I have," she said, as if being caught in a lie were of no consequence. "Please accept my deepest condolences on the death of your brother-in-law."

"That is not why I am here," I said.

"No, I expect not."

"Your man murdered Hezekiah and Deborah Ward." I looked at Stephen, but his face remained impassive.

"That is a serious accusation, Lady Hodgson," Helen said evenly. "I trust you have some evidence of this?"

"You'll not turn this into a legal debate," I replied. "You overstepped your bounds, and by your actions you've made my deputy into a murderess."

To my surprise, Helen Wright began to laugh.

"I am flattered that you think I have the power to transform an innocent maiden into a murderess," she said. "But I could no more do that than I could make her into one of my whores. She left my house the same woman she was when she arrived."

"She was not a murderess," I insisted.

"Nor is she now," Helen replied. "She knew of a crime, and she testified about it. The guilty are hanged. Justice is done. You do not think that Deborah Ward should have been allowed to leave the city, do you? Even if you have no interest in vengeance, ask yourself how many more women she would have killed, even without the help of her lunatic son."

"And what of Hezekiah?" I demanded. "You were an accomplice to both his crimes and his death, weren't you?"

Helen's face became serious as she considered my questions. She nodded slowly and glanced at Stephen.

"I did not know he frequented whores. If I had, we might have ended this sorry business days sooner.

"And I will bear some responsibility for his death," she continued softly. "But it was he who led us down this road. He preached against the very sin he committed, and he dragged his son down with him."

"And you killed him for that?"

"What would you have had us do?" Stephen asked, taking a few steps forward. I don't think he meant to frighten me, but my heart leaped in my chest. If he would kill a famous minister, why would he balk at doing the same to a midwife?

Helen must have noticed the fear in my eyes, for she put a hand on Stephen's arm and drew him back.

"If they had left the city," she said, "they would have escaped justice forever. I have power in York, but my writ does not run all the way to London. I told Stephen that if he could not get Deborah alone, he should hang them both. Of all who died this week, Hezekiah Ward was far from the most innocent."

I could not argue with that sentiment, so I said nothing.

"I am afraid I have other business to attend to," Helen said. "I have no doubt we will see each other again. I hope it is under less morbid circumstances."

It seemed that for the second time in a week, a bawd had dismissed me. The world had indeed been turned upside down.

As I walked home, I puzzled over what Helen had said. No sane man would argue that Deborah Ward should have gone free; God demanded justice and Helen Wright had provided it. But I also dwelled on the murder—could there be another word?—of Hezekiah Ward. What thoughts went through his head as the noose tightened around his neck? What prayers did he say as his feet left the floor? Perhaps he'd thought of his son and daughter, and the horror he'd wrought upon his own family. I hoped so.

In the wake of the inquest into Edward's death, the question that gripped the city was what would happen to Joseph and Will. Nobody could recall such a case, and none could say what should be done. The Lord Mayor kept to his house while he deliberated, as secretive as Papists choosing a new pontiff. My greatest fear was that the godly would convince him that the heat was a sign of God's enduring wrath, and he would order an execution in the hope of appeasing Him.

A few days after the inquest, the Lord Mayor made his decision. As evening approached, he sent a Justice to the Castle to release both Joseph and Will. There would be no formal announcement of their release, and no public trial of either man. Edward's death was an accident, and from that day forward it would be spoken of only in hushed voices.

I did not know all this, of course, when I heard a soft knock at my door. The sun was almost down, and I could not imagine who was out at such an hour. Hannah cried out in surprise when she opened the door, and I hurried in to see what the matter was.

Will stood in the doorway, filthy and shrunken from his time in the Castle. He wore the same blood-soaked clothes he'd been arrested in. As soon as he saw me, his face crumpled and he began to wail like the boy he'd been not so long before. I stepped toward him and he collapsed into my arms, wrung out from grief, fear, and exhaustion. Martha appeared beside me, and Will reached out for her, desperate for consolation.

"Oh God, oh God, oh God," he moaned, tightening his grip on both of us. His body shook as we half carried and half dragged him into the parlor and laid him on the couch. He threw an arm across his eyes and continued to sob.

"Get him some new clothes," I said to Martha. She looked pleadingly at Hannah, who nodded and disappeared upstairs while Martha knelt by Will's side and took his hand. I retreated to the kitchen and put a pot of water on the fire. While the water warmed, I fetched some towels and brought them to the parlor. Will remained on the couch, his eyes closed. Tears washed a path through the grime and blood on his face. Martha held his hand but said nothing.

I looked more closely at his clothes and decided they were beyond saving. When I returned from the kitchen with the warmed water, I brought a pair of scissors, and as gently as I could, cut Will's shirt from his body. Martha and I laid him on the towels and washed the many small wounds that Joseph had inflicted. When we cut away his trousers, I was surprised to find that the wound on his leg had been cleaned and bound with a fresh bandage. Will had opened his eyes and noticed my interest.

"Samuel Short bribed my keeper to let him in," he said. "You'd never know it to look at him, but he'd be a fine surgeon."

I made a note to send thanks to Samuel in the morning.

Once he was clean and dry, Martha and I helped Will upstairs to one of my spare chambers. He'd just laid down when I realized the room seemed cold. I looked out the window to find the city enveloped in a cooling fog. As I watched, the mist slowly gave way to a soft, soaking rain.

For the next few days, we all stayed in as best we could. Part of it was the rain, of course, which lasted nearly a week, as God made up for its long summer absence. But we also wanted to stay close to Will. He showed little interest in leaving his room, to say nothing of venturing out of doors. Indeed the day after his release from the Castle, he spoke hardly a word, and only slowly returned to some semblance of himself.

Hannah and Martha ventured out for food and to gather what gossip could be had. Rather than extinguishing interest in Edward's death, the Lord Mayor's decision to release both Joseph and Will simply inflamed it all the more. How could it be that an Alderman had been slain by his own son, and there would be no trial? Some said that Will (or Joseph) had bribed the Lord Mayor with a share of Edward's fortune. Others claimed that one brother had deliberately killed Edward and then threatened the other into silence.

Two days after Will's arrival, I awoke before dawn and, as quietly as I could, made my way to the kitchen. I thought I was the first one awake, but when I reached the bottom of the stairs, I heard voices from the parlor.

"Will, you don't have to thank me," Martha whispered. "I swore I'd never tell anyone, and I won't."

I stood stock-still as Martha's words echoed through my mind. I told myself that Will's secret could be anything. Perhaps he had fathered a bastard child, or fallen in love with Edward's serving-maid, or found himself with the French pox. But I could not help thinking that Martha knew more about Edward's death than she'd admitted to me or to the jury. Had she seen Will's sword strike the killing blow? I was pulled out of my reverie by Will's next question.

"Will you still marry me?"

My heart leaped at the words. I'd harbored the suspicion that Will and Martha had become fond of each other, but even so, it surprised me that things had progressed to the point of betrothal. Such a revelation explained the violence of Will's reaction when Joseph had struck Martha: he was defending not my maidservant, but his own beloved. Without warning, a tickle in my throat became a cough, and I unintentionally announced my presence.

"There you are, Aunt Bridget," Will called. From his voice I'd have thought that nothing was amiss, and I wondered if the secret he shared with Martha might be entirely innocent. I did not ask what they had been talking about. I knew they would tell me when they were ready.

Will seemed better with each passing day, at least until we learned that Edward's will had been read and his estate settled. Mark Preston brought the news.

"Mr. Hodgson asked me to bring you a letter," he said when I met him in the parlor. "And I have one for Will as well."

I could not help noticing that the cut and quality of his clothes had improved since Edward's death. Were it not for the missing fingers on his hand, one might not know of his bloody history.

"Mr. Hodgson sent it?" I asked. "He included a letter to me

in his testament?" Posthumous letters were not unheard of, but were usually sent from ageing parents to their children. Edward had not known he would die so soon, so why would he write one?

"No, my lady," he replied. "Mr. Joseph Hodgson. He has been kind enough to keep me in his service as he assumes his father's estate."

I knew then that Will could expect little of Edward's wealth. Even in death, Edward had favored Joseph. I opened the letter with my name on it.

> *Aunt Bridget,*
> *In his testament, my late and beloved father made a generous gift to you of 100 pounds, lawful English money. Unfortunately, his estate does not include that much ready money, and I—as his executor and chief heir—cannot pay you at this time. I have enclosed with this letter a bond for the full amount.*
> *Your loving and loyal nephew,*
> *Jos. Hodgson, Esq.*

Except for the speed with which he'd started referring to himself as "esquire," I could not say that the letter surprised me; it might even speak the truth. Trade in the midst of a civil war was no certain thing, and £100 was a lot of money to keep locked away. I also had no doubt that Joseph would pay me, albeit on his own terms and in his own time.

What concerned me most was not the money, but Joseph's claim that Edward had made him his heir— What of Will?

I felt the desire to keep Joseph's letter from Will, for I knew that it could only bring sorrow and anger. But I also knew he would read it eventually and time would not lessen its sting. I called for Will and gave him the letter.

Sam Thomas

He read it in mere seconds then refolded the paper. From his reaction, I'd have thought it had informed him that the sun would rise in the morning. He crossed to the hearth, laid the letter on the fire, and watched while it burned.

"Will?" I said. He shrugged and turned around.

"I'll get almost nothing," he said. "Ten pounds now, but after that it will be however much Joseph sees fit. And I think we know what that will mean."

"You will be fine," I said. I had money and land enough to make up for Edward's neglect and Joseph's malice.

"It would not surprise me if Joseph spreads rumors that— jury or no—I struck the blow that killed our father," Will continued. "What better way to clear his own name?"

"He wouldn't say that," I objected. "Even he doesn't know what happened." My mind returned to the conversation I'd overheard between Will and Martha. Joseph might not know how Edward died, but did they?

"It doesn't matter," Will said. "People will talk about this, and soon they will talk about something else. I don't imagine I can go home, though."

"Well, for now you'll stay with me," I said. "You're the only family I've got, and I'm sure Martha and Hannah would be happy to see more of you."

"Thank you," he said. I could not be sure, but I thought I saw his ears turn pink.

From that day forward, my household found a new rhythm, one that now included Will. Women in travail sent for me and Martha, and we delivered them. We christened children, and attended churchings and sometimes funerals. We went back to being midwives with no concern for murder. If we went out at night, Will came along, but during the day he either stayed home and

304

read or wandered up to the Castle to sit with Tree and Samuel. Sometimes he drank with Samuel, but to my relief he did not return to haunting alehouses. I watched him and Martha and saw signs of their love for each other, but said nothing. For the present at least, Will was in no position to marry.

It turned out that Will's prediction about his brother was right: soon it became common "knowledge" that Will had killed his father, and the Lord Mayor had wanted to try him for murder. Joseph, in the spirit of mercy, had convinced him otherwise. Will took a grim satisfaction in his prescience and made no effort to answer the rumors.

A few days after the reading of Edward's will, Hannah came to me in my chamber.

"Lady Hodgson, a woman is here to see you," she informed me. "I don't know who she is." I met the woman in the parlor. I did not know her either, but from her clothes I took her to be one of the city's poorer inhabitants.

"It's Widow Cowper," she said. "She's fallen and hurt herself. She wants you to come."

Martha and I accompanied the woman to Mrs. Cowper's home. Except for the occasional sign that Elizabeth now lived with her—a doll here, a primer there—it seemed much as it had when we'd delivered Sarah Briggs. Mrs. Cowper lay in her bed, attended by a few of her neighbors. Elizabeth sat by herself in the corner; by the sullen look on her face, I judged she'd been sent there.

"Lady Hodgson," Mrs. Cowper said when she saw me. "Thank you for coming."

I was relieved to find that her voice seemed no weaker than before, and her eyes still shone. Unlike some who passed through their green old age and neared decrepitude, she'd not resigned herself to death.

"How are you?" I asked. "What happened?"

She shook her head. "My crazy body," she explained. "I just fell. I can walk a little, but that is all."

"Do you need a bonesetter or a physician?" I asked. "I can send one to you."

"No, I just need to rest," she said. "But that is not why I asked you to come."

"Do you want me to send Martha or Hannah?" I asked. "I'm sure they would be happy to help you while you heal."

"No, my neighbors will help me." She paused. "It is Elizabeth," she said at last. "I do not know how I will care for her. The neighbors will help until I can walk again, but after that . . ." Her voice trailed off.

"Mrs. Cowper—"

"No," she interrupted. "We must say this aloud. I know not when the Lord will come for me. Nor do I know if He will take me quickly or steal my mind before my body." She looked over at Elizabeth, who had begun to read in a hornbook. "She is a child and does not need to watch an old woman die."

I started to object, but Mrs. Cowper would not allow it.

"I'm not saying I'm going to die today. I'm no fool. But if I don't die from this tumble, it will be the next one, or a winter fever. Elizabeth has seen enough death. She doesn't need to be orphaned again."

"What do you want me to do?" I asked.

"Take Elizabeth and raise her as your own," she said. "I know you lost a daughter about her age, so it won't be too strange for you. She's got no other family. If it isn't you, it will be another ancient widow after me, and then another one after her. And Lord knows you have room for a child in that house of yours."

I looked from Mrs. Cowper to Elizabeth and back. I glanced

at Martha to see if she had any thoughts on the matter, but she was looking toward the child. While I had no doubt that Mrs. Cowper would do her best, I could not deny the pith and marrow of her speech. She was old and poor, and would only become older and poorer. Elizabeth *would* be better off with me. What would that mean for my household? Will seemed to be settling in, and with the cooler weather, Tree had resumed his occasional visits. But even with these additions, I *did* have room for another child.

"We'll bring her back to see you," I said. "You deserve that."

"Thank you, Lady Bridget," she said. "Fetch her over here so I can tell her myself."

Martha crossed to Elizabeth and led her to Mrs. Cowper's bedside. Elizabeth reached out for her, and Martha and I stepped back while the pair talked quietly. From time to time, Elizabeth looked from Mrs. Cowper's face to mine. Tears filled her eyes for a moment, but she fought them back. She embraced Mrs. Cowper, gathered her books and doll, and approached me and Martha.

"Widow Cowper says I'm to live with you," she said. "Is that true?"

Martha and I knelt down beside her.

"If that's what you want," I said. "I have books and toys, and you'll have a bed of your own."

A look of caution crossed her face. "I've never had my own bed," she said. "What if I want to sleep with you?"

"Then you may," I replied.

"Can we play at checkstones?"

"Whenever you want."

"Is she kind?" she asked me, nodding at Martha.

"Very kind," I said. "And you have already met Hannah, but did you know she bakes delicious cakes? And there is my nephew

Will, who can tell you all manner of stories, and a boy named Tree who stays with me sometimes. He is a little older than you."

Elizabeth crossed to Mrs. Cowper, embraced her once again, and kissed her aged cheek. They both wiped tears from their eyes before Elizabeth returned and took my hand. We bade Mrs. Cowper farewell, and then Martha, Elizabeth, and I stepped into the rain and started for home.